Father unto Many Sons

Father unto Many Sons

Rod Miller

FIVE STAR
A part of Gale, a Cengage Company

Farmington Hills, Mich • San Francisco • New York • Waterville, Maine
Meriden, Conn • Mason, Ohio • Chicago

All scripture quotations, unless otherwise noted, are taken from the King James Bible.

Five Star Publishing, a part of Gale, a Cengage Company

LIBRARY OF CONGRESS CATALOGING-IN-PUBLICATION DATA

Names: Miller, Rod, 1952- author.
Title: Father unto many sons / Rod Miller.
Description: First edition. | Waterville, Maine : Five Star, a part of Gale, Cengage Learning, [2018]
Identifiers: LCCN 2018004734 (print) | LCCN 2018009807 (ebook) | ISBN 9781432843748 (ebook) | ISBN 9781432843731 (ebook) | ISBN 9781432843441 (hardcover)
Classification: LCC PS3613.I55264 (ebook) | LCC PS3613.I55264 F38 2018 (print) | DDC 813/.6--dc23
LC record available at https://lccn.loc.gov/2018004734

First Edition. First Printing: August 2018
Find us on Facebook—https://www.facebook.com/FiveStarCengage
Visit our website—http://www.gale.cengage.com/fivestar/
Contact Five Star Publishing at FiveStar@cengage.com

Printed in Mexico
1 2 3 4 5 6 7 22 21 20 19 18

In memory of Joseph Smith, Jr.
who told a story much the same
in a very different way

'Tis a happy thing to be the father unto many sons.

—William Shakespeare

Prologue

Blood and vomit mingled in a puddle between Abel Pate's spattered boots. Head bowed, elbows on knees, he slumped on the edge of the board sidewalk, heaved, and added to the vile stew soaking slowly into the dust. Sweat beaded on his forehead and dripped without splash into the viscous mess. Again and again he heaved until only bile, then nothing but stringy spittle, dribbled from his lips and chin.

Abel's breathing slowed and the spasms stopped. He sat upright and stared without understanding at the knife in his hand, smeared with the blood of his uncle. Turning aside, he wiped the flats of the blade across the dead man's shirt and let it rest on the stain. The body sprawled on the walkway next to him, head dangling over the edge, the deep slit across the throat leering at the boy like a wide scarlet smile.

Using the bandana he had knotted around his neck, Abel mopped his face and pondered his next move. The town was dark and quiet. Abel guessed it would be three or four hours yet until dawn. He picked up Uncle Ben's hat and brushed the dust off it and knew then what he had to do.

He slid his uncle's heavy knife into the shaft of his boot. He worked one arm out of the long linen duster, rolled the body over, pulled the other sleeve loose and tossed the duster aside. Sweat again moistened his brow as he hefted the lifeless feet and rolled the body off the wooden sidewalk that spanned a narrow gap between the stone block building that housed a bank and a wood-frame barber shop. He stepped down and sat on the street, braced his hands behind himself and with both feet pushed Uncle Ben's remains under the walkway. Even for a boy grown to the size of a man, the dead weight made the job difficult. With the side of his boot, he scraped dirt and litter over the blood and vomit, turning it all to dark mud. Abel knew his work made no kind of concealment but figured it would buy him an hour or two come daylight and that would have to do.

Dusting off his backside with both hands, he slid into Uncle Ben's long coat. He lacked the dead man's heft, but hoped it would not be obvious under the duster. Tugging the wide-brim hat low over his brow, he set off for his late uncle's house, trusting the darkness and his feeble disguise to accomplish his mission.

Chapter One

Somewhere in Arkansas, circa 1840

With a fistful of fabric in either hand, Sarah, wrist-deep in the murky creek, knuckled back and forth in an attempt to erase the stains from her only other dress.

And to think I left a wardrobe of finery behind for this. I'm damned if I know why I let that man drag me out here. He has not one lick of sense.

Twisting tight the bodice and watching water spill back to the creek, she tried to blow away a strand of hair troubling her eye, finally swiping at it with her hand and tucking it behind an ear. She unfurled the dress, eyed the stains staring back at her, and plunged it again into the stream, raw knuckles dunking and scrubbing with renewed violence. With all the splashing and thrashing she neither heard nor sensed his approach until covered by his shadow. The haste of her spin upset her balance and she tipped from her squat to a sit in the shallow verge of the creek, soaking her backside.

"Damn you, Lee Pate!" Scrambling to her feet she shook a dripping finger within an inch of her husband's nose while the freshly washed garment streamed water, tinging it with fresh mud where it brushed the ground. "You ought not steal up on a body like that. My heart is pounding like a smith's hammer on an anvil. Like to scared me to death. Damn you!"

"Now, Sarah—there's no need for that. Coarse language does not become you."

The woman wiped another stray strand of hair from her face and gathered the wet dress to wring water from it, muttering something unheard as she twisted and turned the fabric. The man, thumbs in the armholes of his vest, stood tall and thin and watched.

When wrung water diminished to droplets, she shook out the dress, winced at the still evident stains and whispered another obscenity. Eyebrows arched, the man rocked back on his heels and studied the woman.

"It cannot be helped, Lee. I am at my wit's end." Once started, it was as if the bung had been pulled from a vinegar keg. "What am I doing, squatting at this damn stream scrubbing laundry like I was black? Without even a washtub or scrub board! Of course, with naught but two dresses and one threadbare shift it is not as if I require much in the way of conveniences like I had back in Shelby County. I am left to feed four hungry men out of two cast-iron kettles, a skillet and a coffeepot! Oh, the kitchen I left behind. . . . Shops at hand for food and fixin's. Womenfolk to socialize with. Why in hell did we leave it, Lee? Why?"

HIs mouth and jaw worked but formed no words.

"Don't bother—I'll tell you why. All on account of some highfalutin notions about the state of mankind! Damn craziness, that's what it is. That's the why of it!"

He cleared his throat. "A man has to follow his conscience, Sarah, or he ain't no kind of man. Now, I know I ain't got the kind of pedigree you prefer, but I've got my principles."

"Principles! No, Lee, principles is not what you have got. What you have got is a head as hard as a hickory stump! It is not a principled man who stands in the town square of Memphis and warns his neighbors they are doomed to hell. To tell them flat out their city will fall down around their ears on account of their so-called sin of holding slaves!"

"But I know it to be true. It is not given for one man to own another."

"Your own family has done so for a hundred years! More!"

Lee cleared his throat. "An accident of time and place. Nothing more. And it needn't be a barrier to a man's learning better. Besides, I have never held a slave."

"No. But your brother Ben does."

"That's nothing to do with me—nor is anything Ben does. I hardly consider the man family anymore."

"And he, no doubt, returns the favor. But you will not find his wife washing what is left of her wardrobe in a no-name creek in the middle of nowhere!"

He reached a hand to place on her shoulder but she cast it aside, stuffed the wet, wadded dress into his chest, lifted her skirts and left for camp.

Lee watched her walk away, stared at the wet garment in his hand, then followed.

Chapter Two

Spoons scraped enamel plates, raising a ruckus that would betray the camp's presence to any traveler within a mile. Lee Pate set the pattern, face tipped over the plate balanced on his knees, spooning up the thin stew—or thick soup—as fast as his hard-working jaw allowed. Along the length of a log next to the stump on which he sat, his sons, Richard, Melvin, and Abel, followed suit.

Sarah looked on and shook her head in disgust as she gathered her apron and wiped her hands. She pulled a speckled plate from the jumble in the box and spooned up a helping of the meal, such as it was, for herself. A few stringy pieces of snared rabbit meat shared the watery puddle with the mushy roots and slimy greens of plants plucked from the woods surrounding the clearing that had been their home these past two-and-a-half months—give or take, lacking a calendar to mark the passage of days with any precision. Muttering under her breath, she took her accustomed seat on the stump. She spooned up her food without appetite, wondering how her man and their boys—grown men themselves, for the most part—could attack the tasteless mess with such gusto.

Not even salt for seasoning. Such herbs as I can gather a damn poor substitute. Spuds sprouted and rotten. Carrots long since eaten. Onions no more. Like as not we will be stricken with scurvy. If we don't starve first. Nothing that passes for bread, even—hasn't been for weeks.

"Lee!"

All four men snapped to attention.

Lee swallowed. Said, "Sarah?"

"How is your supper?"

The man poked at some unidentifiable fragment of food on his plate, spooned it up, chewed it carefully. "It fills the hole, Sarah."

"Not much!" said Melvin from his seat down the log.

"Now, boy—"

"But it don't, Pa. There ain't never enough of it to fill me up. Been so long since I felt full I can't remember if I was born first or hungry first."

"Melvin, show your Ma some respect."

"I told you—asked you—not to call me that. 'Mel'—that's what I go by now. And my bein' hungry ain't got nothin' to do with Ma. It's you."

"He's right, you know." That, from Richard, firstborn son, seated next to his father. "We eat it, 'cause it's all there is. That don't mean we like it. It ain't like it's food fit for a hungry man."

"Oh, Richard," Lee said, shaking his head.

"Lee!"

Sarah's sharp word this time resulted in three of the four faces looking her way. Abel's remained hidden behind his plate.

"The boys are right. I know it. And you know it, too, if only you would admit it to yourself."

"Why, Sarah, it's not that bad." He leaned forward to look down the log. "Abel, what do you think?"

The youngest of the brood, Abel was just sixteen years old but had already outgrown Richard, who had eight years on him, as well as Melvin, six years his senior. He pulled his plate away from his face, licked so clean it could pass for unused. He looked at his father and smiled. "I like it fine, Ma."

"Aw, hell, Abel—you'd eat a snake and like it," Richard said.

Melvin laughed. "He'd eat a damn bush if he thought there was a snake hidin' in it!"

Abel's brothers laughed, slapping knees and each other on the back.

"Settle down, boys," Lee said. "And watch your language. We ought to be grateful to your Ma for feeding us as well as she does, and be thankful for every bite that finds its way to our mouths."

"It ain't like we ain't thankful, Pa," Richard said. "It's just that there ain't never enough of it."

"And what there is it ain't all that good, truth be told," Melvin said.

"Back home in Tennessee we ate a lot better, that's for damn sure."

"Now, boys—"

"—Let it go, Lee. They're right," Sarah said. "It pains me no end to put this sorry excuse for food in front of you-all day after day. Thinking about all those hams and bacon sides left hanging in the smokehouse—them root crops buried in the cellar—fresh eggs every morning—hell, flour, sugar, salt. . . ." Sarah gathered the hem of her apron and wiped away a tear.

Lee raised his cup as if offering a toast. "We've got fresh milk, leastways."

"For now. The cow's drying up and I haven't seen any gentleman cows hereabouts to get her with calf again." Sarah wiped away another tear.

Lee turned the mug in his hands, studying the bead of milk skating around the bottom. "I don't feel good about it, myself," he said. "But I was moved to be shut of that place. And when I get a sign I am not given to ignore it."

"You and your damn dreams," Sarah said. "Even so, it don't mean we had to leave like thieves in the night with nothing more than we could carry in one trip to the wagon."

Richard stood and dropped his plate and cup in the steaming kettle set beside the glowing remnants of the fire. "She's right, Pa. I'm surprised you took the time to hitch the mules 'stead of making us boys pull the wagon. We left behind a damn good life in Shelby County, and for what? This?" he said as he spread his arms and turned a circle. "Here we sit in the middle of No-Damn-Where Arkansas, all on account of your stupid notions."

Melvin joined the tirade. "Yup," he said, with a nod.

Abel only looked on.

"No need to worry," Lee said. "It is about time we moved on, so we won't be here much longer." He shook out his cup and slid it, with his plate, into the dishwater, and then hitched his thumbs in the armholes of his vest. "But before we go, I've got a little errand for you boys."

Chapter Three

Abel jerked upright. He rubbed his hip where the toe of his father's boot had prodded him awake.

"Wake up, boy. It's near time you were on your way."

The boy's hands scrubbed his sleep-smeared face. He stretched, shook out his boots in case any critters had taken up residence, and pulled them on. He rooted around in his blankets for his shirt and slipped it over his head.

He looked around the clearing in the dim glow of the fire. Ma squatted over a kettle, fanning smoke with one hand and stirring the pot with the other. Rustling branches and leaves announced the arrival of his brothers, stumbling back into the clearing after tending to their morning toilet somewhere off in the trees.

"Come and get it, such as it is," Sarah said.

Richard and Melvin hurried to fetch plates and spoons from the box that served as a cupboard, but waited for their father. Abel joined the back of the line.

"Acorn mush," Sarah said.

"Again?"

"Hush, Melvin," Lee said. "It's better than nothing."

"Not much. And don't call me Melvin."

Sarah said, "It don't matter how many times I leach the acorns, I can't wash out all the bitterness. I'm awful sorry about that, boys." She stared at her husband through squinted eyes as she plopped down a spoonful of the goop, nearly upsetting his plate in the process. "Sugar would help." Plop. "So would molasses." Plop. " 'Course we don't have a speck or lick of either." Plop.

"I'm sure it will be fine, Sarah."

Richard snorted. Melvin laughed.

Dawn was breaking by the time the men finished their breakfast. Lee gathered his sons in a squatted circle to give them final instructions.

"I still don't see why a wore-out family Bible and an old book matters," Melvin said.

"Melvin—Mel—we've been over this before. The Pate family—your family—came generations ago from the north of England. That 'wore-out family Bible' as you call it contains our heritage. In it is recorded births and baptisms and marriages and deaths going back generations. You're in there, and me, and those who came before. And those who will come after, if your brother Richard fulfills his obligation to the family when the Bible comes to him as my firstborn, as it has come down to me. Mayhap it doesn't seem important to you now but someday it will. Or ought to.

"As for the other book, it is the journal of Ezekiel Pate, my grandfather—your great-grandfather—the first Pate to leave the Old Country and come to America, long before anyone had any notion it would become these United States. And he brought with him that family Bible, by the by. His little daybook hasn't the value of the Bible, but it is an important family treasure all the same."

Richard said, "So if them books was left to your safekeeping, how came Uncle Ben to have them?"

Lee picked up a twig and scratched in the dirt for a moment. "When your Uncle Ben built that big house in the town he got himself an iron chest to protect his valuables. Convinced me them books would be safer there, as that lockbox was made of inch-thick cast iron. So I gave them to his safekeeping. Otherwise, they'd have come with us. But, like I said last night, I am given to believe it is time we moved on from this place, and I cannot leave without those books. What I want is for you boys to go back to Shelby County and fetch them."

Richard thought a moment, said, "You want us to bring back any of our other belongings?"

"There ain't but the two mules. With a pair of you riding double or taking turns walking, there won't be no way to pack much of anything. 'Less you-all want to walk."

"I figured we'd take the wagon."

"No. It would only slow you down. It's nigh on to 200 miles back there by my reckoning. Besides, after all this time there won't be much of anything left at the place anyways."

It did not take the boys long to pack—just a matter of rolling up a blanket each. Sarah wept as they mounted up, not only for their leaving, but for their leaving empty-handed with bellies mostly empty as well. She muttered under her breath and wiped away tears with the hem of her apron again.

"You ought to make Little Rock in three, four days," Lee said. "You'll strike the Military Road there. Just follow along and it'll take you right on to the Mississippi opposite Memphis. Another week ought to do it. You-all couldn't get lost if you tried."

Lee led Richard's mule apart from the other and handed him his Kentucky rifle, powder horn, and shot pouch. Then, the father whispered some final instructions to his eldest son.

Richard jerked upright and looked wide-eyed at his father. Lee slapped the mule on the hip and Richard craned his neck, gaze fixed on his father as his mount plodded out of the clearing and into the woods with the mule carrying Melvin and Abel trailing.

Chapter Four

Juice dripped down Richard's chin and congealed in his scraggly beard as he gnawed on a hunk of turkey. Charred on the outside, the meat inside the black crust was all but raw. Disgust, mixed with the grease on his face, did not abate his attack on the double handful of fowl.

"Damn. This bird ain't hardly fit to eat," he said between savaging the meat and bones. "You ain't much of a cook, Mel."

His younger brother wiped his mouth with a shirt sleeve. "Don't seem to be slowin' you down none."

"A man's gotta eat. But it does make you miss Ma's acorn mush."

Mel winced, said, "Abel, what do you think?"

"It ain't half bad," the boy said around a mouthful of meat.

"What about the other half?"

Abel chewed and swallowed. "Can't say. Rich blowed that half of the bird plumb away."

"At least I got him. Otherwise we'd be goin' hungry again."

Abel ripped off another mouthful of meat and chewed for a moment. "You let me have Pa's rifle, I'd a made a head shot and saved all the meat."

Richard snorted. "Why should I give it to you? You ain't but a kid. Besides, Pa trusted that rifle to me."

"Aw, c'mon Rich. You know I'm a better shot than you." Abel wiped his greasy fingers on his pants legs. "Give me the gun and in the morning I'll go get us a deer. Be a lot more filling than a turkey."

"I been lookin' to pot a deer for days and ain't seen nothing but tracks."

"The thing is, Rich, you can't expect no deer to walk out on the road. You got to go where they are 'cause them deer sure ain't coming to find you."

The brothers said nothing more and were soon rolled in their blankets. Food had been scarce since riding away from the family camp—not that it had been in any abundance there. From time to time the trio had stopped at farmsteads and villages along the way, offering labor in exchange for food. But work was hard to come by, and the occasional gift of a loaf of bread or batch of corn dodgers or other small generosity was all that resulted from their efforts.

Richard wasn't awake enough to wipe the sleep from his eyes when a distant shot sat him upright. Melvin was still a blanket-covered lump. Abel's rumpled blanket was the only sign of the boy.

"Mel!"

Melvin scrambled to his feet, staggering in a crouched circle, squinting into the deep gray of the early dawn. "What is it? What?"

"Abel's gone. So's Pa's rifle. I heard a shot."

Melvin dropped to the ground. "Good hell, Rich. That's all? You liked to scared me to death yelling like that. He probably went off to get us a deer, like he said."

"The kid ain't got no right. Pa trusted that rifle to me."

Melvin rolled in his blanket, his back to his older brother. "Shut up, Rich. Hunger'll drive a man to do desperate things. He'll be back. And unless I miss my guess he'll bring in some camp meat."

Abel walked into camp with the first rays of the sun, a young whitetail doe wrapped over his shoulders like a stole. He dropped the deer, then unslung the powder horn and shot pouch and, with the rifle, handed them to Richard.

"Mel!"

Again, the middle brother bolted upright. "What? What is it?" he said, eyes darting.

"Wake up. And calm down," Richard said. "See what you can do about dressing out this deer. Looks like we'll be eatin' good for a few days." With a sharp look at Abel, he leaned the rifle against a tree and threaded the horn and pouch sling over the stub of a broken limb, then stirred up the coals of last night's fire, tossed on some wood and sat staring into the growing flames.

The Pate boys spent the day portioning out the deer and were back on the Military Road the next morning with full stomachs and pockets full of strips of smoked venison. They considered the day spent gorging themselves on fresh meat and letting the remnants cure over a smoky fire as anything but wasted.

Abel rode alone this day, with Richard and Melvin taking their turn riding double.

"We ought to be getting back to Shelby County tomorrow or the day after, oughtn't we?" Melvin said.

"I reckon. Why?"

"You think Uncle Ben will give us them books Pa wants?"

"Won't know till we ask."

"What if he won't?"

Richard let the question lie for a few minutes. "Well, if he don't, Pa told me a way to convince him."

"How's that?"

"Ain't sayin'. Pa said to keep it to myself till the time comes."

The mule stopped short. Richard righted himself in the saddle to see Abel sitting his mule, sideways in the road.

" 'The hell you stopping for, Abel?"

"Figured to give these mules a blow. We've been riding a while."

"I reckon that's all right. Next time, you ask. It ain't up to you to be makin' the decisions for this outfit."

Melvin slid off the back of the mule and squatted against a tree in the shade. Richard dismounted, handed the reins to Abel and followed. "Pull the bits so's they can graze."

Abel did so and joined his brothers.

"Seems to me," Melvin said, "Pa's sent us on a fool's errand."

Abel perked up. "How's that?"

"Ain't no guarantee Uncle Ben'll give us them books. And according to what Rich says, Pa don't think so either."

"What do you mean?"

"You tell him, Rich."

Richard cleared his throat, thought a minute, said, "Well, Pa says if Uncle Ben won't part with that Bible and daybook, I was to fetch something from our place that might change his mind. So, Mel might be right. Pa's got his doubts, and that means all this could be nothing more than another one of his crazy notions."

"Pa wouldn't do that!"

Richard laughed. "The hell you say. Look at us. We been a couple months now wandering through the woods livin' on little more than sunshine and water. We had us a good life in Shelby County—cropland, a few head of cattle, money enough for our needs." Richard sighed. "Left it all behind on account of one of Pa's foolish whims.

Abel sprung to his feet. "Don't you talk about our Pa that way!"

"I swear, Abel, the man's at least half crazy. You just can't see it."

Abel balled his fists and went after Richard. Before he took a second step, Melvin swiped a leg and spilled the boy to the ground. "Calm down, Abel. I know you think Pa can't do no wrong, but it ain't so. Even Ma knows it."

Abel rolled over and sat up, wiping forest duff and litter from his palms. "It don't matter. He's still our Pa. And we need to follow his lead."

"Well, we'll just see about that," Richard said. "I've went along up till now. But I ain't makin' no promises about how much longer I will."

Abel stood, brushed off his shirtfront and pants legs and stalked off to the mules, slid the bit into the mouth of his mount, swung into the saddle and headed off down the trace toward Memphis.

His brothers took their time following.

Chapter Five

Abel smelled the river coming for miles. Knowing their destination was near, the brothers rode on into the night. Save ephemeral reflections on the current from the lights of Memphis on the far shore, smell and sound was all they would get of the river with the moon and stars obscured by heavy clouds.

Wrung out from the long day's ride, Richard declared they would forego a campfire, just stake out the mules to graze and bed themselves down. They slept without dreams until lightning ripped seams in the overcast, releasing thunderclaps and a downpour.

The mules fought their tethers but the picket pins held and Melvin and Abel dragged the animals into the trees while Richard gathered blankets and saddles and their scant camp equipment. The cover was sufficient to ward off the falling rain, but soon the deluge worked its way through the canopy, leaving no shelter from the fast and steady drip and dribble of the storm. The rain quit before long, but water continued leaking out of the trees so the woods were abandoned for a return to the openness of the riverbank. Huddled under drenched blankets, the brothers slept no more that night.

Come morning, the sky was clear and the sun rose bright and warm over the Chickasaw Bluffs across the Mississippi. But the darkness of the night lingered in Richard's mood.

"Almost home, boys. But that's a mighty wide river and we ain't got no way to cross it. Might as well still be in the middle of No-Damn-Where Arkansas for all the good all the ridin's done us."

Melvin wrinkled his brow and squinted one eye and after a moment, said, "Well, what about the ferry?"

Richard's soggy hat slapped down on Melvin's head, then again. "What about the ferry, you fool? We ain't got no way to pay!"

The middle brother cringed, and Abel stepped in front of him, preventing further abuse.

"Stop it, Rich. Your beating on Mel won't help."

"You got a better idea?"

"Maybe. I don't know. This ferry and these other riverboats burn a lot of wood. I say we wander on over to the landing and offer to put up enough cordwood to pay our crossing over and back."

By day's end the brothers had chopped and split enough wood to get them across the river with enough left over for return fare when the time came and a little spending money besides. But it would be morning before the ferry ran again.

Taking their ease around a driftwood campfire, full of biscuits and gravy and fried meat and hot coffee gorged at a Hopefield town eatery, the men contemplated the morning. A round of coin flips chose Melvin to meet Uncle Ben in Shelby County to collect the Pate family Bible and Ezekiel's journal.

Rich and Abel soon slept, but there was no rest for Melvin. Hunched next to the fire, he poked and prodded the glowing coals with a stick of wood as if the answers resided there. How would Uncle Ben react to his arrival? Would he be welcome? What should he say? Would his uncle give up the books? If he didn't, then what?

With the Tennessee shore silhouetted in the growing dawn, Mel toed his brothers awake. They cleared camp, tethered the mules at the ferry landing and hoofed it into Hopefield for breakfast. The whistle blast of the approaching boat signaled their departure from the eatery and the sated men made the landing in plenty of time to load the mules and find a place on deck. The low-hanging sun's long reflection on the river pointed the way to Memphis. As the sidewheel churned and the boat bobbed, Melvin leaned over the rail and left his breakfast swirling away in the steamboat's wake to join the shifting currents of the Mississippi River.

CHAPTER SIX

Benjamin Pate stood on the balcony outside his third-floor bedroom, the shadow of his house stretching before him down the street. He held title to much of what he surveyed in the small town a few miles outside of Memphis. Besides business interests in the town, his holdings included swaths of farmland, most rented out on shares.

A few months ago, he added his brother Lee's abandoned farm to his properties. Pate sipped his coffee and thought it only right. It was, after all, the family farmstead where they were raised. And even though the home place came to Lee as the eldest son when their father died, Ben never stopped believing himself more suited to ensuring its continuing prosperity than his brother.

Time, to his way of thinking, had proved him right. While not born a fool, Lee had grown to become one, he believed. His brother's opinions, always outside the realm of rational thought, had become more entrenched through the years. His flighty notions became more frequent and intense as well until they drove him to forsake all he owned and flee.

Others, Ben knew, shared his brother's addled ideas about slavery and sin. But none, to his knowledge, carried them to such extremes—or allowed them to ruin their lives or those of their families.

Now, owing to Lee's eccentricities, acres of fertile land were being farmed by sharecroppers, a fine herd of cattle had been driven to market, hogs slaughtered and sows sold, and a comfortable house stood empty—since, that is, Ben had stripped it of furnishings and sold them off. And, his brother and his family were off somewhere wandering in the wilderness bound for some make-believe promised land that even Lee didn't know where to find.

A sorry situation, Ben thought as he swallowed the last of his coffee. *On the other hand, it did fatten my purse some, so it ain't all bad.* Within the hour, his banker—one of them, that is—solidified his faith in the thickness of his wallet.

"Mister Pate—Ben—your money could be put to better use than sitting in the vault. I could arrange some investments that would pay off handsomely for you."

"No doubt. And line your pockets as well."

"I've only got your best interests at heart, Ben. You know that. If I can profit a little from making you money, well, there's no shame in that and I won't apologize."

"Thing is, Frank, I don't need your help to make money." Ben reached across the desk, opened the bank president's humidor and helped himself to a cigar and fetched the hunting knife from its scabbard to cut the end. With its heavy blade of Damascus steel and fancy decorated handle, the knife was overqualified for the job, but Ben liked to show off his expensive tool and wielded it at every opportunity. The banker struck a phosphorus match and leaned over to light the smoke. With the cigar lit and puffed and smoldering to Ben's satisfaction, he leaned back in his chair and propped a foot on the opposite knee. "As you are no doubt aware, I have done quite well for myself."

"No one can deny that. But that doesn't mean you couldn't do better."

"I'll leave that to my bankers in Memphis. The cash I keep here is just that—cash. I want to have that money available just in case. If an opportunity comes along, I don't want to have to wait." Ben drew on the cigar and blew a cloud of smoke Frank's way. "So you just keep that money in the vault—it is safe there, isn't it, Frank?"

The banker sat up straight in his chair and tugged the wrinkles out of his vest by the tails. "Most certainly. This bank has never lost a single penny of our depositors' money."

"Good to know, Frank. Good to know." Ben paused for another puff on his smoke. "My reason for stopping by this morning is to let you know I'll be withdrawing 500 dollars day after tomorrow. Got a thoroughbred stud horse coming, cash on delivery."

The banker swallowed. "Must be some horse."

"That he is. Coming off Andy Jackson's plantation up by Nashville."

"President Jackson?"

"The same." Ben stubbed out the cigar and stood, shaking the folds out of the duster he wore. "I've got some good thoroughbred brood mares, and this stud ought to throw some fine colts. I intend to set myself up as a horse breeder in a big way, Frank. And it starts day after tomorrow. Can't recall when last I was as keen on an idea as I am on this one."

Rich men and their playthings, the banker thought when the door closed behind Ben. *I suppose it's good Ben's got something to look forward to.*

With the dinner hour approaching, the banker decided to call it a morning and make his way home for a meal and short nap. He had not covered a block when approached by a disheveled young man.

"Pardon me, Sir, I wonder could you help me?"

The banker took a step backward and made sure his wallet was secure inside his suit coat. He suspected its contents were the reason the man accosted him and had no intention of it leaving his pocket. The man removed his hat and his fingers fiddled with it, rotating it by the brim.

"What is it?"

"Well, Sir, I'm looking for my uncle. Ben Pate, I mean. I went by his house but he wasn't there and the man there said he was goin' to the bank. You are the bank man, ain't you?"

It dawned on the banker that the man was one of Lee Pate's boys. Richard, maybe. No—the middle one, Melvin.

"You're Melvin Pate."

"Yes, Sir. Only folks call me Mel now. I prefer it since I got my growth."

"Yes. Well, Mel, your uncle left me perhaps a quarter of an hour ago. Didn't say where he was going."

Melvin bowed slightly and this time he backed up a step. "I thank you kindly, Sir. Didn't mean to trouble you." He plopped his hat back on and turned to leave.

"Wait!"

"Sir?"

"Ben did say he was expecting delivery of a thoroughbred stallion in a day or two. It's just a guess, but you might find him at his stables out on the old Earl place. You know where that is, don't you?"

"Sure do. I'm obliged."

Lee Pate's boy. I wonder what he's up to.

Chapter Seven

A silhouette stepped into the opening at the end of the barn's alley, interrupting Ben Pate's heated discussion with his stable man. The black man cowered another time as Ben struck him on the shoulder with the quirt looped around his wrist, then Pate shifted his attention to the intruder.

"What do you want?" Ben shouted down the dim corridor, whacking the shaft of his boot with the quirt as if punctuating the question.

"Uncle Ben?" came the reply. "Is that you?"

A pause to consider the "uncle" reference, then, "Who's asking?"

The man removed his hat and stepped into the barn, hesitated, then walked down the alley. "It's me, Uncle Ben. Mel. Lee's boy."

"Mel? You mean Melvin?"

Melvin stopped an arm's length away from his uncle. "That's right. Only I go by Mel now."

"What the hell you doing here, boy? We ain't seen hide nor hair of your family for months. Where you-all been?"

Melvin swallowed, scuffed the hard dirt floor with the toe of his boot, then bowed his head. "Well, Sir, Pa felt the need to leave in a hurry. You know how he is when he takes a notion. Anyways, we been makin' our way across Arkansas."

"Arkansas? What the hell for? Where you-all going?"

"Can't rightly say. All's I know is Pa wants to get shed of the

United States. Talked some about Mexico."

Ben laughed. "Mexico. I hate to say it, Son, but that daddy of yours is addled. Man ain't got the sense God gave a hoe cake. So how come you to be here?"

"Pa sent me. Us. Me and Rich and Abel." Melvin looked at his uncle, glanced at the stable man, then back to his uncle.

Ben dismissed the slave with a warning to do as he was told or he would find himself back in the fields. He shifted his attention back to his nephew, flaring the long tails of his linen duster as he turned. "Well, what is it?"

As cowed as the black man, Melvin bowed his head and rocked from side to side, shifting his weight from one foot to the other. He cleared his throat, swallowed hard. "Pa wants us to fetch some of his belongings."

He paused again, the pawing of hooves and the tooth-grinding of hay and the occasional nicker of horses the only sound. That, and the slow tap-tap-tapping of the quirt against Ben's boot. Melvin grew more nervous in the silence; Ben grew increasingly impatient.

"I don't know what that fool brother of mine has got in mind, but I don't think he's got any belongings left hereabouts. Someone rustled the cattle he left unattended. Pigs stolen. House has been pilfered of anything worth carrying off. Folks have even dismantled some of the outbuildings and hauled them off. Only thing left, far as I know, is the land. And as far as I am concerned, he abandoned title to that when he went off and left it. I've got lawyers working on deeding it over to me. I'm damned if I'll let the farm our daddy and his daddy before him watered with their sweat leave Pate family hands just because your daddy Lee don't care none about it. Family matters to me, if not to him."

Ben had more to say, but paused to catch his breath after the tirade.

Melvin again cleared his throat and stammered into the silence.

"That's—that's—that's the th-thing, Uncle Ben. He didn't send us for no household goods nor cattle nor no other stock. It ain't nothing he left at the home place that he wants." He paused, fingers rotating his hat by the brim.

"Well, what, then? Speak up, Melvin! I swear, you're as thick-headed as your daddy."

"It's just some stuff he gave to you for safekeeping—books is all. He says there's a little book left him by his grandpa Ezekiel, a diary or some such. And a Bible what's got family names and dates and such wrote in it." Melvin lifted his head and met Ben's eyes. "Just family stuff. I guess he does care some about the family."

The quirt lashed out as if of its own accord, striking Melvin's upper arm. He stepped back, grasping the welt.

"Don't you be giving me back talk, boy! And don't pretend you—or your daddy—know anything about family. Far as I'm concerned, there ain't a one of your bunch fit to carry the Pate name."

Speechless, Melvin tried to rub the sting out of his arm. He studied his uncle's face—the flared nostrils, clenched jaw, furrowed brow. "It's just old books. Pa says he's got a right to them, on account of him bein' firstborn."

This time the quirt landed atop Melvin's head, very nearly knocking all awareness out of him. He staggered, covering his head with his arms. The next blow struck his ribs. Melvin managed to shove Ben away.

"Leave off! You got no cause to be beatin' on me!"

Ben raised the quirt, threatening another blow, and stepped toward his nephew; Melvin stepped back in response. "Shut up, you useless whelp! Lee ain't getting one damn thing from me, firstborn or not. Being born first is the only time he ever got ahead of me. All our lives our daddy favored him and he never did one damn thing to deserve it. Now he's gone off and left everything behind. Far as I'm concerned, that's the way it will stay."

"What do you care about a couple of old books, what with all you got?"

Ben laughed. "Fact is, boy, I don't care nothing about them books. Haven't even looked at that bundle of stuff since Lee gave it to me for safekeeping. Been locked in that safe all this time—and that's where they'll stay."

"That ain't hardly right, Uncle Ben. Them books belong to Pa by birthright."

When Ben finally walked away, short of breath and rimmed with sweat, Melvin lay curled up on the packed earth of the barn's alleyway. He could scarcely feel the sting of the welts striping his upper body. The hazy light seemed to grow dimmer as he strained against unconsciousness.

Oh Lordy, Lordy, Lordy. What am I goin' to do now?

Chapter Eight

Abel wrung pink water from the rag and dabbed more blood from the torn scalp above Melvin's ear. It was the only of his wounds to bleed. But the welts and bruises on his arms, back, and ribs would be painful for a time and would likely be slow to heal.

Richard paced back and forth on the porch of the house he and his brothers had grown up in, muttering words the others could not hear. Abel, sitting on the porch step beside Melvin, tossed the tainted water into the dooryard. He stared at the dented and rusty enamel bowl salvaged from a midden beside the house and threw it aside. The clang of its bouncing across the weed-infested yard stirred Richard from his trance.

"You've messed this up but good, Mel. Had you handled things right, Uncle Ben would've handed over them books and we'd be done with this."

"Well I never asked for the job. You could've done it your own self."

"Never thought I'd have to. Figured even a simple-minded ninny like you could fetch a book."

Abel said, "There ain't no need for that, Rich. Mel done his best. Ain't no reason to think you could've done any better."

"Sure as hell I couldn't of done any worse."

Richard resumed his circuit of the porch. Melvin sat wrapped in his own arms. Abel studied the home place. He could not fathom such change in just a few months. There was no sign of life, anywhere. The weeds that spotted the yard grew even taller in the fertile soil of the empty hog pens. The open door of the smokehouse hung tentatively on a single hinge. Half the siding from the barn was missing from the skeletal frame, put to other use elsewhere. The tool shed was gone altogether; only a scattering of rusty parts and pieces witnessed it ever existed. A shallow pit betrayed the former presence of the root cellar. Not even the outhouse had survived—it reclined on its side. The crescent moon cut in the door must have served as someone's target, as bullet holes splintered the wood around it.

The house was likewise plundered. Only shards of glass remained in the few window sashes that still hung. The back door, shattered and splintered from being kicked in; the front door missing. The fancy-carved double-doored wardrobe was gone from Ma and Pa's bedroom. Pantry shelves were empty and pulled down. A length of stovepipe dangled from the ceiling in the sitting room, orphaned from the warming stove that once sat beneath it but was now gone. Missing, too, was the kitchen stove—its only trace the scorched floorboards under where it once stood. The bedroom the boys shared, a lean-to addition to the house, was in shambles; the shingles gone from the sagging roof, one wall missing and another barely standing.

You had to know where to look to find evidence of the family that once—and that only recently—lived here. The door frame between the front room and the kitchen showed a ladder of pencil marks, each accompanied by initials and a year, where Ma marked each boy's growth as part of the family's birthday ritual. There was the rough-carved and painted-over RP on a porch post that resulted in a hiding for the oldest son and a lesson for the other boys. A flattened tin can, tacked over the hole in the kitchen wall from the time Melvin failed his lesson in loading and seating a cap on Pa's old single-shot pistol. Abel searched in vain for the pencil drawing he'd made of the barn—

only pinholes and a torn paper corner remained where Ma had hung it on the wall. He must have been about seven back then.

Abel could not cry over any of it. Instead of sadness, he felt only the hollow emptiness of his former home. He returned to the porch and sat again on the step beside Melvin.

Richard said, "You done moonin' around, baby brother?"

Abel shook his head. After a moment he said, "There ain't much left to show we was ever here. It's kind of sad."

"The sad thing is, we ain't here still. There ain't no good reason on God's green earth for us to be traipsin' around Arkan-damn-saw. We had a good life here, and we just walked away from it, with barely the clothes on our backs."

"It was what Pa wanted," Abel said.

There was no humor in Richard's laugh. "What Pa wanted. Hell, that man don't know what he wants. I swear he's loony as a goose sometimes. And them times gets more regular the older he gets."

"Still, he's our Pa."

"That don't give him the right to ruin our lives."

"He's our Pa."

"Dammit, Abel! Sometimes I think you're as thickheaded as Melvin! You think him bein' our Pa is all that matters on account of you're still a kid. But me and Ma—hell, even Melvin!—we know better. I've gone along up till now but I'm about done with it. If it weren't for Ma, I'd call it quits right now and not even go back."

"You do what you think best. I'm going back. And when I do, I'm takin' them books with me. Just like Pa said."

Melvin said, "How do you figger to get them from Uncle Ben?"

"I don't know," Abel said. "I'll think of something."

"Don't bother askin' him," Melvin said, rubbing the welts on his ribs.

Thought of the beating stirred Richard's already boiling pot. "Sonofabitch," he said. "I can't believe Uncle Ben abused you like that. He's got no right."

Melvin shrugged and winced from the resulting pain. "He thinks he's within his rights on account of he says Pa abandoned all claim to anything to do with the Pate family when he left."

Richard pondered that for a moment. "He's got a point, I suppose."

"Richard!"

"Aw, shut up Abel. I ain't give up yet. There's one more thing we can try—it's what Pa told me about just before he sent us on this wild-goose chase. Something he left behind here at the house that Uncle Ben will want. But I'm of half a mind to forget what he said and just take it back with us instead of them books."

"We'd best do what Pa said."

"Shut up, Abel. Maybe we will, maybe we won't. It ain't up to you to decide, baby brother."

Melvin said, "Well, hell! What is it, anyway?"

"C'mon. I'll show you-all—if somebody ain't stole it like they did everything else."

The brothers passed through the empty doorway into the front room. Richard kicked around in the rubble on the floor and found a bent fireplace poker. He wedged the end between the hearthstone and fireplace and moved the heavy slab an inch or two and cast the poker aside. "C'mon you-all. Give me a hand here."

Twenty-four fingers slid into the crack.

"Ready," Richard said. "Pull!"

The stone resisted but once in motion slid away from the fireplace revealing a shallow hole. Richard swept around in the dirt until he uncovered the leather bag he sought. He untied the thong and unwrapped it from the neck of the pouch and poured the gold eagles inside into a jingling pile on the hearthstone.

"Hell's fire!" Melvin said. "It's a fortune!"

"No, Mel, it ain't no fortune. Ain't but eighty dollars there. It's a goodly sum but far from a fortune. Still and all, it might be enough to convince Uncle Ben to part with Pa's precious books."

Chapter Nine

Ben Pate stared out the parlor window, sucking on a cigar and thinking about nothing. He was alone in the big house, save the presence of his hired man Friday, Peter, who was likely asleep at this hour. He slept in a small room off what Ben's wife called the den, but was more an office, where he and Peter handled business affairs.

He turned away from the window, the rich furnishings in the room triggering thoughts of waste. This place, filled with fancy—and expensive—cabinets and couches, tables and chairs, hutches and highboys, wardrobes and sideboards, mirrors and lamps, draperies and curtains and other fixtures and fittings and finery was all his wife's doing.

And she was seldom here to enjoy it.

Ben's wife, a society girl raised in luxury as the daughter of a Charleston cotton merchant, thought Shelby County a backwater, and nearby Memphis a frontier town—never mind that some 8,000 people now called the place home. And never mind that the money coming in from all his land and livestock, his trade and shipping interests, his stocks and investments, amounted to more than enough to satisfy all the family's needs and wants with plenty left over. Never mind all that. His wife also considered the schools hereabouts inferior, so she packed herself and their now-teenaged daughter and son off to Charleston where they would, she believed, receive a proper education.

And that left Ben to rattle around the big house alone most of the time. Alone, that is, except for Peter and the servants—slaves—a black man and his wife who lived in a shack out back. Exhaling smoke, Ben wondered at the point of it all. What good was this house if he found no pleasure in it? What good was a family that was not here to enjoy?

He thought of his brother Lee, and his family.

Misguided as the man is, his family sticks by him. Lee never had the business sense I've got so he never accumulated much in the way of wealth. But the Pate family farm that came down to him as firstborn son—even though I was more capable of running it—provided a comfortable enough living. And he walked away from it all, the fool!

Still, his family followed him to God-knows-where, and mine won't even stay home. . . .

Ben smashed his cigar into an ashtray, again and again and again, reducing the stub to shreds. He and his older brother had butted heads all their lives. Lee was always the favorite, which made him, the younger son, work all the harder for approval that seldom came. Even now, with their father long gone, he somehow felt inadequate despite outpacing his older brother by any measure.

Of late, their disagreements—and Lee's differences with the world—came down to slavery. Somewhere, somehow, Lee acquired the fool notion it was wrong; sinful even. You would think the man was a damn Yankee instead of Southern born and bred, raised in a slave-holding family. Lee not only turned his own slaves loose, he berated any and every slaveholder he encountered for not following suit. He preached his doctrine at every opportunity and corresponded with newspapers throughout the South, expounding his views.

His brother became a laughingstock.

Especially when his tirades turned to prophesying the ruin of the South, and all of the United States, for their sins. Lee could not say when or where it would come, but he claimed dreams and visions showing a great war of destruction. His notions had finally driven him to quit the country and leave for where he did not know. Good thing, too. Otherwise, the man would be in jail. Or an asylum for the feebleminded.

Plain and simple, Lee was a damn fool if ever there was one. War? Destruction? Bullshit!

Sure, Ben was well aware of the ongoing disputes among politicians. He had heard all the arguments against slaveholding—long-standing arguments hashed and rehashed since the uniting of the States some half a century ago. But that is all they were—political disputes. And, as far as he was concerned, all the time Congress wasted debating slavery meant less time to conjure up ways to hinder trade and commerce, and that suited him just fine. To think it would ever come to war, or that the South could ever be brought to heel, was twaddle. It hadn't come to war when South Carolina adopted its Ordinance of Nullification back in '32, declaring federal tariff laws unconstitutional and vowing not to obey them. Like then, like always, compromise and accommodation would continue to rule.

Ben heaved a big sigh, shook his head in slow disbelief—or, perhaps, discontent. He turned down the lamp, watched the flame shrink to a dim glow, and shuffled off to his empty bed.

Come midmorning, as Ben sat at his desk studying contracts, Peter knocked at the door and walked in uninvited, as was their custom.

"Some, uh, gentlemen here to see you, Sir."

Ben rocked back in his swivel chair and clasped his hands across his belly. "Who?"

"I did not get their names, I'm afraid. They claim to be family—'Tell him Lee's boys is here,' they said."

Ben lurched forward, slapping his hands on the desk.

Lee's boys! What the hell? I thought I'd made it clear to that muddleheaded Melvin to go away and leave me the hell alone!

"They know I'm here?"

"Yes, Sir. I said as much. Although I did tell them you were quite busy and, without an appointment, you may be unable to see them."

Ben pushed away from the desk, swiveled his chair and looked out the window, seeing nothing of what it framed.

"Go ahead and show them in, I suppose."

Chapter Ten

Five gold eagles sat stacked on Ben's desk. He had to admit they made a pretty picture. But $50 meant little to a man such as himself. Not that he would turn it down in most circumstances. But this time—well, this time he would forego a further entry in his account books in the interest of keeping his no-account brother from getting what he wanted.

"Where the hell did you-all come up with fifty dollars cash money?"

Richard cleared his throat. "That ain't your business, Uncle Ben. All's you need to know is, you give us them books Pa wants and it's yours."

"That Bible and that journal diary ain't worth anywhere near fifty dollars."

"They are to Pa," Abel said.

"Well now, ain't that just like your Pa. My brother, bless his soul, never did have an idea of the value of things. Offering that kind of money for them books just goes to show how rash the man is."

"Ain't no need for you to be bad-talkin' our Pa," Abel said, stepping toward the desk with fists clenched.

Richard grabbed him by the elbow. "Don't bother, baby brother. It ain't like he's wrong."

Abel jerked his arm free and turned his anger toward his brother.

Ben laughed. "Sounds like you've growed up enough to see

your daddy for what he is."

"What's between me and my Pa ain't any of your business. Whilst I can think of a hundred better ways to spend that money, it's Pa's money and he said to use it to get them books he wants. So do we got a deal or not?"

Ben rocked back in his chair and swiveled around until his back was to the boys. "See that safe there in the corner?"

"We ain't blind."

"Well, here's the thing. That box—all the sides and the door—is made of inch-thick iron. You couldn't open the thing with a pickaxe. There ain't but one key to it—well, there's another one, but it's locked up in the vault at the bank—and the onliest people on all the earth that knows where that key is, is me and Peter. You-all met Peter, didn't you? He's the one answered the door," Ben said as he swiveled back to face the boys.

He talked on. "That book and Bible your daddy gave me for safekeeping is locked in that safe."

Richard, irritated by all the talk, said, "That's fine, Uncle Ben. It's good of you to keep them in your damn safe. Now, why don't you unlock it and give us them books and we'll take our leave."

"Let me finish. As I said, them books is in that safe." Ben looked at each of the boys in turn, locking eyes until each, save Abel, looked away. "And that's just where they're going to stay."

Both Richard and Abel protested, but Ben hushed them with a wave of his hand. "Now, boys, I suggest you-all get the hell out of here and go back to your daddy—wherever he is—and tell him he ain't got no claim to any part of the Pate family. Including the name, as far as I'm concerned."

Richard huffed and reached for the stack of coins.

"No," Ben said softly, his hand beating Richard's to the pile and covering it. "The money stays."

"The hell!" Richard said. Abel stepped up beside his brother, voicing his own protest. Melvin stayed where he stood, propping up the far wall.

Again, Ben hushed them with a raised hand. "Hold it, boys. As I said, the money stays."

"But that ain't nothin' but thievery!" Abel said.

"It ain't right!" Richard said.

"We'll go to the law!" Abel said.

Again, the humorless laugh rolled out of their uncle. "Boys," he said. "You-all stop a minute and think about it. I'm a respected citizen hereabouts as you know—from this town all the way to the courthouse in Memphis. You-all ain't nothing but drifting vagrants. I could have you in jail by dinnertime."

Abel reminded him who was breaking the law, but it had no effect on Ben. He repeated his claim of standing in the community. And said that the reputation of their father reflected on them, and not to their credit. He pointed out again that he could have the boys arrested for vagrancy. Or, come to it, accuse them of trying to rob him in his own house, with Peter as a witness.

"Now, boys, just who do you think the law is going to believe?"

His nephews offered no answer, but their eyes betrayed their thoughts. Richard looked angry, but defeated. Melvin, cowed, as usual. Abel's eyes burned with hatred.

That boy might bear watching.

The boys left Ben's house and did not speak until reaching the river, where their mules were corralled in an abandoned pen that backed onto an empty shack. It was Melvin who broke the silence.

"Rich?"

An irritated look was his older brother's only response.

"I'm wonderin' why it was only five of them gold eagles Uncle

Ben took from us. There was eight of them under that fireplace, wasn't there?"

"Oh for God's sake, Mel! I kept out three of them so's we won't go hungry on the way back to Ma and Pa. Or when we get there. We been hungry long enough on account of Pa's foolishness, and this money will stave it off, at least for a time."

"But Pa said—"

"Shut up! I know what he said. But Uncle Ben wasn't no more likely to give up them damn books for eighty dollars than he was for fifty. So why don't you just forget about it? We'll get on the ferry this evenin' and that'll be the end of it."

"No."

Richard whipped around and stared wide-eyed at Abel. "What?"

"I said no. This ain't over. You-all can do what you want, but I ain't goin' back without them books. Pa sent us here to get them and I aim to do just that."

"Pa! Pa this, and Pa that! I'm sick to death of hearin' you carry on about Pa. Had you the sense God gave a bottle cork you'd see he ain't give us nothing but trouble, with more to come."

"Say what you want—he's still our Pa and we ought to do what he says. I'm going back and get them books for him."

Before Abel could draw another breath, he found himself prone on the riverbank, the wind knocked out of him—whether from his brother's two-handed shove to his chest or from the landing that resulted. He sucked air in but could not release it and the feeling of strangling panicked him.

A kick in the ribs from Richard's boot solved that problem as it rolled the boy from his back to his belly. Richard wound up for another kick, but Abel had come to himself enough to roll out of the way, and when Richard followed up with a stomp, he grabbed his foot and upended him, then scrambled to his feet, fists cocked.

With a leer on his face, Richard rose and rushed in, only to have his direction and momentum reversed by a blow to his nose from Abel's fist. Blood streamed, and Richard's face reddened to match.

"Grab him, Mel! Hold him!"

Melvin hesitated. "But Rich—"

"Grab him, I said!"

But Mel lacked enthusiasm for the job and was too slow. Abel interrupted his attempted bear hug from behind with an elbow to his tender ribs and Melvin went down. But Abel's attention to Melvin gave Richard a chance to land a blow, and he made the most of it. Abel went down and when he did, Mel, now in the fight with fervor, rolled on top of his younger brother and pinned his wrists to the ground. A blow to the boy's head from Richard's boot rattled his brain. Another kick landed on his shoulder.

"You little sonofabitch!" Richard said between gasps. "I've had a belly full of you trying to lord it over me!"

As Richard wound up for another blow with his boot, Abel jerked and bucked, loosening Melvin's hold on his wrists. With an open hand, he smacked Melvin above the ear, opening the wound he had bathed only yesterday. His brother screamed and rolled off and away and Abel was soon on his feet.

"Leave off!" he told Richard.

"Like hell," came the reply, accompanied by a flying fist.

Abel ducked away, landing a blow to Richard's gut. His brother bent double and Abel's wild uppercut landed on his chin, standing Richard upright if only briefly, as he collapsed in a heap. Abel turned to Melvin, sitting spraddle-legged with blood leaking between the fingers of the hand held over the gash on his head.

"You had enough, Mel?"

Mel nodded.

Abel rummaged around the one-room cabin and came out with a rusty bucket and a rag that looked to have served as an apron. He dipped the bucket full from the river and half the water leaked through the bottom before he got back to Melvin.

As he had done before, he mopped away the blood and cleaned the wound as best he could. He rinsed the rag, folded it, and told Melvin to press it against the cut. Refilling the leaky bucket, he hurried to where Richard lay and dumped it in his face. His brother wagged his head back and forth, spitting and snorting as he came awake. When finally his eyelids cooperated and lifted, he saw Abel standing over him. Anger darkened his eyes but it faded with echoes of the blows his youngest brother had delivered.

"Now, you two listen to me," Abel said. "I meant it when I said I'm going back to get them books."

"How do you aim to do that?" Richard said.

"I don't know. I'll figure out something, somehow."

"I suppose you want our help."

"No. I want you-all to stay here and wait for me. If I ain't back by morning, go on ahead back to Pa. Tell him I tried my best."

CHAPTER ELEVEN

Once a grassy clearing among the trees, the campsite was trampled down to dust. When it rained, that meant mud. Gathering firewood forced Lee always deeper into the forest. Likewise, Sarah's foraging for roots and greens and berries and seeds sent her ever farther afield. Any rabbits or squirrels in the immediate vicinity who hadn't found their way into the cooking pot by now had quit the area long since.

Amber sunlight filtered through the trees, softening the harshness of their temporary home. But it did nothing to dampen Sarah's increasing ire at the state of her affairs.

"We'll move on once the boys is back," Lee said for the hundredth time.

Sarah stirred the watery stew with more enthusiasm than the chore required, the spoon ringing the sides of the cast-iron kettle like the clapper in a bell. She swiped a stray strand of hair away but to no avail; it again draped over her face until she tucked it persuasively behind an ear. "Like as not them boys has been set upon by thieves or killed by Indians or succumbed to some other untoward end."

"Now, Sarah—"

"Don't 'Now Sarah' me! Had you not sent them off on such a senseless errand they'd be here right now, where they belong." She clanged the spoon clean against the rim of the pot. "No, I tell a lie. They'd be here, all right, but it damn sure ain't where they belong. Ain't none of us ought to be here." Sarah wiped her hands on the hem of her apron and again slid the unruly hank of hair behind her ear. "You and your damn-fool notions. . . ."

"Coarse language is becoming a habit with you, woman. And such talk don't tote up to your advantage."

"Shut up," she said, dabbing her eyes with the apron. "Just shut up."

Clouds of dust followed her out of the clearing. She sat on a rock on the bank of the stream. Not the most comfortable seat, but over repeated visits her backside had somewhat conformed to its hills and valleys and angles and slopes. The whisper of rushing creek water did not wash away her fears or anxiety, but it did soothe them to some extent. And, unlike Lee, the stream heard her complaints without comment or correction or contradiction.

"What's happened to the home place?" she said under her breath, so only the creek could hear. She thought again of the spindle-back rocker in the front room and the contented hours spent there with needle and thread, darning egg, or knitting needles. Or, at times, a favorite book.

"I wonder if whoever's cooking at my stove has learned to regulate the heat, what with that finicky damper." She thought of the pantry, the crocks on its shelves brimming with the fruits of their labors. Dried apricots and cherries, prunes and raisins. Pickled cucumbers afloat in brine, sacks of onions, bags and boxes of herbs and spices. Dry beans. Rice. Flour and sugar. The cellar, with its trove of root vegetables and stored apples. She swallowed saliva at the thought of salty ham and bacon from the smokehouse. "Oh, Lord," she whispered, "what I would not give to see the yolk of an egg running across a plate."

Sarah stood, brushed off her backside and smoothed her apron and walked back to the cook fire to dish up a supper of weak broth for herself and her husband.

"Mighty tasty, Sarah," Lee said, licking his fingers.

She only looked at him.

"Once the boys get back," he said, his tongue catching a drip on the heel of his hand, "we'll go on to Fort Smith. Can't be more'n a week's travel."

"Then what?"

Lee handed her his plate and spoon and wiped the palms of his hands against his thighs. "I reckon me and the boys will rustle up some work for the winter. With four of us makin' wages we ought to could earn a pretty good pile. Outfit us real good, come spring, then roll on west."

"Where to?"

"Don't rightly know, as yet. It'll come to me 'fore the time comes."

" 'Nother one of your fool notions, that what you're saying?"

He looked at his wife through sad eyes. "Call 'em notions if you will, woman. Man's got to follow his heart."

"It's your heart you're following, is it? Well, one thing's for certain sure, Lee Pate—it ain't your brain."

Sarah lowered herself to the ground, legs folding beneath her. She studied the empty plate in her hand and set it aside. Tucking a stray lock of hair behind her ear, she wiped away a tear runneling down her cheek.

Lee's eyes widened in wonder. "Why, Sarah! What is it?"

"It's everything, Lee. Everything." Wiping more tears with the hem of her faded apron, Sarah repeated much of her conversation with the creek to her dumbfounded husband. She confessed her shame at the meager fare that left her family unfilled and unsatisfied. She repeated her fears for the well-being of her boys. And she punctuated it all with a frenzy of racking sobs.

Sliding off the log on which he sat onto his knees, Lee crept the few steps to Sarah and enfolded her in his arms. "I am a thick-headed man, Sarah. I knew you was upset, but I did not know it went beyond your annoyance with me."

It took some time, but Lee's embrace relieved Sarah's quaking. Whispered apologies felt useless as they fell from his tongue, but he knew no other course.

Chapter Twelve

Something about his meeting with Lee's boys bothered Ben Pate. He didn't feel guilty about what he'd done; not exactly. But he didn't feel good about it, either. He'd fussed and stewed over it, picked at dinner, then fretted about it some more. Finally, he told Peter to tell the cook he wouldn't be needing supper—he was stepping out for a drink and would find something to eat in town. Peter watched him hunch into his long-tailed duster, tug on his wide-brimmed planter's hat and leave the house like a troubled man with much on his mind.

But Ben never did eat supper. He did have a drink. He did not stop after the first one, or the third, or many others to come. Long past midnight and well into the wee hours, the bartender decided to lock up. He shooed a few men with no particular place to go and in no hurry to get there out the door. Then he tried to rouse his last holdout out of somnolence. After lifting Ben's limp head off the table three or four times and watching it sag back into a stupor when the bleary, bloodshot eyes failed to make sense of his surroundings, he realized Ben—or Mister Pate as he called him when the man was conscious—would not be walking out the door on his own.

"Antonio!"

The old man who worked as a swamper in the saloon looked up from the sink where he was up to his elbows in glassware.

"C'mon over here and help me get Mister Pate out the door."

Antonio dropped the dirty rag he'd dried his forearms with

on the table where Ben sat and, arms akimbo, studied the man. "He no look so good."

"Ain't no wonder," the bartender said. "He's swallowed enough of what passes for whiskey in this place to float a steamboat."

"You think he make it home on his own?"

"Oh, he'll be all right. Let's take him outside. Fresh air will do him good."

The bartender propped Ben's hat on his head and each man hitched an arm under one of Ben's and half-carried the stumbling, mumbling man out the door. They leaned him against a sign advertising nickel beer hanging beside the door of the saloon and held him there.

"Mister Pate!" the bartender said, shaking the unsteady man by the lapels. "Mister Pate! Wake up!"

Ben stirred and lifted heavy eyelids enough to manage a few slow, quizzical blinks until the world came into a soft but penetrable focus. He looked at the men holding him up, and seemed disturbed at their presence. "Go 'way," he slurred. "Le' me 'lone."

"You going to be all right, Mister Pate?"

"Damn right," Ben said, weakly swatting at the men.

"You sure?"

"Get the hell out of here!"

"Looks like he's comin' around, Antonio. Let's leave him be. I'm plumb tuckered and beggin' for a bed."

The men went back inside and the bartender closed and latched the saloon door. Ben stayed where he was, not trusting his rickety shanks to support him without assistance. Deep, deliberate breaths of the damp night air slowly brought him back to semi-consciousness and he set off for home, staggering along the board sidewalk. He dragged one hand along the walls of the buildings he passed to steady him along his path.

He stopped for a breather before attempting the narrow gap between the bank and the barber shop where no support was offered, leaning against the stone building and scrubbing his unfeeling face with the palms of his hands.

"Uncle Ben? That you?"

Sobered considerably by the surprise of the question, he shouldered his way upright and thought he felt his brain slosh around inside as he jerked his head back and forth to locate the source of the voice in the darkness.

He found it, a few steps away. A shadow-shape of a man, standing on the dusty street in front of the barber shop.

"Who is it?"

"It's me, Uncle Ben. Abel Pate."

Ben's awareness came rushing back with a sharp intake of breath.

"What the hell you doing here? Didn't I already send you and your brothers packing? More than once, as I recollect."

Abel walked a few steps closer. "I estimate you know why I'm here."

"I told you you ain't gettin' those books."

Abel stepped up onto the sidewalk and stopped scant inches from his uncle. "And I'm telling you I ain't leaving without them."

The older man was no taller than Abel, but considerably bigger by every other measure. The boy had no idea how he would fare in a fight with his uncle, and hoped it would not come to that. Ben had a different idea.

Before he even knew the fight had started, Abel found himself back on the street, sitting on his backside, his jaw throbbing. He shook the cobwebs out of his head and stood up.

"I don't want to fight with you, Uncle Ben. You don't appear to be feeling all that good."

Ben laughed. "I ain't never felt so bad that I couldn't lick the likes of you. What I ought to do instead is turn you over my knee and give you a good spanking. If that no-account daddy of yours had done that more often, you wouldn't be here disrespecting your elders like you are. But I guess I can't expect much better from one of Lee Pate's boys."

Abel waded in with fists flying, but even in the man's dissipated state Ben did not yield. The boy's blows seemed to have no effect on his whiskey-numbed opponent. The only part of the man that moved was his big-brimmed hat. Knocked askew by Abel's fist, it tipped off Ben's head, rolled off his shoulder and fell to the walkway.

With a roar, Ben staggered out of his stupor and lashed out with heavy fists. He pummeled the boy's body with bruising blows and a walloping uppercut slammed Abel's head against a wooden post that propped up the bank's porch roof.

But the attack was all Ben could muster and, gasping for air, he knew he had to end it then and there. He groped at the front of his duster, trying with an uncooperative hand to find his knife in the scabbard on his belt. A man in his line of work needed no such weapon, but vanity told him its heft and jeweled handle conveyed evidence of his wealth.

Slipping the knife from its sheath, he grabbed a hank of Abel's hair and tipped back his head. Wobbly and woozy, Ben lifted the knife. But just as the blade's razor-edge reached the boy's neck, he mustered the strength to hoist a knee and plant it in his uncle's crotch. With a gasp and whimper, Ben staggered and dropped to his knees, the knife clanking to the sidewalk beside him. Abel seized the opportunity along with a handful of shirtfront, hammering Ben's head with his other fist until blood streamed from his crushed nose, trickled from his ears, and seeped through mashed lips.

Abel's blows grew weaker and he stopped, turning his uncle loose. Ben fell forward and rolled to his back, head dangling over the edge of the plank sidewalk. The boy dropped, gulping air. Crawling on hands and knees, he gathered the knife and slowly, but without hesitation, sliced a wide and deep scarlet arc across his Uncle Ben's throat.

Chapter Thirteen

Daniel Lewis whoaed up the team to have a look around. Fort Smith did not appear to be a big town, but it surely was a bustling one.

"Righty-o girls. Looks like we are here."

Mary, Martha, Emma, and Jane joined their father at the first of the family's two wagons, each drawn by a pair of oxen.

"Is this where we will be staying, Father?"

"Ah, no, my Jane. It is Texas we are bound for. But if the prospects look good, perhaps we shall lay over here for the winter."

At thirteen, Jane was the youngest of the girls. Emma, at fifteen, never let her sister forget she was the baby of the family. Martha and Mary, at eighteen and nineteen, considered themselves beyond such childish obsessions, and what with doubling up in an attempt to fill the role of a dead mother, they had little time for it.

The Lewises stood beside the wagons watching men scurry about like insects under a lifted rock. They hauled carts burdened with bricks, pushed wheelbarrows full of mortar, drove wagonloads of saw logs going one way and milled lumber the other. High-wheeled freight wagons lumbered by, loaded with goods under canvas. Indians paraded in and out of the agent's office, soldiers drilled under arms, roustabouts unloaded cargo from riverboats, drovers herded small bunches of cattle, sheep, and pigs. Everywhere the girls looked, it was a chaotic cavalcade of men. Some pretended not to look as they passed, others couldn't help staring. Some doffed hats, others stopped dead in their tracks at the unfamiliar sight of the female of the species.

Spying a uniform with enough embellishments to imply importance, Daniel advised his daughters to stay put, then hustled after and hailed the army officer.

"Begging your pardon, Sir, I wonder if I might impose upon you for a bit of information."

The officer, a captain, looked Lewis over, noting worn shoes, dust-covered trousers, and worn shirt rolled at the sleeves. "What can I do for you?"

"As you might have surmised, my family and I have only just arrived here. It has been a long road from Missouri. Where might we go in search of accommodations?"

"Accommodations? Of what kind?"

"Well, my good man, a rental house, perhaps. Or a house taking boarders if it comes to that. Even a hotel, on a temporary basis. We have been traveling these four weeks and are weary and in need of a comfortable place to rest for a time."

The captain smiled, then shook his head. "I don't know that you'll find what you're looking for here in Fort Smith. As you can see, we have more people than we have town at the time."

"It does seem busy. For what cause?"

"The government is funding the rebuilding of Fort Smith—the military base, that is. What with all the Indians the War Department is removing to Indian Territory, the Arkansas politicians lobbied that soldiers be garrisoned here for protection."

"I see."

"So, we've had to bring in workers from New England to do the work. They've built a sawmill, put up a brickworks, dug wells—well, all that won't matter to you. What does matter is that there wasn't much in the way of public lodgings in the first place, and with all these extra men, you won't be finding a room to rent, let alone a house—or even a bed to share."

Daniel, hands clasped behind his back, lips pursed and brow wrinkled, considered his next question. "Is there work available for a body hereabouts, then?"

"It shouldn't take a man more than five minutes to find a job as a laborer. If you've any skills, not even that long."

"Would we find a place to establish a camp? Perhaps build a cabin?"

"Plenty of room. Were I you," the captain said with a nod toward Daniel's wagons and the Lewis girls standing by, "I'd find me a place outside of town, well away from Belle Point. Those young ladies will for sure attract unwanted attention otherwise."

Daniel soon discovered the accuracy of the captain's comments on the housing situation in Fort Smith—and the magnetic nature of his daughters. Looking to the south, he found a campsite on Mill Creek. He fitted up a platform of milled lumber and erected a walled tent atop it, purchased from army surplus. With the few pieces of furniture and rugs unpacked from the wagons, and a small potbelly stove purchased in town, the shelter proved cozy.

Mary, Martha, Emma, and Jane arranged sleeping pallets on the tent floor; Daniel spooled out his bedroll in a wagon bed. A wagon sheet served as a kitchen fly and a rocked-in fire pit the cook stove.

Work was easy to come by. Daniel hired on at the brickyard, simple stoop labor as an off-bearer, hauling pallets of molded bricks to the drying yard, where they lay until ready to be kiln-burned. His daughters took in laundry and the workmen kept them so busy that even after buying extra buckets and tubs and paying for delivery of cordwood they turned a tidy profit. Soon they invested in a town buggy and horse to pull it to make pickup and delivery and running errands more efficient.

At every opportunity, Daniel haunted any gathering of men he could find, seeking information about Texas. Other than stories about the revolution—Goliad, the Alamo, San Jacinto—he learned little about the Republic. Most of the men in Fort Smith came from the southern states or the East; only a few had seen Texas firsthand. He did learn there was cheap land for all takers, and prospects were good for those willing to face the tenuous political situation there—Mexico threatening to fight to regain possession, some Texians petitioning for annexation by the United States, others for maintaining independence from both powers. Liking what little he heard despite possible setbacks, come spring Daniel Lewis planned to continue his quest for Texas.

It would take some doing to change his mind.

Chapter Fourteen

Blood sprayed from Ben Pate's slashed throat, then streamed, slowed to a dribble, then seeped with only an infrequent drop absorbed by the syrupy bog soaking in the dust.

Abel sat in a sagging heap on the edge of the sidewalk, his own strength seeming to dissipate along with Uncle Ben's blood. The knife, heavy in his hand and heavier on his mind, stuck to his fingers as he tightened and loosened his grip on the ornamented handle. His mind ricocheted from shock at what he'd done to wonder at what he would do, to fear of the course his life would take as a result—pinging wildly from one frenzied thought to the next. Getting out of town, out of Shelby County, out of Tennessee, was a given. But how to get what he came for before leaving was not.

He picked up his uncle's hat and brushed it off. He looked it over, turning it in his hands, staring into the crown as if the answer he sought might be hiding there like the rabbit in a magician's top hat.

And then he knew.

For a while, he would become his Uncle Ben. Cloaked in his uncle's long coat and wide-brimmed hat, with the aid of the dark of night, he just might pull it off, if only for a moment. That, he hoped, would be time enough.

Abel shrugged into Ben's linen duster and pulling the borrowed hat low, he walked down the quiet streets toward his uncle's house. He maintained a deliberate pace, fighting the urge to run and compromise the disguise. With hunched shoulders and bowed head, he mimicked his uncle's inebriated gait.

Every step pounded the killing deeper into his unsettled mind, spawning fears that in taking on the evil man's countenance he had also absorbed his soul. Grabbing a gatepost for support, he paused outside Uncle Ben's dark house as his insides once again attempted to void themselves.

With a deep, shuddering breath, he eased open the door.

"Peter!"

The stillness of the big house echoed with the call Peter was not sure he had heard. With eyes slowly blinking themselves awake, he lay listening in his bed.

"Peter!"

This time, there was no doubt. Peter swung his feet out of bed and felt around the floor for the carpet slippers there. Slipping on the robe that hung from a hook on the back of the door of his small room, he opened the door and looked into his employer's office. The faint odor of sulfur matches tickled his nose.

Against the dark window, he made out the darker silhouette of a man in a wide-brimmed hat seated at Ben's desk. "Ben? Is that you?"

The only answer was a grunt.

"What is it? What do you want, Ben?"

"Get the key to the safe," the slurred voice said.

Drunk. Again. Peter retreated to his room, fetched his keys, and returned with a lit lantern. He raised it high, saw Ben swiveled in his chair, facing the window. He set the lantern atop the lockbox, fiddled with his ring of keys for the one he sought, and opened the lock.

"Now, step away," came a voice—not Ben's, and cold sober.

Peter turned to see the borehole of a pistol in the hand of the man standing over him. He recognized the shadowed face under the hat as that of one of the men who were here earlier—yesterday, now—arguing with Ben. He moved away from the open safe and stood, the pistol following his rise. The gun, he saw, was one of a pair of caplock revolvers—some of the first manufactured by Samuel Colt—that were Ben's pride and joy. He saw the other pistol on the desk, taken down from the wall where the boss displayed it and its mate.

"Wh-what do you want?"

"You know what I want. Get that Bible and that other book out of the safe," Abel said as he ratcheted back the hammer.

Without a word, Peter dropped again to his knees, rustled around in the safe and came up with the books. Abel gestured with the pistol, and Peter handed them to him, one at a time. Abel slipped the books into a coat pocket. *These books ain't all that big, given all the trouble we went to to get them.*

"I suppose you want the money, too," Peter snarled.

"No. I got what I came for. Now, get up."

"Where's Ben?"

"Don't you worry none about that."

"He's dead, isn't he?"

"I said don't worry about it." Abel gestured again with the pistol. "Get dressed."

"Why? What are you going to do to me?"

"You're coming with me. Need you out of sight for a few days. Now, get dressed."

Abel stood in the doorway of Peter's room, watching him pull on clothes and shoes. "Ain't you got any boots?"

"No. Why?"

"Them city shoes ain't likely to hold up where we're going."

The blood left Peter's face and his eyes went wide.

"Where are we going?"

"Don't worry about it. Let's go." Abel stepped back from the doorway to let his hostage through. He stepped to the desk and pocketed the other revolver. "I will take these guns," he said. "Ben won't be needing them."

Peter blanched again. "You killed him, didn't you?"

Abel did not answer.

"How? You're not much more than a boy."

"Man enough, I guess," Abel said. "Now, where does Ben keep powder and caps and balls for these things?"

Peter gestured with his chin toward a drawer chest beneath where the pistols hung.

"Get them."

Peter did, and handed them gingerly to Abel, who stuffed the pouches into the coat pocket with the second pistol. "Let's go."

Peter led the way out the door and into the still-quiet, dark town. Abel, hard on his heels, nudged him now and then with the pistol barrel.

Neither man knew what would happen next.

Chapter Fifteen

Blue dawn hung heavy over the Mississippi River. Even the songs of the morning birds seemed listless to Melvin as he sat on his blankets, listening to Richard's sleepy breathing. The tethered mules were growing restless, rattling their halters and hoof-scratching at the ground. He contemplated stirring up a fire from the gray ashes in the fire pit and boiling coffee but cast the thought aside.

Tired to the bone after a fitful night, Melvin could sleep no more. He worked his shoulders slowly, wincing at the pain. Twice in two days he had endured severe beatings, both at the hands of family, first Uncle Ben and then little brother, Abel. All owing to the foolish notions of an addlepated Pa.

Some family.

The mules stirred. Melvin followed the direction of their alert ears, and movement on the path toward the campsite lifted him from his torpor. Two men approached.

"Rich! Wake up!"

Richard rolled to his stomach and raised to hands and knees. He wagged his head, snorted, turned to sit on his backside. "What? What is it?" he said, scrubbing his face with the palms of his hands.

"Somebody's coming."

"Who? Where?"

"Two men. Look!"

Melvin's stomach roiled at the sight of the man in the long

duster and wide-brimmed planter's hat.

"Damned if it ain't Uncle Ben!"

"What?" Richard said, his sleep-smeared eyes still trying to focus.

"Uncle Ben. And it looks like that man what works for him. You know—the one what was at the house."

Richard flipped back over to his hands and knees and scrambled to grab the rifle where it leaned against a tree. He pulled back the hammer and checked the seating of the cap. He turned over to sit, shouldered the weapon, and found the approaching men at the end of the barrel.

Melvin whispered, "You suppose they've killed Abel?"

Richard laid his cheek against the rifle stock. "Don't know. Serve the little bastard right if they did." He took a deep breath hoping to steady his heart, pounding from the suddenness of the men's approach. "Stop right where you are!" he hollered.

The men stopped, studying the situation. Abel raised his hands. "Put the gun down, Rich. It's only me."

Richard lowered the rifle barrel, staring without comprehension at his little brother, looking for all the world like his Uncle Ben. He lifted the barrel upright, and used the rifle, buttstock on the ground, as a prop to get himself upright.

Melvin, too, found his way to his feet, flinching at the hurt. "Abel? What the hell? What you doing in Uncle Ben's clothes?"

Abel and Peter walked on toward the camp.

Richard said, "Mel, gather some wood and get that fire going."

"But Rich! I—"

"Do it! Now!"

Muttering in indecipherable annoyance, Melvin set about gathering driftwood. Abel, weary from the long walk through the night, skirting most of Memphis, lowered himself to a seat on Mel's blanket. "Might as well sit," he told Peter.

The captive collapsed in a rumpled heap, unaccustomed to so much strenuous walking for so long a time or so far a distance. Head hung low, he swayed slowly where he sat.

"What the hell's he doin' here?" Richard said.

"Had to bring him along," Abel said. "Otherwise, we'd have the law on us by now."

"What happened?"

"I got Pa's books. That's all that matters."

"The hell you say! What about the law bein' after us?"

"I don't believe they will be, yet. But they'll be coming."

The steam whistle on the ferry boat sounded from the landing.

"Mel!" Abel called. "Drop that wood and get on back here." To Richard, "We had best be on that ferry."

Richard bristled at the orders coming from his baby brother. But, sensing a ticklish situation, he set resentment aside and the brothers gathered their camp goods and rolled them into bundles, piling the plunder on hastily cinched saddles atop the mules. Richard and Melvin grabbed the lead ropes and set out for the landing.

With the toe of his boot, Abel prodded his listless hostage. "Get up!"

Wide-eyed and slack-jawed, Peter looked his way and said, "What? You're making me go with you across the river?"

"Get up. We've got to get going."

"What are you going to do with me?"

Abel hoisted him to his feet by the collar and shoved him along after the mules. "We ain't got time to worry about that right now. Light out for the ferry and don't dawdle."

Once the brothers and Peter were settled on board, questions came in a torrent. Abel told how he had stumbled upon Uncle Ben in town while on the way to his house. How Ben, so drunk he could barely stand, attacked him nonetheless and came within an inch of slitting his throat. How he managed to get the best of him and return the favor.

The telling made salt and bile rise once again in Abel's mouth and his stomach turned. He interrupted the story and sat with head bowed between his knees, waiting for the nausea to pass. Peter, sitting near enough to overhear Abel's account, looked as white and disturbed as the foam in the paddle wheeler's wake.

Impatient and edgy, Richard urged Abel on. "Good Lord, Abel. That was nothin' short of murder."

Abel's head jerked upright at the accusation. "It was him or me! You didn't feel the steel of that knife blade against your throat."

" 'Course not. I got better sense than to keep after a man who already told me no. God knows what kind of a fix we're in now."

Abel stewed on that for a moment. He pulled the Bible and journal from the pocket of the duster. "Pa sent us for these books. We come all this way for them. I meant to carry out Pa's wishes, and I did. You-all ain't nothing but cowards and quitters."

Richard swatted at Abel with his hat, but Abel snatched his wrist and turned the blow aside. He continued twisting the arm until his brother cringed, then cast it aside. Rubbing at the offended wrist, Richard said, "You had best watch yourself, little brother. Fact is, you killed a man. Even as far gone as Pa is, I don't reckon he'll take kindly to you killing his brother."

"I did what he asked me to do," Abel said, then stood and stomped off down the deck.

Chapter Sixteen

By the time Richard and Melvin unloaded the mules and made the Arkansas shore, Abel was waiting.

"Where's Peter?"

"How the hell would I know?" Richard said. "Come to that, why the hell would I care?"

Without a word, Abel ran up the stage onto the boat. After a few minutes, he returned, Peter in tow.

"What do you want him for, anyway?" Melvin said.

"Think it over, big brother. He stays on the ferry and gets back to Shelby County, what's the first thing he'll do?"

Melvin pursed his lips and wrinkled his brow, but came up with no response.

Abel said, "He'll go to the law, that's what."

"You mean to keep him with us?" Richard said.

"Well, sure. Leastways till we're out of reach of Shelby County law."

Peter witnessed all this in silence, but could hold out no longer. "Wait a minute! I do not intend to go one step further with you-all."

"You don't have any choice in the matter," Abel said.

Richard said, "Aw, hell, Abel. Let's let him go. We don't need him draggin' along with us all the way across Arkansas—feedin' him and all!"

"Think about it, Rich. By now somebody's probably found Uncle Ben's body—if not, it won't be long. I hid it best I could, but it ain't like it will be hard to find, bein' as it's right on the main street of town. And once they find him, him being who he was in Shelby County, they won't waste a minute looking for who killed him."

"They will find me missing!" Peter cried. "The blame will fall on me!"

"Maybe, maybe not. If they do, that's not such a bad thing to my way of thinking."

Peter's breath came in short gasps and his face turned pallid; Richard provided contrast with his complexion tinged with red. No one spoke as the men studied one another in turn.

All but Melvin, who appeared disconnected from the whole situation. He swayed slowly back and forth for a time, then broke the silence, and the spell. "I'm hungry. When we goin' to get something to eat?"

After breakfast in a Hopefield eatery, the brothers set about planning their return. With the three gold eagles Richard held back from the money offered Ben, he allowed they would make the trip without going hungry. They purchased beans, bacon, flour, cornmeal, salt, rice, dried fruit, coffee, a cooking pot, skillet, coffeepot, and a tin plate, cup, spoon, and fork apiece. Packed in canvas sacks hung from the saddle skirts and slung across the seat and atop it, the provisions left no room for riders.

Richard tugged the last leather tie tight. "Looks like we're all a-hoofin' it all the way this time, boys."

Melvin said, "I don't mind, long as I get something to eat regular-like."

Abel looked things over, smiled and shook his head.

"What is it, baby brother?"

"Well, Rich, it's these mules of Pa's."

"What about 'em?"

"By the time we get back to Ma and Pa, they won't know if

they're draft mules, saddle mules, or pack mules."

Even Peter thought the observation worth a chuckle and joined the chorus.

"We had best get a move on," Abel said. "The law likely don't know who they're looking for or where to look as yet. I'd as soon we were long gone and forgotten before they figure it out. Any luck, they never will."

"We'll go, all right," Richard said. "But don't you be gettin' in the habit of givin' orders around here. It might have slipped your mind that you're just a kid, but I ain't forgot."

Step by step, mile by mile, day by day the brothers and Peter followed the old Military Road across the swampy lowlands of eastern Arkansas, towing the laden mules along. One evening by the campfire, Peter massaged blistered feet, soothed somewhat from a long soak in a stream feeding the Arkansas River, but still sore and worn from the unaccustomed walking. "We are a long way from Tennessee, gentlemen," he said. "How much longer do you intend to hold me captive?"

"You really want to be turned loose to fend for yourself out here?" Richard said.

"No. Not really. What I meant to ask, I suppose, is what you intend to do with me."

Richard kneaded his whiskery chin as if he could work out an answer that way. "Don't know. We ain't far from Little Rock. We'll see about it then. For all we know, first thing you'll do is set the law on us."

Abel walked out of the woods, silhouetted in the fading twilight. Peter lurched upright.

"What's the matter?" Abel said.

Peter relaxed and settled back into his stoop. "It's that hat and coat. I thought for an instant there you were Mister Pate. Ben, I mean."

Melvin said, "Gives me a start myself now and then. You aim

to keep them clothes of Ben's?"

"Don't see why not. It's a good hat. And I like this here duster. Lots of pockets and whatnot."

Richard said, "What you got in them pockets, anyway?"

Abel pulled a bundle from one side pocket and unwrapped the cloth he had wrapped around the Bible and diary, then rewrapped them and put them back in the pocket. "I reckon these is as safe here as anywhere." From the opposite pocket he pulled one of Ben's Colt revolvers.

"Holy hell!" Richard said. "Where'd you get that?"

"It was Uncle Ben's. Got another one, too," Abel said, pulling the other revolver from an inside pocket. "They was hanging on the wall in his office there, so I borrowed one to persuade Peter here to cooperate."

"That so?" Richard said.

Peter nodded, and told the brothers how he had been fooled by Abel's disguise into opening the safe. "Once he had obtained those books, he held me at gunpoint and forced me to come along."

Abel laughed.

"What's so funny?" Melvin said.

"What he don't know," Abel said with a nod toward Peter, "is that that gun wasn't even loaded. Wasn't then, isn't now, ain't never been."

Peter reddened at the revelation.

Richard, equally florid, said, "You've had them pistols all this time? You ought to've give them to me!"

Abel's only response was a questioning look.

"Damn it, boy! I'm the oldest one! You got no right deciding who gets what around here—that's mine to decide."

Abel shook his head. "If you wanted something from Uncle Ben, you should have went yourself and got it. I'm the one that got what Pa sent us for, not you. These here pistols helped me do the job, so I helped myself to them."

Richard sprung to his feet and stood toe to toe with Abel. Locked eyes blazed. Neither brother backed off.

"Aw, c'mon, Rich," Melvin said, wilting under the tense heat of the encounter. "Leave off. We'll let Pa decide once we get back."

"Right. And Pa'll say to let Abel keep them. He's Pa's pet, you know." Richard placed a hand on Abel's chest and gave him a push—enough to make a point but not enough to elicit a response—then walked away.

Melvin said, "Y'know, Abel, there's two of them pistols. Seems like you could give one to Rich."

Abel did not reply.

"Shut up, Mel," Richard said from across the fire. "Go check on the mules."

Abel squatted by the fire next to Peter. Peter said, "When do we get to Little Rock?"

"Tomorrow, maybe. Maybe the next day. You think them feet of yours will make it?"

"Oh, for certain. They still pain me, but they are toughening up. The reason I ask, is, your brother thought perhaps you would release me once we arrived in Little Rock."

Abel mulled it over. "Wish I knew, Peter. Wish I knew."

Across the fire and at the edge of its light, Richard rustled around in the supply sacks. He found what he was looking for, rolled in a bag padded for protection. He sat in the dark, uncorked the jug and took a long, slow draught of whiskey, all the time eyeing Abel.

Chapter Seventeen

Sarah Pate knelt and lowered the bucket into the creek, tipped the open mouth upstream and watched it sink as it filled. She hefted it out of the water as she stood and listed into the weight as she carried the heavy pail back to camp.

As she stepped into the clearing four men and two mules trailed in from the opposite direction. Water geysered out of the dropped bucket when it hit the ground, but it remained upright. "Lee!" she said in an attempt at a yell, pinched off by her caught breath. "Lee!" she said again.

Her husband backed out of the bed of the wagon with axe in hand. He had crawled in to fetch it, bent on replenishing the wood pile. "What is it, Sarah?"

"The boys! The boys are back!"

Lee followed the direction of her pointed finger. "Land sakes! We was startin' to wonder if you boys would ever make it back," Lee said.

Finding herself, Sarah rushed into Richard's arms. He lifted her off her feet and spun her around in a hug. She tore herself away and clinched Melvin and kissed his cheek. Then it was Abel's turn, and he embraced his mother then held her at arm's length. "Ma, you look fine! We sure been missing you—Mel, well, he ain't much of a cook."

Lee stood back, watching the welcome. "Boys," he said, "it looks like you come back with more than you left with. Who is this fellow?"

Richard and Melvin looked at each other, then at Abel. Abel looked at Peter, then at his father. "That's Peter, Pa."

"Peter?" He squinted his eyes and wrinkled his brow and studied the man. Recognition dawned. "Peter—ain't you the office man who works for Ben?" Peter removed his hat and nodded. "What on earth are you doing here?"

Abel said, "It's a long story, Pa. I'll tell you-all about it later." He pulled the wrapped bundle from the pocket of his duster and offered it to his father. "Here's something else we brought back that you'll be more interested in."

Lee stared at the bundle in his hands, found his way to a stump that served as a camp chair and sat. Carefully laying the bundle on his lap, he unwrapped it slowly and deliberately. He smoothed the cloth wrap against his thighs, eyes locked on the little journal. He opened the cover and thumbed through the pages of the slim book then slid it under the Bible and did the same with it, running his eyes over the names and dates recording the history of his people. Rewrapping the bundle, he stood and set it on the stump.

"Boys," he said, wiping the dampness from the corners of his eyes with the ball of his thumb, "I don't have the words to thank you."

Sarah had plenty to say about the supplies the mules still carried. She fussed and fluttered about the sacks and bags of food as the boys unloaded them. Knowing their folks had had no way to replenish their scant stores in their absence, and having grown accustomed to a more abundant diet, the brothers restocked supplies in Little Rock. They, as much as Ma and Pa, would appreciate having a little something to put in the pot.

Humming tunes and occasionally voicing snatches of song, Sarah flitted about the camp and the fire and her few cooking pots like a honeybee. She told the boys to get on down to the creek, declaring that if they expected a seat at her table—knowing full well the family lacked the luxury of a table—they had best clean themselves up.

The brothers finished unloading the mules, unsaddled them, led them down to the stream to drink and staked them out to graze, then pulled off their shirts and scrubbed up as best they could—paying particular attention to the parts that showed. Peter did the same. With fresh-shaved faces they trooped back to camp.

The boys settled into their accustomed places along the log, Pa on his stump, and Peter making do cross-legged on the ground. Ma scurried around, filling and refilling their plates with bacon, boiled rice smothered in gravy whipped up from flour and bacon grease, corn dodgers, and topping off the meal with refilled cups of coffee and stewed dried apples.

"Sorry I didn't have time to make a pie crust, or even batter for a cobbler," Ma said. "And I lack cinnamon spice. Still, you-all got the best part of an apple pie."

Lee tried, with limited success, to stifle a belch. "It was right fine, Sarah. Don't know when I've enjoyed a meal more." He stretched and yawned and squirmed into a more comfortable seat on the stump. "Now, suppose you-all tell me about your visit with your Uncle Ben."

None of his sons seemed eager to tell the story, looking from one to the other expecting someone else to start. Lee waited, sipping his coffee, but the tin cup clattered to the ground when Melvin finally burst out with, "Abel killed him, Pa!"

Once Pa caught his breath, the story unfolded. Richard told how Melvin went to see their uncle and asked for the books and took a beating for doing it. He told how they recovered the stash of gold eagles from the farmhouse and offered them—most of them—to Uncle Ben in exchange for the books, and how he had run them off and kept the money.

"We'd of let it go at that, Melvin and me. But Abel was

determined to go back and I couldn't stop him no matter what." Richard neglected to mention how he and Melvin attacked their younger brother but got the worst of it.

Lee sat quiet for what seemed a long time but could not have been more than a minute or two. Then, "Abel, I guess you better tell me about it."

Abel told how he had set out in the night from their makeshift camp on the river, skirting most of Memphis on the way to the town where Ben lived. He told how, by sheer luck—good or bad—he found his uncle drunk in the empty street.

"I wouldn't of done it, Pa, had I seen any other way. Uncle Ben was so drunk he couldn't hardly stand up, but he mustered the strength to almost kill me. I guess seeing that knife blade so near my throat, I just kind of lost my head. I feel awful bad about it, Pa. Real bad."

With that, Abel hoisted his pants leg and pulled Ben's heavy knife from the shaft of his boot and handed it to his father. "That there's the knife that nearly killed me—and did kill Uncle Ben."

Lee studied the knife, turning it over and over and admiring the fancy carving and inlays on the handle. "I remember this knife," he said. "Ben was right proud of it. Carried it around in a belt scabbard all the time, like he was fixin' to skin out a deer—even when he was sitting at his desk in town." He studied the knife some more. "Well, Son, it's a fine knife. I reckon you're the one to keep it if you want to, what with what you went through to get it."

Melvin said, "That's it, Pa? That's all? Abel kills Uncle Ben and all you got to say about it is he gets to keep the knife?"

Lee's brow wrinkled at the question. "I don't get what you mean, Melvin—Mel. I sent you boys to get them books and Abel done it. What else is there to say?"

But it was Richard who answered. "Good hell, Pa! He killed

a man! Our own kin! And he kidnapped Peter!"

Lee shook his head sadly. "Sometimes, boys, you just got to do what you got to do. Sure, Ben's dead. But he brought it on hisself, sounds to me like. He could have just given you-all the books in the first place. Abel only did what he had to—and he got the job done."

Later, Peter told the part of the story he knew. And again voiced his wish to be set free.

Lee pondered it for a while, then said, "Where would you go, if we was to turn you loose?"

It was Peter's turn to ponder.

"I cannot say, Sir. At first, I would have returned to Shelby County. But, without the job with Mister Pate, there is nothing to hold me there. I did not leave anything behind but a bank account, and I can obtain those funds no matter where I wind up. And, truth be told, working for Ben—Mister Pate—wasn't all that pleasant. I see that now that I am away from it. Richard suggested earlier I might be released in Little Rock, but Abel decided otherwise."

Richard interrupted Peter's story. "That's another thing—Abel comes more and more to think he can tell me and Mel what to do. The boy can't remember his place."

Lee said, "It looks to me, Richard, like you and Melvin might do well to pay attention to your younger brother."

He thought another minute or two as his older sons fumed, then spoke to Peter. "Well, Peter, I don't know what to do with you. Abel's got a point that you might go to the law the minute we set you free."

"I would not do it, Sir. You have my word."

"Would you swear to it on that Bible?"

"Absolutely, Mister Pate."

"Well, come morning we'll pack up and go on to Fort Smith. Maybe by the time we get there we'll have an idea what to do."

When they packed, the journal and family Bible, wrapped in sacking, went into the wagon's jockey box.

Chapter Eighteen

Emma Lewis stood breathless on the makeshift dance floor. She, like practically every other female residing in Fort Smith, including her three sisters, found it all but impossible to sit out a dance. Women were at a premium in the town, especially with the influx of army troops and workers imported to rebuild the military post.

Her previous partner had scarcely dropped her hand and bowed when another stepped in, took her by the hand, and requested the pleasure of the next dance. It had been so all evening for Emma and the other women—from the sixty-two-year-old wife of a merchant all the way down to Emma's sister Jane, who was only thirteen.

The dance floor, an almost-level platform of nailed-up planks sprinkled with candle shavings, was lit by the dim glow of lanterns hanging from corner posts and bonfires laid in stone circles at each side of the rectangle. The two fiddlers, the banjo-playing soldier, and a woman with an accordion—the only female not on the dance floor—were as weary as the dancing women from playing nonstop through the evening. One of the fiddlers announced the next song would be the last, as the hour was late and the men all had work the next day.

The Lewis girls, too, had work the next day. Morning found them, as usual, filling wooden washtubs, adding boiling water and lye soap slivers, scrubbing soggy garments against wash-boards or stirring and beating them with a dolly stick in a dolly tub, rinsing, then hanging laundry from the web of clotheslines strung about the creek-side work area.

The job was not easy, but the nature of it allowed all the time the girls needed to compare notes about last night's dance and the men they took a turn around the floor with.

"That Lieutenant Anderson dances like he has wings on his shoes."

"Oh, but Matthew Adams from the brickworks, he is lighter on his feet still."

"That soldier Griffith—I disremember his Christian name—he danced well early in the evening but later, well, too much drink made him tangle-footed."

"Did you see the two who came to blows? I don't know their names, but they were going at it hammer and tongs. It must have been a dozen men it took to pull them apart."

"I suppose such behavior is to be expected. Many of the soldiers are from the South, and the brick makers and builders are New England Yankees."

"Aye, and add whiskey to the mix and trouble will not be avoided."

"Still and all, the men here are better behaved than those Missouri Pukes we lived among, times past."

"Emma, I do believe that Sergeant Beauregard is sweet on you."

"Oh, Mary, he is not!"

Martha said, "Pa won't hold with any of us taking up with an army man. Especially not with war coming."

"Nonsense. There will be no war," Mary said.

"Some say so."

"Aye, Martha, and they have been saying so for years."

And on and on they talked until midafternoon when a man unfamiliar to them came along. He looked to be about their father's age and stood waiting, hat in hand, until the girls paid him attention.

"Good afternoon, Sir," Mary said. "Is it clean laundry you are wanting?"

"No. No thank you, ladies. I'm lookin' for a gentleman who goes by the name of Daniel Lewis. I was told he has set up housekeeping hereabouts. Do you know him?"

"Aye. He is our father and this is his home, such as it is. I am Mary Lewis, his oldest."

"Is your father about?"

"I am afraid not. He is at work in the brickyard. But you will find him here this evening should you care to call again."

"I will do that. Thank you," the man said with a slight bow. He set his hat upon his head and turned to go.

"A moment, Sir," Mary said. "Can I tell father who came calling?"

"Of course. My name is Lee Pate."

"We shall see you later, Mister Pate. I assure you father will be expecting your visit."

With another bow, Lee walked back to near Fort Smith where he had left his family and Peter waiting with the wagon earlier that day. Peter was still there. And Sarah. And Abel. Richard and Melvin, however, were nowhere in sight.

"Where are the boys?"

"They've gone on into town to have a look around," Sarah said.

"Should have waited, like I said."

"Oh, they won't come to any harm. It's been tiresome waiting. What did you learn in town?"

Lee took off his hat, pulled a rag from his pocket and mopped his forehead and the hat's sweatband. "No shortage of work here. Finding a place to live, now that's another matter. Army's putting up a new fort and the workers have taken every place with a roof."

Sarah said, "What are we to do, then?"

"I was told of a family—man with three or four girls, I think—came to town a while back with a pair of wagons. They set themselves up in a nice camp on Mill Creek. Went to have a look, and see if we could join them."

"And?"

"Daniel—that's the man's name, Daniel Lewis—is workin' in the town. Girl of his said come back this evening. Why don't you come along with me, see what you think?"

Sarah nodded. "I suppose. I do tire of living out of this wagon and cooking on an open fire."

"Might be the best we can do, for now."

Sarah laughed without mirth. "No. The best we could do we left behind in Shelby County."

Lee called for Abel and sent him to Fort Smith to fetch his brothers. "Take Peter with you, if you care to. But keep an eye on him."

"Thank you, Mister Pate. I swear I won't cause any trouble for you-all," the captive said.

It did not take long to locate Richard and Melvin. After trying the streets, grog shops looked to be a likely prospect. In the second saloon they tried, Abel and Peter found Richard and Melvin propped at the far end of the bar. A bucket of beer sat before Melvin, residue of its foamy contents clinging to his scraggly mustache. Richard drained off the contents of a shot glass and refilled it from the whiskey bottle at his elbow.

"Well lo and behold! If it ain't my baby brother, Abel. Come to have a drink with us, did you, Abel?"

"You know better than that."

"How 'bout you, Peter?"

"No thank you, Rich. I would not care for anything right now."

Richard tossed back the contents of his glass and refilled it.

"What brings you-all out on this fine afternoon, then?"

Abel said, "Pa wants you two back at the wagon."

"Some particular chore he's got in mind for us?"

"He didn't say. He just said he wanted you-all back, and that ought to be enough."

Abel looked at Melvin. Melvin looked at the floor. Richard swirled his glass around and around on the bar, watching the whiskey climb the sides. He stopped and poured the shot down his throat.

"Well, it ain't good enough for me. You tell the loony ol' coot I'll be back when I'm damn good and ready."

Abel reddened at the insult to their father. "C'mon, Rich! He's your Pa!"

"That he is. But I ain't a kid anymore and I ain't dancin' to his tune 'less it suits me."

"Rich. . . ."

"Abel. . . ."

"How about you, Melvin?"

Melvin sipped his beer, wiped his mouth with his sleeve, and tried—without much success—to stifle a belch. "I told you not to call me Melvin. I go by Mel now."

"You comin' or ain't you?"

Melvin looked at Richard. Richard gave his head a slight shake.

"No, Abel, I don't guess I am. I'll stay here with Rich."

Abel left the saloon with Peter on his heels, wondering all the way back to the wagon what he was going to tell his father.

Chapter Nineteen

Lee squatted low, head leaned into the cow's flank. The milking almost finished, he grasped the teats between thumb and forefinger and in turn stripped the last of the milk from the udder. He looked into the pail. *Not deep enough in there to drown a field mouse.*

He stood, patted the cow on the hip, and carried the bucket to Sarah. She shook her head at the milk—little more than a puddle. "It's a good thing we're not relying on that cow to feed us or we'd starve for certain."

"They tell me work is easy to come by here. With me and the three boys working, we ought to have money enough to eat well."

Sarah poured the milk into a skillet sizzling hot on the fire with grease from the bacon she'd just fried. When the milk boiled, she tossed in a handful of flour and stirred until it thickened into gravy. She plopped biscuits for herself and Lee onto plates and spooned gray over the top then forked on slices of bacon. They sat on the wagon tongue, plates on their laps, and ate.

Sarah saw Abel and Peter coming back from town, gestured their direction with her fork and said, "What about Peter? We planning to keep on feeding him?"

Lee watched them coming for a moment. "Can't say. We'll have to figure something out. Maybe he'll find work and pitch in something for the pot." He chewed his food and waited for

Abel and Peter to make it back to the wagon. They did, and stood in silence. "Well, Abel?"

Abel took off his uncle's hat and hung his head. "We found 'em, Pa."

Lee waited.

"They didn't want to come back with us."

Lee said nothing.

Abel stood the silence as long as he could. He turned the hat slowly in his hands. "They was in a saloon."

Lee clenched his jaw, shook his head slowly. "Drinking?"

" 'Fraid so. Rich is drunk, but he ain't silly-stupid so. You can't tell with Mel—you know how he is."

"That sound right to you, Peter?"

"Yes, Sir. Rich was adamant about not coming back. Even angry, you might say."

Sarah said, "Lee, you ought not expect those boys to do your bidding without question anymore. They're not children, you know."

Lee stared at her in disbelief. "They may not be children, Sarah, but they are still our boys. You know as well as I do they weren't brought up to be drunkards."

"They might not of been raised drinkers, but these past months puttin' up with you and your craziness could sway anyone to take it up."

The comment stunned Abel. Even Peter was taken aback. Only Lee appeared to take it in stride. He removed his hat, smoothed his hair with the palm of his hand and resettled the hat. "We'll deal with this later. Right now, I'm going to visit Daniel Lewis and see if we can set up camp near him. Sarah, you're welcome to come along."

She stood, took Lee's plate and stacked it on her own and set them on the wagon seat. She smoothed her apron front, did her best to tuck stray locks of hair back under her bonnet. "May as well, I suppose. Abel, Peter, there's food cooked. Help yourselves. I'll worry about cleaning up when we get back."

"Yes ma'am," Abel said. He put on his hat and watched his parents walk away.

Their day's laundering done, the Lewis girls bustled around the area of camp that served as kitchen and dining room attending to their father, keeping his plate and cup full. Mary saw Lee and Sarah coming and walked out to greet them.

"Welcome back, Mister Pate. As you see, Father is at home now and if you don't mind talking as he finishes his supper, he will be pleased to see you." She turned her attention to Sarah. "I suspect this must be Missus Pate."

Sarah confirmed it with a slight nod of her head. Lee said, "Yes, Miss, this is Sarah."

"Pleased to meet you—"

"—Mary. Mary Lewis." By now the other three sisters were lined up beside Mary. "These are my sisters, Martha, Emma, and Jane." The girls dipped with slight curtsies in turn.

The girls escorted the Pates to the table under a canvas fly where Daniel Lewis sat at his supper. Sarah looked enviously at the thick slabs of bread, the cold roast beef sliced thin, cheese, and pickles.

Daniel wiped mouth and hands with a napkin, then stood, bowed slightly to Sarah and offered a hand to Lee. "Daniel Lewis." Lee shook the hand and introduced himself and Sarah.

"My daughters warned me of your coming," Daniel said. "My apologies for your catching me tucking in, but I'm just home and hungry. Would you care to join me?"

"Looks tempting, Mister Lewis," Lee said with a glance at his wife. "But me and Sarah, we just ate ourselves."

Daniel nodded. "Sit, please. Now, what is on your mind?"

Lee explained they had come from Tennessee and hoped to lay over in Fort Smith for the winter, to work and earn money in preparation for pushing on in the spring.

Daniel smiled. "I find myself in much the same circumstances."

Sarah, eyeing the well-outfitted campsite and the two wagons, and seeing the four oxen lying on their bellies contentedly chewing their cuds, could see the Lewises' "circumstances" far exceeded their own.

"What we were wondering, Sir, what with houses and such scarce as hen's teeth, is if you would allow us to set up camp here along the creek. Looks like you've chosen a right fine place to pitch your tents."

Mary bustled around gathering the supper leftovers and dinnerware, trying not to intrude but not wanting to miss a word. The other daughters, equally curious, hovered nearby.

"It has proven providential," Daniel said. "We are near enough to town for convenience's sake, but far enough away to assure privacy. For the girls, don't you see."

"Them girls might be the fly in the ointment," Lee said. "See, I've got three boys—not boys anymore, men—and there's another man who—well, he's—I guess you could say he's been travelin' with us. You might not want them boys so close by."

Daniel laughed. "Not to worry, Mister Pate. My girls can take care of themselves when it comes to fending off unwanted advances. They—all except Jane, who is too young as yet to attract that kind of interest—are well and truly experienced at handling menfolk."

"So you don't mind?"

"Not at all. As they say here in America, it is a free country."

Lee stood and this time offered his hand. Daniel gave it a vigorous shake. Lee said, "Thank you kindly, Mister Lewis. I reckon we'll be joining you-all here tomorrow."

Chapter Twenty

Twilight darkened into night as Lee sat on the doubletree astraddle the wagon tongue, head resting against the wagon box, watching stars prick holes in the dome of the sky. Only glowing coals remained of the campfire. A ways off, he could hear the staked-out mules grinding grass and the occasional jangle of halters when they shook their heads, and he heard Sarah's rattly breathing from inside the wagon where she slept.

He heard Richard and Melvin long before he saw them. He tossed a couple of pieces of split firewood onto the coals and flames flared up. In the nearing distance, Richard would say something Lee could not make out, Melvin would laugh and snort, then Richard would laugh, and the performance would repeat. The brothers walked into the dim light, Richard grasping an uncorked and mostly empty bottle of whiskey.

"Pa!" he said. "Thought you'd be snorin' up a storm long 'afore now."

Melvin thought that funny.

Lee cleared his throat and spat. "When I went into town today, I thought I told you boys to wait here by the wagon with your Ma."

Richard drank from the bottle. Melvin poked him in the ribs and Richard passed the bottle along. "We waited some. Got to feelin' like I was growin' roots so we decided we'd go take a look-see at Fort Smith."

Lee said, "It weren't but a few hours you-all was asked to wait."

"It was long enough. Too long."

"You-all had pressing business in town, did you? So what did you-all see? Anything other than the bottom of a whiskey glass?"

The brothers glanced at each other and then seemed to take an interest in the dirt at their feet.

"You-all know I don't hold with drinking."

"Aw, Pa," Melvin said, hands in pockets and scratching at the dirt with the toe of his boot. "You been known to take a drink."

"That's true, Melvin—Mel. But only to be sociable. And never to put myself in such a state as I see you two in."

Richard raised his head and glared at his father, snatched the bottle from Melvin and took another pull, draining the bottle.

"I don't know what's to become of you boys. You-all could stand to take a page from your brother Abel's book."

Without a thought, Richard flung the empty whisky bottle at his father. It missed, shattering against the wagon.

Lee stared at the shards of glass on the ground glinting in the firelight. "I will disregard that, seeing as you ain't in your right mind, Son." He stood, hitched up his britches. "Come morning, we'll be moving camp. I expect you two to be up and around and helping." With that, he walked behind the wagon to the trees under which the men's bedrolls were spread out. He sat down on his bed and pulled off his boots. Abel and Peter were quiet, but he did not think them asleep.

After a moment, Lee crawled into his blankets, laced his fingers behind his head and studied the stars, thinking they should glow brighter than they had earlier and wondering why that did not appear to be the case. Perhaps there was a storm moving in.

He had no more closed his eyes than the snap and crackle of an axe splitting firewood awakened him. For a few minutes he did not move, listening to the sounds of morning filtering through the twilight. After sitting up and pulling on his boots, Lee scrubbed his face with the palms of his hands then walked into the woods to relieve himself. When he came back, he toed Richard and Melvin in turn with his boot. Melvin did not move; Richard burrowed deeper into his blankets. Lee toed them each again, this time with more determination. "If you boys are fixin' to fill your bellies, you-all had best roll out. There's work to be done, on an empty stomach or otherwise."

Abel had eaten and was throwing harnesses onto the mules when his older brothers came to the fire. They walked slowly, placing their feet gently with each small step. Neither had the stomach for bacon and corn dodgers, and the coffee they sipped roiled inside.

"You-all look like something a dog dug up," Lee said.

Richard's head jerked up to glare at his father, but the scowl failed to form when the sudden motion caused him to wince and squint. Melvin only slowly wagged his hanging head. He mumbled, "Why for we got to be up so early, Pa? Sun ain't hardly showin' at all."

"Like I told you-all last night, we're moving camp today, and there ain't no time like the present. I reckon there'll be plenty to do to get us settled in."

Melvin groaned.

Richard hacked and spat, nearly gagging himself as he did so.

Sarah shook her head in sympathy. "Lee, I don't see as there's all that much hurry. Let these boys set a spell and get their wits about them."

"Now, Sarah, these boys bargained for this suffering, and I ain't the one to deny them their reward. There ain't no reason they can't stir their stumps and help you and me and Abel and Peter get this stuff stowed in the wagon and on the way. No reason a-tall."

Abel drove the mules ahead of the wagon and as soon as he backed the team over the tongue, Lee lifted the yoke and fastened it to the collars while Abel hooked the traces to the singletrees. Peter hefted the kitchen box into the wagon. Lee sent Melvin to fetch the milk cow and Richard after their bedrolls.

Within minutes, Lee was on the wagon seat with Sarah beside him, snapping the lines and kissing up the mules to move. Peter and the brothers followed behind, Abel joking with his captive and Richard and Melvin moving slow and silent, still doing their best to avoid jarring their heads with each footfall.

As the wagon rattled its way toward Mill Creek and the Lewis camp, Lee watched the sky, wondering what the gathering clouds had in store.

CHAPTER TWENTY-ONE

The Lewis camp was all a-bustle when the Pate wagon rolled by. Mary and Emma bent over steaming washtubs working workmen's clothing and army uniforms against scrub boards while Martha dipped garments out of rinse water, wrung them out, and pegged them to clotheslines. Jane fed the fires and folded dried shirts and trousers on a plank table.

Lee and Sarah waved and the wagon continued on to the campsite they and Daniel Lewis had chosen. Richard and Melvin and Abel and Peter stopped as if at the end of a tether and stood watching the Lewis girls at work. No one spoke, but all four of the young men managed to remove their hats and hold them against their chests. The Lewis girls stopped work and looked the men over, but soon each was back at her task.

The wagon turned a narrow circle and Lee whoaed up the mules. He and Sarah sat smiling at the boys for a moment. He hollered, "Rich! Mel! Abel! Peter! You boys unhobble yourselves and get on over here!"

That calling of names was as close to introductions as there would be that day. When the wagon was unloaded, plans laid and orders given, Lee and Sarah drove into Fort Smith to arrange credit on lumber and surplus army tents and such supplies as they could bargain for. The boys set about grubbing brush and leveling the ground and digging fire pits and the like while the Lewis girls kept to their jobs, doing their best to ignore their new neighbors, but the camps exchanged furtive glances and curious stares throughout the day.

It was late in the day when the loaded wagon creaked and rattled back into camp. Sarah set about arranging supper as Lee and the boys unloaded and stacked lumber and emptied the wagon of the foodstuffs it carried. Just as the last of the load came out the endgate, Daniel Lewis joined them. He walked into the campsite, hitched his thumbs in his pockets, rocked back on his heels and said, "Well, neighbors, it looks like you are about getting your bits and bobs well organized. Lee, did the merchant I recommended suit your fancy?"

"He sure did, Daniel. Got most all we need on good terms. He says that with work goin' wanting he ain't the least bit concerned about us makin' good, what with four able-bodied men to draw wages."

Daniel nodded. "For certain there are jobs to be had. If I know my onions—and I believe I do—you gents could find work one and all at the brickyard. Then there are jobs digging foundations, working with brick masons, out in the quarry at Belle Point—and I am told the warehouses supplying the army need help. If you should care to, and your wagon is fit for such work, there is a constant need for drayage."

The men listened in interest. Peter said, "It looks as if a man can choose his circumstances."

"Aye, that is for certain." Daniel studied Lee's sons and smiled. "I've not seen such opportunity in donkey's years for a man of ambition. Your boys look strong, Lee, but these two look like they've got the collywobbles," he said with a nod to the two oldest boys.

Richard and Melvin reddened and took a sudden interest in the dirt between their feet. Lee said, "Nothing that won't pass. Them boys snuck into Fort Smith yesterday and struck up an acquaintance with John Barleycorn. Got to know him a mite too well. But I will sweat it out of them."

Melvin kept up scuffing the dust. Richard glowered at his father and walked away. But he did not go far and the men worked until dark and sleep.

Before the sun set on another day, the Pates had cobbled together a suitable, if temporary, home. Following Daniel Lewis's pattern, they erected two surplus army wall tents on wooden platforms. One would serve as sleeping quarters for the boys and Peter, the other would house Lee and Sarah and most of the provender and other supplies. Neither lodging included a stove, but if winter proved too harsh, those implements could be installed later. The wagon sheet, lashed to one side of the box, stretched upward to planted poles providing cover for kitchen work and a rough table with benches for eating. The cooking fire, positioned to reflect heat off the canvas, would afford some warmth as well.

Sunday would come with the sunrise so there would be no work at the camp, and no looking for jobs in town. Lee allowed the brothers and Peter leave to visit Fort Smith for the evening, admonishing against sampling the wares on offer at the saloons.

As shank's mare took the boys to town, talk turned to prospects for the evening. Peter allowed a walking tour would be time well spent. Abel agreed. "It'll give us some idea of the lay of the land," he said. "See where this brickyard Mister Lewis talked about is at, have a look at the fort they're building and whatnot."

Richard laughed. "You-all go on ahead, boys. There's a couple of barkeeps I've not met yet."

"Pa says not to!" Abel said.

"I don't give two hoots in hell what Pa said. It's Saturday night and I don't aim to waste it."

"But Pa says—"

"Oh, dry up about what Pa says. Look where his words has got us so far. Half of what he says is plumb crazy and the other half ain't worth listenin' to."

Abel bristled and only the jingle and rattle of an approaching wagon prevented his attacking his older brother. He unclenched his fists and turned to the trace behind. It was the Lewises' town buggy coming, Mary at the lines, Jane beside her, with Martha and Emma in the back seat.

Peter and Richard removed their hats and the men stepped aside to let the buggy pass, but Mary reined up beside them. "Good evening, gentlemen. On your way to town, I expect."

Abel, eyes locked on Emma, did not think to answer. He finally found the presence of mind to remove his hat, but did not find his voice. Melvin, tongue-tied on the best of occasions, reverted to his usual hidey-hole in the dirt between his boots. Abel elbowed him and gestured for him to take off his hat, which he did. Richard swallowed hard and stammered some, but no words would come. He, too, stared at Emma. Most men found her the fairest of the sisters, but none of the Lewis girls could be described as anything but attractive—including young Jane, just beginning to blossom.

It fell to Peter to speak. "Good evening to you as well, ladies. You surmise correctly—Fort Smith on a Saturday night is our destination."

Jane, at age thirteen knowing no shyness, piped up. "We're a-goin' to the dance! How 'bout you?"

"Dance?" Abel said, surprised at the sound of his own voice.

"There's a dance every Saturday night, almost! Them soldiers and other men even ask to dance with me!" Jane said.

Mary confirmed her sister's claim and mapped out the location of the dance floor in town. As she put the horse and buggy into motion, Martha spoke. "I hope we'll be seeing you gentlemen at the dance."

Emma did not speak, but Abel believed ever after that she gave him the slightest of smiles as she rode away.

Chapter Twenty-Two

Richard did not make it to the dance. At least not until too late. Unable—or unwilling—to resist the lure of liquor, he was drawn into the first set of swinging doors he encountered. Melvin, as was his wont, followed his older brother like a passive pup.

Abel and Peter navigated the town streets on the way to the dance, which they found as much by sound as sight, and joshed and joked in anticipation of meeting the neighbor girls. Finding the Lewis girls—and much of the rest of the population of young women of Fort Smith—was not difficult. A deep ring of men surrounded the females, thin at the edges and ever-more concentrated as it approached the women at its center. Many in the crowd sported well-worn but clean working clothes—some laundered at the Lewis camp—in contrast to the proper army uniforms—many of those cleaned courtesy of Lewis hands as well. The music players continued their preparations as men bargained for turns with the girls of their choice.

Elbowing their way through the mob, Abel and Peter found Martha. She dismissed with a smile and a promise the soldier who had her attention and turned it to her new neighbors. "Gentlemen. How nice to see you. You found your way without incident, apparently."

"We did," Peter said, doffing his hat. "Allow me, please, to introduce myself formally. I am Peter Neumann, late of Shelby County, Tennessee—" A sharp elbow in the ribs interrupted the introduction, and a pointed look from Abel reminded Peter to go no further in revealing his past. "I am pleased to make your acquaintance, Miss Lewis."

"Martha, please. And who is this man in the long coat?"

"His name is Abel Pate."

Abel bowed slightly. "Miss," he said, then put his hat—Uncle Ben's hat—back on.

Martha glanced around for her sisters and hailed Jane and Emma to join them. "I don't see Mary, but she's the one you spoke to earlier—the one driving the buggy."

With smiles and apologies, the other two sisters brushed off the attentions of several men as they made their way to join Martha.

"This," Martha said, taking Jane by the hand, "is our baby sister, Jane."

"I am *not* a baby!"

"Of course not, dear. Jane, say hello to Peter Neumann and Abel Pate." As Jane curtsied, Martha turned to Emma. "And this is our Emma—likely to be the belle of the ball tonight if history holds."

Emma blushed at the description. "Mister Neumann," she said with a nod. She turned to Abel and offered her hand. "Mister Pate."

Now it was Abel's face that flushed. "Call—call me Abel, please."

"As you wish, Abel." He reddened again at the sound of his name on her lips. "And you must call me Emma. No need for formality among neighbors, I should think."

"Yes, Miss—Emma, I mean."

Abel searched for more words and was relieved when Martha came to the rescue. "Where are the others who were with you? Brothers, I assume?"

"Yes, Miss Martha. My brothers, not Peter's. He's—he's—well, Peter has been traveling with us. Richard is the oldest.

Mel, the big one, is next. He don't say much. They might come along later."

"I hope so. It will be a pleasure to meet them."

"Maybe so," Abel said.

The pleasure did come, but not until much later. In the interim, the Lewis girls were in great demand and Emma, as Martha predicted, was pursued all evening long. Still, Abel and Peter found opportunity to dance with each of the Lewis sisters, even Mary.

Richard still had his wits about him when he and Melvin arrived, but they were severely impaired. Rather than carrying around an obtrusive bottle of whiskey, he sipped from time to time from a pocket flask. Melvin's state of sobriety was more difficult to determine.

The dance was at an end when the brothers found Abel and Peter talking with the Lewis girls at their buggy.

"Well, would you looky here," Richard said as he approached. "Got the whole neighborhood right here in one place."

"Richard," Abel said.

"C'mon baby brother, meet us up to these fine-looking ladies."

Abel introduced each of the sisters in turn.

Richard stood, hat over his chest, leering bleary-eyed at the girls. "Lemme see if I've got you-all sorted out." He pointed at each sister and said, "Mary, the boss. Jane, the baby—"

"I am *not* a baby!"

"—Martha, and Emma. I got to say, Emma, you are as cute as a spotted pup."

"Richard!"

"What is it, baby brother?"

"Mind your manners."

Richard plopped his hat on his head, turned to Abel, and prodded his chest with his forefinger. "Listen here, Abel," he said, punctuating each word with a finger poke. "I've told you for the last time not to be orderin' me around."

Abel grabbed the finger and held it immobile. "And Pa has told you more than once to behave yourself."

"The way I act ain't none of his affair, not no more. I'm a grown man and don't intend to take orders from him any longer."

Melvin stood back, eyes darting to follow the conversation. The Lewis girls quietly loaded into the buggy, with a hand up from Peter.

"As long as you're eating at his table you'll do as he says." He tossed Richard's hand aside and turned to the girls in the buggy. "Ladies, our apologies. Richard is not himself."

The girls drove away.

Richard stepped into Abel near enough to smother him with liquor-laced breath. "Don't you be apologizing for me, you little shit!"

Abel pushed him away. "You have embarrassed yourself, Rich. Our whole family, as far as that goes."

With a sharp intake of breath, Richard unleashed the fist of his right hand. Abel dodged and the blow slid off his shoulder.

"Stop it!"

"Why, you—" Richard reloaded for another blow but before he could unleash it, Abel smashed his brother's leering lips with a swift, straight punch.

Richard sat, landing with his head rattled and breath bursting out in a sour cloud.

"What's going on here?" a uniformed soldier on security duty asked as he hurried over.

"Ain't nothing," Abel said. "Family squabble is all. Mel, help Richard home. Pa will have something to say about this."

Richard, head weaving, managed to glare at his brother and slurred, "I'll be damned if I'll be listening."

Abel and Peter started for home. It would be some time before Melvin and Richard arrived at camp. When they did, Richard was accompanied by his newfound friend—the half-pint glass pocket flask.

Chapter Twenty-Three

The incident after the dance was set aside, if not forgotten. The Pates and Lewises settled into a comfortable routine, passing time together as occasion allowed. Many an evening they shared a meal or simple conversation. The young men's tongues eventually loosened in the presence of the girls and friendships formed. Lee and Daniel, in particular, found themselves companionable, enjoying conversations that sometimes lasted long into the night.

The Lewis girls invited Sarah to join their laundry enterprise, but she allowed that having raised three boys and through all her years of marriage to Lee she had washed more than enough men's clothes. Sarah did, however, agree to take over most of the cooking for the Lewis family, allowing the girls to devote more time to their work without the distraction of preparing meals. She even learned to cook up some family favorites from across the sea like Shepherd's Pie, bangers and mash, mushy peas, and pork pies.

As anticipated, the men had little difficulty finding work. Lee signed on to help the brickmakers at the brickyard. After the molded bricks Daniel and others arranged and rearranged and stacked in the drying yard sat for a couple of weeks, they were ready to be fire-hardened. Experienced brickmakers directed Lee and other laborers to stack green bricks in beehive-style arches with an opening to build a fire inside, so the bricks created their own kilns for firing.

Small wood and coal fires inside the arch cooked the water out of the bricks for a couple of days until they stopped steaming, then Lee and the other helpers plastered the outside of the arch with mud and built up the fires as the temperature inside the kilns rose to nearly 2,000 degrees, sweating the bricks dry. The fires were kept stoked for a week or so until the experts determined the time was right to seal up the fireholes and allow the kiln to cool down.

A goodly number of the bricks Lee helped fire eventually found their way to Melvin, who hired on as a hod carrier, or "hoddie." His strength allowed him to handle the work without much effort, toting a dozen bricks at a time in his hod to the two bricklayers he was to supply, and sometimes feeding a third. Melvin also used his hod, a three-sided box with a four-foot pole attached, to carry mortar.

Unaccustomed as he was to hard physical labor, and with a mind trained in different pursuits, Peter sought and found a position as a clerk in a warehouse owned by a merchant and trader supplying the quartermaster at Fort Smith, along with other commercial pursuits.

Abel hired on for the same employer, working as a warehouseman. Unloading crates and barrels from riverboats, storing them in warehouses, repacking items for local distribution, and accompanying deliverymen offered enough variety to keep the work from growing monotonous.

Richard went a different way, taking a job as a night watchman at the brickyard. The nature of the work allowed free evenings to congregate with newfound friends in the grog shops, and as long as he arrived at work on time and in a reasonable state of sobriety, his employer didn't worry much. If the night got too long, he might even sneak a nap between making his rounds. And although Richard worked alone, he was seldom without the company of his flask.

Over the weeks, the friendship between Lee Pate and Daniel Lewis flourished. Lee learned the Lewis family emigrated from Manchester in England when they converted to the Mormon church. Daniel's wife, the girls' mother, died of dysentery during the crossing. The Lewises joined their fellow Saints in Missouri and unexpectedly found themselves in the midst of conflicts with the old settlers bordering on all-out war. Although the family still held to the faith to some degree, Daniel chose not to join the exodus out of Missouri to re-settle with the Mormons in Illinois, opting instead to head south and try his luck in the Republic of Texas.

For his part, Daniel learned of Lee's distaste for the practice of slavery; an aversion that grew to revulsion. When Daniel broached the idea of the Pate family going with him to Texas in the spring, Lee refused to even consider the idea.

"The Texians embrace slavery just as our Southern states do. It is no less an evil in their republic than it is in ours," Lee said. "Besides, word is that Texas will join the Union soon. In any case, I'll not reside among slavers again."

Daniel said, "I am no supporter of slavery. The Prophet Joseph opposes it and has denounced it in his preaching. He does not count himself an abolitionist, but his views contribute to the persecution of our people."

"*His* views. But what about *your* views, Daniel?"

"To be honest, I have not given the subject much thought. I must say it seems an established practice here. Be a good bloke, Lee, and admit that your banging on about it is but flogging a dead horse."

Lee laughed. "Sometimes it seems so, and I almost believe it myself. But I cannot in good conscience come to terms with such evil. There is no choice for me but to remove myself and my family from it."

"And what do they think?"

Again, Lee laughed. "They think me—what's that word I've heard you use? Barmy?"

This time Daniel laughed. "Barmy may well describe it. So, where do you propose to go to remove yourself?"

"Mexico."

"Mexico! Lee! I believe you are off your nut! 'Tis a Papist nation, and I do not believe you count yourself among the Roman Catholics."

"No. But in the northern reaches of their territory I am told they pay little attention to religion and a man is allowed to follow his own convictions—if not by law, by practice."

On another occasion, Lee invited Daniel to come along with him to Mexico.

"I confess I know little—nothing, really—of the geography of which you speak. Where do you propose to go in Mexico? And how does one get there?"

"Aim for the sunset and you'll get there. There's a trail of sorts—not much of one. Go on up the Arkansas a ways till you strike the Canadian River. They say following that'll get you most of the way to Santa Fe—a city that's been a source of Mexican trade with the States for years."

"But what of the Indians?"

"It's Choctaw and Chickasaw country much of the way, all right. But I am told if we hold to the river and keep moving we should not be molested."

Daniel furrowed his forehead and pursed his lips. "Your proposal bears pondering, friend Lee. I shall take it under consideration."

Chapter Twenty-Four

Richard claimed another advantage owing to his contrary work schedule as a night watchman—the ability to spend hours in the company of the Lewis girls. Wet to the elbows, the girls scrubbed and wrung and rinsed and hung laundry through his visits. Always polite, but reluctant to engage, there were invariably tubs to refill, soap to shave, clotheslines to clear, shirts to sort, and a host of other tasks demanding attention.

One day, in yet another attempt to start a conversation, Richard said, "What do you-all think of Mexico?"

"Mexico?" Martha said. "Have not thought about it at all. Should I?"

Richard smiled. "Might be good to give it some thought. Could be you'll be living there soon."

Jane said, "Nah. We're a-goin' to Texas."

The smile held. "Then I guess you-all don't know that my Pa is worryin' your daddy like a dog with a bone, trying to talk him into followin' him to Mexico."

Fires snapped and popped, hung clothes flapped in the breeze, water still boiled and bubbled, but scrubbing and rinsing and wringing fell silent as four sets of eyes fixed on the visitor.

Mary found her voice first. "Why on earth would Father do that? He has been set on Texas for quite some time. He has said nothing to us of a change of heart."

"Could be he ain't interested. But Pa thinks he's got him

hooked like a catfish on a trotline."

"I do not understand," Martha said. "What is the attraction of Mexico? The Texians only recently fought a war to be shed of Mexico."

Richard shifted on the stump he sat on, removed his hat and raked his fingers through his hair. "Mexicans don't allow no slavery. Pa thinks slavery is so awful it will destroy the United States. Been sayin' so for years. Says he can't tolerate livin' among such sinful ways no more." He reset his hat and gave the brim a tug. "What do you think, Emma?"

Emma's eyes widened. "Well. . . . I do not know. We have heard much talk for and against slavery since coming here from England. And there is always talk of war, but most folks do not put much stock in it."

Martha said, "But Emma, you know the prophet Joseph Smith has predicted a war over slavery."

Richard laughed. "Some prophet! The man must be as crazy as my Pa."

"We will thank you not to speak ill of Joseph," Martha said.

"Sorry, ladies. I meant no offense." Again, the smile. "Emma, one of these days you'll have to tell me all about this Joseph Smith and the Mormons."

Mary answered for her sister. "Not today. There is work to do, girls, and we had best get back to it. Good day to you, Mister Pate." She hefted a basket of soiled laundry and tipped it into a steaming tub to soak. Emma immersed her arms up to the elbow in the tub before her and set to scrubbing an army tunic against the washboard.

That evening, when Daniel returned from work, his daughters bearded him with questions about Mexico.

"Father, what is this we hear about Mexico?"

"Have you given up on Texas?"

"Are we really going to Mexico?"

"Have you changed your mind, Father? Your heart?"

"Tell us, what are your plans?"

When the deluge subsided, Daniel answered Martha's question, "Did you intend to consult us about this, Father?"

"Girls! Please! Allow me to catch my breath and have a bite of supper. I have been working all day and am knackered. We will talk later. I will share my thoughts and you shall all have your say."

And so they did.

Daniel passed along the gist of his many conversations with Lee. Their neighbor's desires, he said, were not so much in favor of Mexico as they were disfavor of the United States. "The man makes a convincing argument against the institution of slavery and its inherent evils. I find it impossible to disagree. He assigns the same sin to the Republic of Texas, as slavery is permitted in their Constitution. And he, like many, contends that Texas will soon be annexed into the United States and such an eventuality will heighten sectional differences."

Mary thought a moment. "But Father—we have been living among slaveholders since coming to America. Surely we can continue to do so, whether here or in Texas."

"Perhaps, Mary. Perhaps. Many are of the opinion—Lee among them—that the abolitionists will continue to agitate, slaveholders will continue to resist, and war will result."

"Such rumors were rampant in Missouri, and we still hear them here," Martha said. "Many say they are but rumors, and that nothing will come of it."

Daniel agreed. "But many others believe war is inevitable. And remember, girls, to number the Prophet Joseph among those who hold such beliefs. Like Mister Pate, he contends that when war comes it will be destructive beyond contemplation and the very nation shall fall."

"Do you believe that, Father?"

"I do not know, Emma. Were it only Mister Pate and such ordinary folk who say so I would not be swayed. But when the Prophet says as much, well. . . ."

Martha said, "But father, Joseph calls the Saints to gather to Zion for protection against such storms—not run off to Mexico. Or Texas, for that matter!"

"This is so, but we know from sad experience that gathering with the Saints presents difficulties of its own. It offered no refuge in Missouri."

The girls, thoughtful, said no more until Jane spoke. "Are we a-goin' to Mexico, then, Father?"

"I do not know. I do believe it is an idea that merits consideration. But it need not be decided this evening. Will you think it over, please, girls, and we will speak of it again. But for now—to bed."

CHAPTER TWENTY-FIVE

As fall turned to winter and the months wore on, so did the discussions. There were debates about Mexico. Talk about Texas. Conversations about Fort Smith. Within and between the families and among their members, advantages and disadvantages were weighed and measured, pros and cons considered, and a variety of conclusions reached and decisions made and minds changed.

Lee never once wavered in his desire to remove himself and his family from the trouble the sin of slavery would bring—eventually, inevitably—to the United States and its people, and could not be convinced otherwise.

Sarah stayed steadfast in her desire to return to Shelby County and a life that no longer existed. Every day carried a reminder of her depressed circumstances, and bitterness with her situation festered. And, despite her complaints and pleadings, Lee seemed oblivious to her pain.

Richard remained determined to cast off his father's influence and make his own way. He had no idea what that way would be or where it might take him. But his lack of respect for his father owing to his dreams and delusions, combined with the favoritism toward Abel, led him to rebel more and more in matters large and small.

Melvin did not form opinions and did not concern himself much with the future. He, like Richard, was taken aback by Abel's attempts to assert authority—although he was not certain why it should bother him. He leaned on Richard for direction and was easily swayed by his older brother's opinions and actions.

Abel, alone in the family, revered his father. He was not troubled by his quirks and foibles, nor did he doubt the rightness of his father's desires for the family. If anything troubled the youngest of the Pates, it was the intransigence of his brothers and the insolence of his mother concerning his father and her husband. For Abel, it was simple: if Pa told him to do something, he did it, no ifs, ands, or buts.

Peter had come to like Fort Smith and his prospects in the growing city and hoped to remain. His life with Ben Pate was behind him and of no concern; the death of his former employer a fading memory. And while his being held hostage continued, it was more a matter of habit than fact. Peter had no intention of going to the authorities to report Abel's crimes and the Pates knew it. But while his presence among the family had become comfortable, Abel and Lee encouraged him—in no uncertain terms—to stay close, at least until they quit the country, just in case.

Daniel waffled. One day, he defended his decision to decamp to Texas. On the morrow, he promoted Mexico.

Mary seldom voiced an opinion, save that she could not wait to set out for any place—any place—that would get her hands out of a washtub.

Martha had but one opinion: the belief that ambition equals success and success equals happiness and geography did not enter into the equation.

Emma sometimes paused at her work, wash water settling around still arms as she stared at nothing and smiled for no apparent reason.

Jane was all for adventure and experience, and could not wait to load the wagons and get up the oxen. She did not care much about the trail they took.

But not all conversation centered around emigrating from Fort Smith. The Lewis women were young and feeling their oats; the Pate men—and Peter—were young and ready to sow some. The proximity of the families provided ample opportunity for pursuit. And so Richard pursued Emma doggedly, and until enlightened by Mary, was unaware his attentions were all but unnoticed.

"I know you have your eye on Emma," she said one evening. "But she has her heart set on Abel."

Richard sputtered and stuttered. "Abel ain't said anything about Emma—why, far as I know, he don't care a thing about her."

"I cannot speak for Abel. But I do know Emma's taken a liking to him. With his being a man and all, he will catch on sooner or later."

"Damn!" Richard said, uncorking his flask and tossing back a mouthful of whiskey. "That boy ain't nothin' but a bother to me. Pa thinks the sun rises and sets on him. And now you say he's takin' Emma away from me and he don't even know it."

Mary poked at Richard's flask. "I am not saying that is the reason for her lack of interest in you, but I am certain it will not further your cause so far as Emma is concerned. Our faith frowns on partaking of strong drink to excess and Emma takes the advice seriously, for herself and others."

Richard took another sip. "She's young. She might grow out of such notions."

Mary sat in silence for a few minutes as Richard sipped his whiskey. Finally, she said, "Do you find it difficult being the oldest child?"

After laughter with no hint of humor in it, Richard said, "Not so's you'd notice. Pa ain't never give me much responsibility or respect, even though it's owed. Abel's his pet and he gets all

Pa's favor. I try not to let it get to me—leastways, I used to try. But having it throwed in my face day after day is more than I can bear." He took another sip from the flask.

"It is different with me. Mother died aboard ship during our passage from England, and Father has expected me to fill her shoes since, although I am barely older than Martha. I do not believe I am well suited to it. And I believe I understand your frustration concerning Abel."

"How's that?"

Mary spent a moment composing her thoughts. "I am the 'odd man out' in our family, so to speak. Martha is much smarter than I, Emma much prettier, and Jane—well, she is coddled as the baby of the family—besides, she is still a child for the most part." Mary sighed. "It seems all I am good for is taking on the responsibility for most of the work."

The whiskey left in the flask was barely enough to swish around the bottom. Richard watched it swirl, poured it down his throat, pressed the cork into the bottle with the palm of his hand, and slipped the flask into his pocket.

"I had best be goin'," he said. "I've got a stop to make in town 'fore I go to work."

Richard did not make it to work that night. While making his so-called stop—refilling his flask at a saloon—he tipped back several glasses in an attempt to wash away any reminder of his conversation with Mary. And so he drank some more. The New England accent of a bricklayer at the bar grated on his nerves until he attempted to stop the sound with his fist. It did not work. The bricklayer let loose a Yankee bellow then he and Richard battered each other and broke up a good bit of the saloon while they were at it. Since witnesses all agreed Richard instigated the fight, he spent his night shift locked up in the Fort Smith city jail.

A shaft of morning sunlight cut through the high, barred

window in the cell and Richard squinted closed eyes tighter and turned away. Rolling over hurt. He lay still, flexing and tightening parts of his body in turn. He could not decide where or what hurt worst.

And then Abel showed up, saying he had been sent by Pa to fetch him home.

Chapter Twenty-Six

Lee managed to smooth things over for Richard at the brickyard. He could not bring himself to lie for his eldest son; only said that Richard was "indisposed" and unable to work. It seemed to him a reasonable explanation of his son's condition, and, owing to Lee's good reputation with their employer, it saved Richard's job.

Richard spent most of the day in the tent sleeping. Sarah awakened him midafternoon with an offer of food.

"Sorry, Ma," he said, sitting on his bedroll and kneading bleary eyes with thumb and forefinger. "I ain't got the stomach for it just now."

"You've got to eat, Richard. C'mon. It'll make you feel better. Give you strength." She handed him a plate.

He looked it over. "What is this?"

Sarah sat down on a box and tucked stray locks of hair behind her ears then adjusted the bun at her nape. "It's what I fixed for the Lewises' supper. Something they gave me the recipe for. Call it 'bubble and squeak.' "

"Don't *sound* like nothin' to eat. What is it?"

"Mostly potatoes and cabbage fried up. A few leftover vegetables stirred in, and some sausages."

He still looked suspicious.

"It's pretty good. Try it."

Richard poked around the plate and forked up a small bite. He sniffed at it, slid it off on his tongue, and finally chewed and swallowed. After a moment, he tried another bite, then another, then emptied the plate as fast as his fork would work. "You're right, Ma. That stuff ain't bad."

She studied her son for a moment, noting his reddened eyes, sallow face, bedraggled hair, unkempt whiskers—and split lip, bruised cheek, and black eye. "Richard, I don't aim to rant like your Pa does. But the way you're goin' leads no place but trouble."

"Aw, Ma, don't you be gettin' after me too. I ain't a kid no more."

"You've got your growth, for certain. But that don't mean you're growed up."

"What's that supposed to mean?"

Sarah waited until the anger left her son's face. "All this drinking, Rich. It's no good. From what I've seen in my years, most of the troubles that come to men come on account of whiskey."

"Plenty of men drink. Most do."

"True enough. But some men, well, it takes ahold of them and won't let go. They drink too much and too often. I'm afeared that's the way you're going."

Richard said nothing.

"What is it you intend to do, Son? Time's drawin' nigh when Pa's goin' to be loadin' the wagon and lighting out for God knows where."

Richard laid back, turned on his side and curled up. "I don't know, Ma. Wish I did. If I was to come along, Pa would keep on givin' me trouble, expect me to take orders from Abel—you know how he is."

"I know it. But you got to know it ain't all his fault."

"What the hell's that supposed to mean?" he said as he sat up.

"The thing is, Rich, you're just as contrary as your Pa is. No matter what he asks of you, you argue with him. If he wants something done one way, you insist on doing it some other way. Sometimes you don't finish a job. And Melvin—well, you know how he is. He does his best, bless his heart. It's just easier for Pa to have Abel deal with things, don't you see? You got to admit, the boy's reliable."

"That's one way of lookin' at it, I guess."

"That's Pa's way, for certain sure."

Richard hugged his elbows and shook his head. "I can't figure how to overcome it, Ma. I remember when me and Mel was little tykes. We'd run and play—even learn to work some—and you and Pa doted on us. Then Abel come along and, well, after that it's like us older boys was only half there. You folks never had time for me and Mel after baby brother got there."

"Oh, Richard, we never meant to neglect you. Fact is, I never knowed you felt we did. But a baby—Abel, or any baby—needs near constant care. And you boys liked runnin' wild. Your independent streak showed even back then."

"Maybe so. But after Abel it was sort of like I was on my own—me and Mel, that is. Didn't seem to matter what we did. Abel was the only one you and Pa—especially Pa—ever paid any mind to. He never bothered with me, save it was to remind me I wasn't good enough."

Sarah wiped away a tear, smoothed her apron, gathered Richard's plate, and stood to leave.

"Ma?"

She waited.

"What do you think of all this? This talk of Mexico? Askin' the Lewises along?"

Sarah stared at Richard's plate, slowly scraping at the food residue with the fork. "I don't know, Son. I wish I knew what's come over Pa these past years. He never used to have such foolish notions—at least not so powerful. If it was up to me, we never would have left Shelby County. We left behind a good life for no good reason. I wish we could go back—but from what you boys found, there ain't nothin' to go back to. And, with what Abel done, we couldn't go back anyhow."

She turned and lifted the tent flap, stopped again. "I just wish I had a stove again, Richard, 'stead of cooking over a campfire all the time. I'm gettin' so I don't much care where that stove is at."

Sarah turned again, stopped again. "And a bed that ain't in the back of a wagon or a tent would be nice, too."

Evening was well on its way when Richard left his bed to again meet the world. Stiff and sore, he stepped delicately down to the creek, knelt, and laved water over his head and face. Supper was over, but Ma had put aside another serving of the meal she served the Pates and the Lewises. He chewed the food gingerly with his pained and now stiff jaw and teeth. "Y'know, Ma, a man could get to like this stuff. What is it you call it again?"

"Bubble and squeak."

"That's sure a funny name for food," Melvin said from the stump where he sat whittling a big stick into a smaller stick. "But Rich is right—it tastes pretty good."

Lee toweled off the plates Sarah handed him from the wash water. "Richard," he said, "your boss is expectin' you back at work tonight."

A sharp glance from Richard was the only response.

"You expectin' to be there?"

Richard nodded, turned his attention back to his plate and poked at the bits of food still there.

"It would behoove you to show up sober. And you'd be well advised to leave that whiskey flask of yours at home, too."

The silence was so thick in the camp it seemed to dampen the rattle of the dishes in the pan. Peter sat upright and when he slapped both hands on the table, the others flinched. With a smile, and perhaps louder than necessary, he said, "A delightful meal, Missus Pate. If there are no objections, I believe I shall pay a call on our neighbors."

"Any neighbor in particular?" Sarah said.

A flush crept up Peter's neck. "I will be pleased with the company of them all. But I intend to have a word with Daniel."

The response brought a sly smile to Sarah's face, but only blank looks from the men.

Abel sat at the table across from Richard, the light from a lantern hanging on the side of the wagon illuminating the family Bible he paged through. The rhythms of its archaic language mesmerized him, but the contradictions in many of the stories confused him. Take David, who swayed from good to evil to good to evil as if swinging from a rope. Then there was Abraham's bewildering approach to family loyalty, allowing his useless nephew Lot every advantage yet willing to snuff out his own son's life. And the deceptive and debauched dance between Judah and Tamar.

Unable to come to terms with a grownup version of morality for himself, he determined safety lay in following his father's course until he could.

Peter watched the boy scrutinize the book for a moment then interrupted his reverie when he said, "Would you care to come along, Abel?"

The boy looked up, startled and surprised. "What?"

Peter smiled. "I am on my way to the Lewis camp. Want to come with me?"

The furrows returned to Abel's brow. "Why, no, I reckon not. I don't have any business with the Lewises."

"Suit yourself. But what shall I say to Emma if she asks about you?"

Abel's bewilderment deepened as he watched Peter walk away.

Chapter Twenty-Seven

Like the Pates, the Lewises had finished with supper and were enjoying the break from labors the evening offered. No one stirred when Peter walked into camp. Without a "howdy" or any other greeting, he walked over to where Daniel sat and removed his hat. "Mister Lewis. I wonder if I might have a word."

"Of course."

Peter cleared his throat, and glanced about at the attentive, curious girls. "In private, Sir?"

Daniel nodded, stood up and put his arm around Peter's shoulder and led him a short way from the camp. "What's on your mind, lad?"

"Sir. I—I—I would like your permission to call on Miss Martha."

Daniel smiled. "Do tell! Am I incorrect in thinking you have been calling on her for some time now?"

Peter flushed. "What I mean, Mister Lewis, is—well, Sir, I assure you my intentions are honora—the thing is, I hope one day to ask for her hand in marriage—if she'll have me—with your permission, of course. . . ."

Daniel continued smiling inside as Peter squirmed. "Marriage, you say? My Martha? Why, she is only a girl!"

"I believe she is eighteen, Mister Lewis—not that you don't know the age of your daughter, Sir. . . ."

With a loud laugh and a few hearty pats on the back, Daniel said he was pleased to give his permission, but could not speak for his daughter. He then turned serious. "Tell me, Peter. Do you intend to follow the Pates westward to the Mexican territories and take my daughter with you?"

Peter pursed his lips and wrinkled his brow as he thought what to say. "I hope to remain in Fort Smith. If possible, that is."

"And why would it not be possible?"

"Well, Sir, I have certain, uh—obligations—to the Pates. But I intend to broach the subject of my remaining here with them soon."

"Why do you wish to stay here?"

"I have a good position, Sir, and my employer finds my services valuable. I am confident that in time I will advance in the firm. In fact, I don't think a partnership is out of the question. Then there's Fort Smith itself. There are already five companies of infantry assigned here, and I believe there will be more to come as more of the eastern tribes are removed to Indian Territory. The city is bound to grow, and I believe commercial prospects are good."

"It seems you have thought this through thoroughly."

"Yes, Sir. I am not inclined to go off half-cocked, as they say."

"Much like Martha, in that regard." With another pat on Peter's back, Daniel said, "Let us go talk to the girls. They have a say in this, as well, I suppose." He stopped, and stopped Peter with a tug on the sleeve. "Another question concerning the Pates and Mexico and such. Lee—do you think he is barmy?"

"Barmy, Sir?"

"You know, daft. Off his nut. Crazy."

"Oh, no, Mister Lewis! Lee—Mister Pate—has as good a heart as any man I've met. He is somewhat impetuous, I suppose, and perhaps inclined to follow his emotions. And I believe his assessment of the slavery situation is somewhat overblown.

But he is by no means 'barmy' to use your word."

"Thank you, Peter. And now into the maw, so to speak. Girls! Martha!" he said with raised voice as they neared the camp. Then, "Peter here has asked to call on you, Martha. On a more formal basis, that is. What do you think? Is he to be trusted, or is he just another 'Jack the Lad' with dishonorable intentions, of which there are so many in these parts?"

Martha blushed.

Jane giggled.

Emma smiled.

Mary, arms akimbo, said, "Mister Peter Neumann! What could you possibly see in a girl like Martha?"

"Well, I—I—you see, I—"

"You *what,* Peter? I suppose a more apt question is, what could Martha possibly see in a man such as yourself?"

Martha's flush deepened and she tugged her older sister's skirt. "Mary!" she whispered.

Mary laughed and clapped her hands. "If it is my blessing you're wanting, Peter, you can certainly have it."

With a slow release of held breath, Peter extended a hand. "Martha—Miss Lewis—would you care to walk with me?"

"I should be honored, Mister Neumann."

Hand in hand, the young couple strolled down the road and into the evening.

The evening was over and night well established when Peter returned home. The camp was dark and quiet, save Abel, still sitting at the table by the wagon by lantern light. But rather than reading, one of Ben Pate's Paterson Colt pistols gleamed on the table, the other scattered around it in pieces. With an oil-soaked rag he cleaned and polished the frame, cylinder, barrel, breech, lock springs, and other parts.

"Ben's guns," Peter said as he took a seat on the table bench opposite Abel. "You've taken quite an interest in them."

Abel only nodded. Peter was right. Abel had disassembled and cleaned and rebuilt the revolvers so many times he could likely do it blindfolded. He believed, in fact, that both pistols could be taken apart and left in a jumbled heap before him and he could—aided by Colt's innovation of interchangeable parts—put together two working revolvers in a matter of minutes. He had long since mastered the task of removing and loading the five-chambered cylinders with his eyes closed. With practice, his accuracy with the handguns had become precise as well.

"You know," Peter said, "sometimes when I see you in his hat and duster, I still think you're him. It can be unnerving."

Again, Abel nodded. He snapped the bolt spring into place and set the pistol frame aside and looked off into the night. "I see him too," he said after some time, barely above a whisper. "Sometimes I wake up in a sweat. I see in my dreams Uncle Ben hanging off that sidewalk with his throat gaping open." He shivered, and went back to assembling the revolver. "It don't hardly seem real, what I done."

After a time, Peter said, "He was a hard man, your Uncle Ben. Not always easy to work for."

Abel, head bowed over his work, raised his eyes to look at Peter. "That don't forgive what I done."

"No."

"If I had not killed him, he would of killed me. I know that for certain. Still, looking back, there must of been a better way to get them books Pa wanted."

"Were—are—those books so important?"

"That ain't up to me to say. Pa sent us to get them. Might not of been the best way to do it, but when all's said and done I did what Pa sent me to do."

They sat in silence for a time and Abel finished putting the pistol together. He gave it a final wipe with the oiled rag and laid the revolver on the table beside its mate, lantern light glimmering off the oil and metal.

"What about me?" Peter said.

"What about you?"

"Well, your father is determined to move on to Mexico. The time for leaving isn't that far off."

"What do you aim to do?"

"That's what I'm asking."

Abel thought a moment.

"What would you like to do?"

Peter squirmed in his seat. "I'd like to stay here. In Fort Smith."

After mulling it over, Abel said, "I don't reckon there's any reason for us to keep dragging you around with us. If you was of a mind to cause me any trouble, you would of done it by now."

Peter nodded.

"We'll talk it over with Pa."

"Good enough. One other thing. . . ."

"What's that?"

"I spoke with Mister Lewis earlier. And with Martha. We hope to be married, she and I."

Abel smiled and reached across the table and grabbed Peter by the shoulders, giving him a firm squeeze and a couple of shakes. "That's fine, Peter! That's right fine!"

"We believe we can make a good life here in Fort Smith."

Abel gave him another shake. "I reckon so."

Peter said, "Let's hope your Pa agrees."

Chapter Twenty-Eight

Every evening found Peter and Martha walking out, discussing the life they hoped to make together. And so several days passed before Peter and the Pate family sat down to talk about that same—or, perhaps, a different—future.

When finally they did find themselves all together at the rough table under the wagon fly after supper, Peter told of his intention to wed Martha Lewis, news met with much delight and little surprise.

"You-all, if course, have much to say about what is to come," Peter said.

"I suppose that's true," Lee said. "You must know we would not wish to upset your apple cart."

"Sakes alive, no!" Sarah said. "We hope you young'ns will be happy as can be."

Peter smiled at their enthusiasm, then sobered. "The day is soon to come when you-all will pack up and move on. You have already started laying in supplies for the journey. What is to become of me? Am I to accompany you?"

Lee thought a moment, and said, "You know, Peter, we've grown right fond of you, Sarah and me. In some ways, you're like another son to us. We put you in a hard way, but you never let it get the best of you. Your going on west to Mexico with us would suit us just fine. I do believe Daniel is of a mind to travel with us—and his girls, of course—so you and Martha—"

"—What is it that you-all want?" Sarah said.

"Martha and I, we're of a mind to stay here in Fort Smith." Peter went on to explain his reasoning behind his desire. "So that leaves the question of whether or not you will allow it. I—and Martha—hope you will. If not. . . . Well, I don't know. . . ."

"We appreciate your understanding our worries," Lee said. "Although we don't expect it, there is still the prospect of your going to the law. As much as we hold your future in our hands, you hold Abel's in yours. Maybe more so."

Richard snorted. "Far as I'm concerned, Peter can turn baby brother in and he can rot in jail."

"Now, Richard—"

"Don't 'now Richard' me, Pa! Abel done got us in this mess and I'm sick to death of us livin' with one eye on our back trail."

"Now, Richard," Lee said. "You know it ain't that bad. There ain't been a speck of trouble and there ain't likely to be."

"Besides," Sarah said, dropping her bonnet on the table and sweeping a lock of hair off her forehead, "our bein' here is your Pa's doing, not Abel's. This is all his fault. If it weren't for his cockeyed ideas and dreams—"

"—Sarah, we've been all over that. Leave it go."

"Please," Peter said. "What of me and Martha?"

Abel said, "If I can speak, Pa—and Ma—I've already told Peter I trust him. If he was apt to have me arrested he'd have done so long since. Far as I'm concerned, he can go his own way."

Lee thought for a time. "I reckon you're right," he finally said. "Any of you-all object to the idea of leavin' Peter to do as he pleases when we move on?"

"Of course not," Sarah said.

"No, Pa," Abel said.

Richard shook his head and Melvin shrugged.

"That's it, then. Peter—you—and Martha—are welcome to

come along west, or stay here in Fort Smith as you please."

"We would dearly love to have you-all stay with us," Sarah said. "I'm sure the Lewises would like that, too. But you-all do what you feel best, and the Pates will wish you-all much happiness."

Peter stood. "Thank you. If you-all don't mind, I will go now and tell Martha."

Sarah smiled. "It's late. You be sure to comport yourself like a gentleman and behave yourself—and get back here right soon."

"Yes, Ma'am."

On his way to the Lewis camp, Peter passed Daniel on his way to the Pate camp. They stopped and talked and Peter passed along the Pates' approval of his plan to remain in Fort Smith. Daniel allowed as how he would miss Martha but understood young folks had to make their own way.

The Pates were still gathered at the table when Daniel arrived, and he slid into the space on the bench Peter recently vacated.

"Daniel," Lee said. "What brings you around?"

"I have arrived at a decision, Brother Pate. The girls and I—less Martha, as you are aware—will accompany you to the Province of New Mexico. We have decided our prospects for a good life there should be equal to those in Texas."

Lee stood, clapped his hands together once and placed them on the table and leaned toward Daniel. "I am happy to hear it, my friend! You-all coming along will make the journey more pleasant. And time will prove your decision a wise one." He extended a hand and when Daniel grasped it, pumped it with enthusiasm.

Sarah said, "Mister Lewis, I am delighted! I've grown fond of those girls of yours and, Lord knows, they know how to work."

"Indeed. With their industry in running the laundry enterprise, they've quite a packet to help outfit us. But, I confess, they will be delighted to get their hands out of wash water."

Lee and Daniel talked over preparations. They had compared and contrasted the use of mules and oxen to pull wagons, and agreed to disagree. Daniel would yoke up his oxen and Lee harness his mules. Daniel's four head of oxen were in fine fettle after a long season's rest, and the Pate mules were much the same. Lee debated and decided to invest in a saddle horse to aid in hunting and scouting the trail. Sarah insisted he rid them of the dry cow, and Abel arranged a trade—with money to boot—for a heifer with calf. The Lewis girls purchased a half dozen hens and lashed together willow withe cages to hang on the wagons.

"Toodle-pip," Daniel said with a wave as he walked into the darkness. "We leave this place two weeks hence!"

CHAPTER TWENTY-NINE

Richard's frustrations mounted as the day of departure drew ever nearer. At work one night, his flask long empty, he fidgeted and fussed and finally recruited and paid a man wandering the streets to fetch him a bottle.

The whiskey settled his nerves—and all the rest of him—to the point that when the brickyard workers arrived in the morning, they found Richard curled up next to a warm kiln fast asleep. His boss gave him the sack and told him not to bother coming back for his time—the money owed him would be given to Lee and he could collect it from his father on payday.

Richard staggered home, slapped his way through the tent flap, sagged to his knees on his bedroll, then collapsed in a heap. He did not move until Melvin toed him awake at the end of the day.

"Rich," he said. "Rich—wake up!"

Richard rolled to his stomach, hoisted himself on hands and knees, and shook his head like a dog worrying a caught coon. The pain of the sudden move prompted him to turn onto his backside and drop his chin to his chest and grasp his head with both hands to stifle its throbbing.

He groaned. "Oh, hell, Mel. I wish I was dead."

"You just might get your wish. Pa's plenty mad."

With effort that flexed his whole face, Richard managed to open his eyes, partially and intermittently at first, and when finally they stayed open, their sagging state ever threatened their closing again. "What time is it?"

"Past work. Me and Abel and Pa and Peter is all home and Ma's 'bout got supper fixed."

Richard still sat, swaying slowly.

"What you goin' to do, Rich?"

He scrubbed his face and scalp slowly with the palms of his hands. "I don't know, brother. What the hell can I do?"

He would soon find out.

Supper was a silent affair, with the hungry workmen laboring hard to fill the holes in their bellies. Richard only picked at the food on his plate and barely sipped his coffee. With the meal cleared and coffee mugs topped off, Lee broached the subject permeating the camp like a miasma.

"Anything you'd like to say, Richard?"

The dissipated son only shook his head.

"I believe we're owed an explanation."

"Aw, hell, Pa. What good would it do? What's done is done and jawin' about it won't change nothin'."

Abel shook his head in disbelief. "That's it, Richard? That's all you got to say for yourself?"

Richard glared at his brother through bloodshot eyes. "Shut the hell up, Abel."

"Aw, c'mon, Rich! What were you thinking?"

"I said shut up! Any more sass out of you and I'll kick your ass!"

"Boys!" Sarah said. "Enough! You-all fighting ain't goin' to help."

Silence persisted for a few minutes. Lee broke it. "Here's what's going to happen. There's plenty to be done to get ready to pull out. Richard, since we all are still working and you ain't, that job falls to you."

Richard sat, sullen and silent.

"Ever' morning, Ma and me will give you a list of things that need to be done. It'll be yours to do. Understand?"

Richard nodded.

"When occasion calls for you to go into Fort Smith, you're to do what you're sent to do and come back. No visits to no grog shops, no refilling that infernal pocket bottle of yours, no nothin'! Is that understood?"

Again, Richard nodded. Then, "One thing, Pa."

"Oh? What's that?"

"I'll help get things ready to go. But I'm tellin' you right now I ain't goin' with you-all."

Sarah stopped her scrubbing in the dishpan. "Richard!"

"I'm sorry, Ma. I followed Pa's foolish notions this far—hell, I even went all the way to Shelby County and back again for him—but I won't do it no more. I'm done with him." Richard turned an ugly stare on his father. "If the rest of you-all had any sense you'd quit him too."

Abel stood, nearly upsetting the table, with fists clenched and breath hissing fast between clenched teeth. Lee placed a hand on his arm. "Sit down, Son. It's all right."

Then, Lee said, "Richard, I don't know what you got in your head. I've tried to fathom it, but I can't. Makes no sense to me whatsoever. We'll not talk on it any more tonight. Just be ready to go to work come morning—if not for me, then for the rest of the family, for your Ma."

Richard did not go to bed that night. Instead, he nursed tepid coffee, stewed and fretted, and nodded off where he sat at the table. Sarah shook him awake when she arose to fix breakfast.

"You'd best get on down to the creek and freshen up some," she said. "You smell like somethin' the dogs dug up and don't look much better. Vittles'll be ready by the time you get back."

He tossed aside the dregs of coffee gone cold and shuffled off toward the stream. When he returned, his father and brothers and Peter were bowed over their plates, forking up biscuits and gravy and slabs of bacon. Richard filled a plate and slid onto the bench at the end of the table. Melvin watched his older brother, but no one spoke during the meal.

When Abel and Melvin and Peter finished, Sarah handed each a sack holding a pair of pork pies—another dish she learned cooking for the Lewises—for their midday meal. Before they started off down the road to Fort Smith, Lee handed Richard a slip of paper with a list scrawled on it.

"Here's what you're to do today, Richard. We'll talk when I get home from work."

Richard spent the day mending and checking harnesses, building a trough and soaking wagon wheels in linseed oil, greasing axles, tightening the king pin, tongue bolts and hounds, adjusting the reach, aligning brake blocks, tightening bow staples, and other tasks to ready the wagon.

He did not make it all the way through his father's list but made a good start by the time his father and brothers returned home. Lee looked the wagon over and found the work good. "You've done well, Richard," he said, grabbing the sideboard and giving it a shake. "This old wagon looks like it just might make the trip."

After supper, Richard took Melvin aside. "I could sure use a drink, Brother. How 'bout let's go to town and I'll buy you a beer."

"I don't know, Rich. Pa says you ain't to be drinking."

"You let me worry about that. Besides, he ain't said nothin' about you drinking."

Melvin hitched his thumbs in his waistband and studied the ground he scratched with his boot. "Nah, I don't think so. I don't want Pa mad at me."

Melvin's eyes widened when Richard put a hand in the middle of his chest and shoved. "You're a damn milksop, Mel.

When you goin' to grow up and be a man?"

With that, he turned and walked out of camp.

Chapter Thirty

Richard thought better of going to Fort Smith. Instead, he walked to the Lewis camp. He stood in the waning light watching Emma—and Martha and Jane—talking and laughing as they sat with needles and thread stitching minor repairs into laundered shirts and trousers. Daniel and Mary sat at the table apart from the girls, Mary with pencil in hand, making notes from her conversation with her father.

After a few minutes, Richard walked on into the camp and approached the girls. He took off his hat. "Miss Emma," he said. "Could I have the pleasure of your company on a short walk?"

Emma looked at Richard. She glanced at Martha and Jane. Looked to where Mary and her father sat. Dropping her hands and handwork to her lap, she said, "I am sorry, Richard—I have work to do."

"Aw, c'mon. It's gettin' too dark to do that."

"I know that. There is not much time left this evening to get it done. That is why I have to keep at it," Emma said, casting glances at her sisters, then fixing her eyes on the tear in the shirt in her hands and the needle in her fingers dragging thread through the fabric.

Richard stood for a moment, shifting his weight from one foot to the other, then turned and walked to where Daniel and Mary sat. He asked permission to sit, and did so.

"Mister Lewis, I guess you-all know I ain't workin' nights no more."

Daniel hesitated. "Yes," he said, but said no more.

"Well, Pa's got me gettin' things ready for the move over at our camp. I've got the wagon mostly in shape. There's plenty more to be done, but I reckon I could give you folks a hand if you could use the help."

Daniel folded his arms and furrowed his brow. "I do not know. Nothing comes immediately to mind. What do you think, Mary?"

Mary smiled. "It is kind of you to offer, Richard. We have been making ready all along, so much of what is needed is already prepared. I do not doubt we will need some help as the move grows nearer. I will surely ask for—and appreciate—your assistance when the time comes."

"Thanks, Miss Mary." Richard stood, studying the inside of his hat. "I wonder, Mary, if I might have a moment. Alone."

"Father?"

"Certainly," Daniel said with a wave of his hand. "Absolutely."

Richard and Mary walked into the woods bordering the campsite. He sat on the trunk of a fallen tree and she stood before him. After an awkward silence, Mary said, "What is it, Richard?"

He cleared his throat. "About my not workin' at the brick-yard. . . ."

"Yes?"

"I suppose you-all know why."

"Yes."

"Emma, too?"

"Yes. . . ."

After a moment, "Mary, I know you done told me she ain't interested in me."

"Yes. It seems your brother Abel is the only man who

intrigues her."

"Abel. He ain't but a boy."

Mary laughed. "Oh, Richard! Abel is every bit as much a man as Emma is a woman."

"He ain't but sixteen."

"And Emma is fifteen."

"But it's different with girls."

Mary swept her dress against the back of her thighs and sat next to Richard.

"No, Richard. It is not. Oh, with some it is, sure—everyone grows up in their own time. But there is no question that both Emma and Abel are of an age to be counted grownups."

Richard sighed and crushed his hat in his hands. "You can't know what it's like, Mary. Me bein' the oldest and having feelings for Emma, and then my baby brother—hell, it ain't even him—he don't even see Emma for what she is—but to lose out like this to that little. . . . Oh, never mind. You don't understand."

Mary laughed. "Richard, Richard! How blind you are!"

"What do you mean?"

"You forget that I am the older sister in our family. The circumstances may not be the same, but I assure you it is no easier for me."

Richard looked so perplexed she explained. "Look at Emma. The girl is a natural beauty and attracts men like moths to a lantern. Imagine what it is like to watch men pass me by without a glance for the chance to be near her. Then there is Martha. When not standing next to Emma—who makes other women invisible—Martha is attractive as well. And when it comes to intelligence, whether book learning or just plain common sense, I cannot hold a candle to her. She is to be married to Peter. Emma could marry any man she chose whenever it suited her. That leaves me—Mary Lewis, spinster."

"Aw, Mary! You ain't no old maid!"

"You said I do not understand how you feel. It is you who does not understand."

Richard sat mulling things over. Mary waited.

"The thing is, Mary, when Pa and your family pulls out of here next week or the week after or whenever, I don't aim to go along."

Mary's eyes widened at the words. "Does your family know this?"

"Yes. I've said as much." Then, "I want to ask Emma to stay with me. We could stay here in Fort Smith, or go somewheres else—whatever suits her."

Mary stood. "You can ask Emma if you want. It is not my place to answer for her. But I believe I know what her answer will be." With that, Mary walked away in the darkness.

After a time, Richard started for home, staying to the edge of the woods until well clear of the Lewis camp. When he arrived at the Pate camp, he found his father sitting on a stump in the glow of the dying fire.

"You're back early," Lee said.

Richard did not answer.

"You been in town?"

"No."

"Where, then?"

"I been over visitin' with the Lewises. Not that it's any of your affair."

Lee let that settle for a minute while he tossed a stick of wood on the fire and watched the sparks rise to meet the stars. Then, in little more than a whisper, "Son, as long as you put your feet under my table, it is my affair. For all we—me and your Ma—knowed, you was off in Fort Smith drinking and making another mess for us to clean up."

"Well, Pa, it ain't goin' to be a problem much longer. Once

you're gone from here, you won't have to worry about me no more."

"It saddens me to hear that, Son. Your Ma will likely be heartbroken."

"Can't be helped."

"Sure it can, Richard. All you got to do is keep in mind that it ain't just you that matters—you're part of a family."

"That would be a whole hell of a lot easier if my part was as big as Abel's. Sometimes you act like you ain't got but one son, Pa."

Lee thought for a minute. "I reckon it might seem like I favor the boy. It ain't by intention. Me and you—well, we butt heads like a pair of randy billy goats. I just ain't got the will to fight you every step of the way. I want the best for all my sons. But if you ain't willing to obey or abide correction—well, Son, I wish you'd see the light. And I wish you'd leave off tryin' to drag your brother Melvin off into the dark with you."

"Mel's got a mind of his own."

"True enough, I suppose. But ever since you two was little tykes, he's been prone to let you do his thinkin' for him."

"Can't be helped."

"That's where you're wrong, Richard. You could help Melvin no end if you'd lead him in the right direction instead of the wrong one."

"Who's to say what's right and what's wrong? You?"

Lee used the ball of his thumb and forefinger to rub the moisture from the corners of his eyes. "I can see I've failed you, Son. I'm awful sorry about that."

Chapter Thirty-One

Over the days to come, Richard approached his work at a more deliberate pace. He trimmed the mules' hooves and tacked on new shoes. He sharpened the axe and hatchet and shovel and checked and re-checked other tools to ensure their serviceability.

He laid in leather and awls and stout waxed linen thread for harness repairs, cordage and ropes, tin buckets, spare canvas, picket pins and tent pegs and a mallet for securing them, and powder and lead and caps.

Sarah ordered and received additional cooking equipment to supplement the sorry selection she tossed into the wagon before leaving Shelby County with little notice. An assortment of pots and kettles and pans and accouterments to make camp cooking more convenient were added to those already acquired.

Delivery of goods and supplies to the camp—as well as to the Lewis camp—was most often arranged by Abel and he made several trips with his employer's wagons. But on a few occasions, Richard harnessed up the mules, pulled down the kitchen fly, hitched up the wagon and drove the team to town. No trip was complete without a visit to a saloon where he hoisted a few and refilled his flask.

But those trips were too few and far between to satisfy his thirst and come Saturday night he cajoled Melvin into a trip to Fort Smith with the stated intention of taking in the evening's merriments at the dance.

Lee was less than enthusiastic with the idea but realized—despite evidence to the contrary—Richard was a grown man and entitled to a certain amount of independence. Besides, his firstborn son had performed well the work given him in readying for the move. "Richard, Melvin," he said, "you-all enjoy yourselves. But, for heaven's sake, stay out of trouble."

Melvin said, "Sure, Pa." Richard did not answer.

When they were gone, Lee said, "Abel? You going into town?"

"Hadn't planned on it, Pa."

"Not that I don't trust your brothers, but if you was to go along and sort of watch out for them—and maybe keep them from mischief—I would be grateful."

"Sure, Pa, if that's what you want. But you know Rich don't appreciate my being around."

"Well, just try and take it easy. Besides, the Lewis girls will be there and from what I hear, Miss Emma might appreciate your being around."

Abel reddened, ducked his head, hauled on Uncle Ben's duster, pulled his hat low, and hurried out of camp to catch up.

As predicted, Richard wasn't happy to have Abel tag along. When his brothers veered off into the first saloon in town, he went in with them but propped himself against the wall inside the door. He watched workmen and soldiers and businessmen and saloon girls laugh and talk and sing along with the jangly piano. His brothers joined right in while Melvin nursed his beer and Richard downed several shots of whiskey. But when his demeanor started shifting from high-spirited to sullen, Abel opted to intervene.

"Mel, Richard—let's go to the dance."

Melvin tossed off the rest of his beer. "Sure. Let's go. Rich?"

Richard thought it over, said, "Why the hell not?" He checked to make sure his flask was full and tucked it into the inside pocket of his coat.

The sun slid below the horizon as the brothers walked to the dance. The bonfires were burning, the lanterns lit, and the musicians strumming and sawing and squeezing out dance tunes when they arrived. The Lewises' town buggy jingled to a halt beside them and Abel grabbed the cheek piece on the bridle to steady the horse. He scratched the horse's forehead and watched as Richard stepped up to lend the girls a hand out of the carriage.

"Ladies," Richard said, removing his hat with a sweeping bow. "What a pleasure to see you-all here." One by one, he grasped chapped hands. When Emma's came into his grip, he held on after she lit. "Miss Emma, I hope you'll save a dance for me."

"Perhaps, Mister Pate."

"Maybe later, I can walk you home."

"I do not think so. It has been a long day and riding with my sisters will get me home to bed much sooner."

Mary was last. "Richard. You are well, I trust?"

"I reckon so, Miss Mary."

"You seem dejected."

"Oh, I'll be fine," he said as he pulled out his flask and hoisted it as if in a toast.

"Drink will solve none of your problems, Mister Pate."

He took a sip. " 'Mister Pate' now, is it? What happened to 'Richard'?"

Before she could answer, there was a stir when Peter hurried up. "Martha!" he said between quick breaths. "Looks like I just made it. Working late."

Ignoring social convention, Martha wrapped her arms around the breathless man. "I am so glad you made it, Peter! Let us sit so you can catch your breath. Then, we shall dance!"

Emma slipped up behind Abel. He started when she spoke. "Abel—it is good to see you."

"Oh! Thank you. Nice to see you, too," he said, pulling off his hat and clasping it to his chest. "And your sisters."

"Will you be asking for a dance this evening, Abel?"

"Don't know. Maybe. Later."

"But we have danced before—did you find the experience unpleasant?"

"Oh, no, Miss Emma. It's just—well—I—" He looked around wide-eyed, as if expecting someone to throw him a lifeline. Mary came to his rescue.

"Abel, may I impose upon your time and ask you to see to our horse and buggy?"

"Yes, Miss. Happy to." With a quick nod to Emma he plopped his hat on his head, grabbed the lines just behind the bridle bit and turned the horse away and off into the darkness. He took his time with the unhitching, unbuckling the breeching straps from the shafts, unhooking the traces from the whiffletree, and sliding the shafts out of the tugs. He unbridled the horse, slipped on a halter and tied the horse to the back of the carriage. From a bag he found on the floor of the buggy, he poured a small heap of oats on the ground and stroked the horse's shoulder and withers as it ate.

When finally he made it back to the dance, the musicians were taking a breather. The dance floor was empty and soldiers, workmen, and women were gathered in clumps all around. Loud voices from a cluster on the other side of the platform caught his attention and he saw Melvin pulling uniforms aside and moving to the center of the circle. Abel stepped onto the dance floor and ran across. He found Melvin on his hands and knees, head down with blood-tinged drool dangling from his mouth. Richard was backed up and trapped uncomfortably close against a bonfire with half a dozen soldiers closing in.

Abel shouldered his way past the soldiers and, pulling a pistol from his pocket, turned to confront the attackers. "You-all had best back off!"

The men stopped, eyeing their new adversary, taking note that he was armed.

"You can't shoot us all, farm boy," a soldier said.

Abel rolled back the hammer with this thumb and the Paterson's trigger reached out to find his finger. "I got five shots here. I reckon my brother Rich can take care of the one of you-all I can't."

In a confrontation of this sort there can be but two kinds of men. One kind looks at the odds and sees they are not in his favor and imagines himself already shot. The other kind somehow assumes he will be the one spared and presses the attack. In this particular assemblage of soldiers, all were of the first kind. Each slowly stepped back.

By now, Melvin had regained his feet. He shuffled toward his brothers and, with bloodied mouth, turned to face the soldiers. Still, it was the Colt revolver on which the bluecoats' eyes were riveted.

One of the soldiers glowered at Richard. "This is not over, jackass." Then, as if in close order drill, they turned in unison and walked away.

Abel released the breath he had been holding and carefully lowered the hammer on the pistol. "Rich, what the hell's going on here?"

"Just a little disagreement, brother. No need for you to stick your nose in. Me and Mel had it handled."

"What? They'd have tore you apart had I not been here!"

Richard stepped close to Abel and said through gritted teeth, "Abel, you stay the hell away from me. I don't need nothin' you got. If you're a-scared of a few damn soldiers, just go on back to camp. I suppose Pa will protect you."

Melvin, confused, looked on. And when Richard turned on his heel and shoved his way through the crowd, he followed his older brother.

Chapter Thirty-Two

Two days before scheduled departure, preparations were all but complete at the Pate camp. Everything that could be packed was packed, everything that could be stowed was stowed. With no inclement weather on the horizon, even the wall tents were struck and rolled and loaded. Richard's belongings stood apart, evidence of his determination to stay behind. Melvin waffled yet about whether to stay with the family or stay behind with his brother.

Arrangements were mostly complete at the Lewis camp as well. The oxen were shod, the wagons refitted, the town buggy and horse bartered for goods, the laundry paraphernalia sold off. One wall tent still stood on its platform and some camp equipment remained in service. Peter and Martha had gone before a preacher and taken wedding vows. They would continue to live at the camp until more permanent accommodations could be acquired.

Feeling ever more free of family fetters, Richard spent more time in town. This evening was no exception. He persuaded Melvin to come along and they walked into Fort Smith and through familiar saloon doors. Over drinks, Richard tried to convince Melvin to stay with him.

"I don't know, Rich. Ma and Pa might need my help."

"Oh, hell! You know as well as I do that so far as Pa's concerned Abel can do anything. He don't need us no more than a milk cow needs six tits."

"What'll we do for money? What'll we eat?"

Richard emptied his shot glass and signaled for a refill and watched the bartender pour. "You got a job, Mel."

"Already told the boss I was leavin'."

Richard laughed. "Don't worry 'bout that, brother. They'll be tickled to keep a big, strong hoddie like you around. And I can find me another job—not at the brickyard, maybe, but there's other work around." He swallowed his drink in one gulp and called for yet another. "We ain't neither one of us too handy with a cookin' pot, but we sure as hell won't starve."

The saloon doors banged open and every patron in the house turned at the noise. Two army privates, well along in their evening of drinking, stood smiling and studying the clientele. One of the soldiers spotted Richard and his smile turned upside down.

"You!" he yelled, pointing at Richard. "You sonofabitch!"

Surprised, Richard looked around to make sure the man was pointing at him. Then he realized it was one of the soldiers from the altercation at the dance. He slid his chair back from the table and stood.

The soldier was at him in three long strides. "I told you it wasn't over."

Later in the night, Melvin staggered into camp, heaving for air after a long run. "Pa," he said between gasps, "we got trouble."

Lee bolted upright in his bedroll, trying to make sense of the world. "What? Melvin? What is it?"

"Richard. He was in a fight. The town marshal's got him."

Lee sat across the desk from the deputy on duty at the jail. He squirmed in the wooden ladder-back chair seeking a comfortable seat. The deputy, seated in a swivel chair with his feet propped on the desk, whittled a chunk off a plug of tobacco. He chewed for a minute to moisten the cud, tucked it in his cheek, and leaned over to spit in a battered cuspidor by the desk.

"Marshal'll be back soon. He's over to the fort talkin' with some officer there."

"Do you know what happened?"

The deputy spat again. "It was a hell of a fight. That saloon looked like a herd of buffalo had passed through. Never thought two men could make such a mess." He spat again.

"Richard's locked up?"

The deputy chewed and spat and nodded, wiping a splash of brown juice off his chin.

"Where's the other man?"

"He was a soldier. He's in the infirmary over to the fort."

The door opened and the marshal walked in. The deputy dropped his feet to the floor and stood, stepping away from the desk to stand against the wall with his hands clasped behind his back.

The marshal sat in his already-warm chair and studied his guest. "You must be Lee Pate—Richard's father."

Lee nodded.

"Hell of a boy, him. Seen a lot of him these past weeks."

Lee cleared his throat. "I'm awful sorry about that. He wasn't raised that way."

The marshal moved a stack of papers on his desk aside, pulled a single sheet from a drawer, placed it on the desk and carefully aligned it with the palms of his hands. "No," he said, staring at the paper and adjusting it slightly. "I don't reckon so. Sometimes boys go their own way, no matter their teaching."

"Can you tell me what happened?"

"Near as we can tell, your boys was having a few drinks and minding their own business when this soldier came in—him, and another soldier, already liquored up. Seems he knew who Richard was on account of some altercation they had at a dance

Saturday week. They started fighting and didn't quit till they'd wrecked the place and neither one of them had any strength to go on. Beat each other up pretty bad."

"Is Richard hurt?"

"He's plenty bruised up, and bleeding out of a few places. But the doc took a look at him and said there weren't nothing busted and he'd heal up fine, given time."

"And the soldier?"

The marshal leaned back in his chair and turned and stared at the front door for a minute. Then, he turned back, leaned forward with elbows on the desk and interlaced his fingers. "That's the thing. That soldier boy's broke up pretty bad. Your boy picked up a busted table leg and whaled on him till he tired out. Good thing he was already pretty well spent, or he would have beat that soldier plumb to death."

Lee shook his head in disbelief. "Will he be all right?"

"Too soon to say. Army doc at the infirmary says it could go either way."

The men sat silent for a time. Then the marshal said, "Word is, you folks are leaving town."

Lee looked surprised. "Yes. Yes, we are. Day after tomorrow. Well, I guess it's tomorrow now."

"Here's the thing. Witnesses at the saloon all said the soldier started the fight. Came in the door and went right after your son. So I ain't inclined to file any charges. Army'll stand for the damages, on account of their boy started it." He paused. "But if that boy dies, well, things will be different. The army could insist I keep Richard locked up and hold a trial. I don't think any jury in Arkansas would convict him—but if that soldier don't make it and we don't try your boy for killing him, well, the army could make it right uncomfortable for me. And I don't want that."

Again, the men sat silent. Finally, Lee said, "What is it you're saying, Marshal?"

The marshal turned and looked at the deputy, who continued to stare straight ahead. He turned back to Lee. "Now, I would never advise someone—officially—to leave town in such circumstances. But we could not put a man on trial if he wasn't here. And I doubt, given the nature of the fight, that anyone would bother to track him down." He paused, then, "Besides, like I said, Mister Pate, I've been seeing too much of your son—and I don't want to see him anymore."

Lee and the marshal locked eyes, and, in a moment, Lee nodded.

The marshal turned to his deputy again. "Go get the boy."

"Yessir."

A few minutes later, Richard shuffled through the door to the cells. Lee took him gently by the arm and led him out into the night.

Chapter Thirty-Three

Ten days out, the Pate and Lewis wagons stopped where the Little River joined the Canadian. A few miles up the tributary lay Edwards's Post. Over the first 140 or so miles of the journey here, they encountered Choctaw Agency a long day's travel out of Fort Smith, then a handful of small Choctaw and Cherokee towns and farms scattered along the way. But this place, run by a white man named Edwards and his Creek wife, was the last settlement until reaching the Mexican towns around Santa Fe nearly 700 miles later.

Lee and Daniel decided to lay over a day at the Edwards place to rest the stock and make a final inventory of supplies and provisions. The trail ahead—such as it was—would be long and lonely and they could rely only on their own resources. Hardtack, flour, coffee, tea, sugar, bacon, cornmeal, salt, rice, beans, and dried fruits were measured out and replenished. On the advice of Mister and Missus Edwards they added a new—to them—kind of trail food: pemmican. The mixture of pounded buffalo meat, berries, and animal fat was nutritious and traveled well, they were told by the storekeeper.

Richard, still tender in spots but ever more mobile since getting off the wagon after the first three days and hoofing it, albeit with a slight limp, found occasion to slip away to Edwards's store. After his return, his bedroll secreted a number of bottles of whiskey, wrapped in burlap bags for protection—both from breakage and discovery by clinking and rattling.

Rested and restocked, the family wagons were rolling by sunrise following the day of rest. Sarah sat on the wagon seat and drove the mules with Lee walking alongside, the saddle horse and cow tethered to the back of the wagon.

The Pate's mule-drawn wagon could make good time, but the plodding oxen set the pace for the train. Daniel trudged along beside the team on the lead wagon with a goad and a rope attached to the near-side ox's nose ring. The second wagon followed, the team content to walk in the tracks of the first. Still, Daniel always kept one of his daughters on duty with that span, just in case.

Richard, Melvin, and Abel walked along with the wagons save when one of the boys went out hunting meat, or rode ahead on the saddle horse to choose a suitable site for nooning or an overnight campsite.

The families kept a communal kitchen, with Sarah and the Lewis girls pitching in to prepare meals efficiently. When time for the midday layover approached, it became routine for the Pate wagon to swing around the ox teams, the mules allowed to step out ahead to provide Sarah the opportunity to have a cooking fire ready when the Lewises pulled in.

Abel rode back to the rolling wagons late one afternoon and passed along word to his father and Daniel that they would soon cross a small creek a ways ahead, and on the other side find a clearing for the wagons and good grass for the animals. Lee climbed onto the wagon seat and Melvin clambered up the back and stepped over the endgate when his father urged the mules ahead. Between the three of them, camp would be well underway when the others arrived.

Abel swung out of the saddle and led the horse to walk beside Emma behind the Lewis wagons. "How you holdin' up, Miss Emma?"

"Just fine, Abel. And you?"

"Same. Only that every day is just like the one before."

Emma laughed. "And, most likely, the one to come."

Abel smiled and they walked along in silence. With the sun's intensity waning, Emma untied her bonnet strings and pulled it off, freeing her hair to cascade down her back. Abel noticed its sheen in the angled sunbeams that peeked through the trees. He sought something to say, but the opportunity was lost when Richard made them a trio.

"Emma," he said with a tip of his hat.

"Richard."

"I sure do like the looks of your hair when it hangs down like that."

Emma rolled her eyes at the intimacy of his comment. "It is a bother, actually," she said. "All the time gathering dust, getting tangled in the wind and all."

"Looks pretty, just the same." He waited a minute, then said, "Say, Abel, why don't you ride on ahead and make sure Pa stops at a good place."

Abel cocked his head to look at his brother. "Already found a good place."

"Well, you know Pa. The old fool's likely to start daydreamin' and pass it right by."

Abel walked on several paces wondering at a reply. "I don't think so, Rich. Pa can take care of things just fine."

"Oh, sure, little brother. Like he's been doin' all along. Ever since we left home." With a snort, he said, "Go on ahead, Abel. I'd like to have a little talk with Emma."

Abel turned to Emma and his arched eyebrows asked the question.

"Stay here, Abel—please. Richard, Abel and I were already talking."

Another snort from Richard. "Hell, Emma, he ain't got nothin' to say. He's just a kid."

"Well then, I guess that goes for me, too. Me and Abel are close to the same age. I am younger. And even if he does not talk much, he is a good listener."

Abel's blush was his only contribution to the conversation. But the crimson of embarrassment soon shaded to the scarlet of anger.

Richard grabbed Emma by the elbow and gave it a tug bordering on a jerk. "C'mon, Emma! Why bother messin' with a boy when there's a man to be had?"

Abel dropped the bridle reins and pivoted around Emma and planted himself square in Richard's path. Richard drove the palms of both hands into Abel's chest, with the only result the younger boy taking half a step back. Richard tried again, but this time Abel thrust his forearms up and out, fending off the attempt. He followed up by duplicating his brother's move, and his shove sent Richard sprawling. He found his way to his feet and dusted off his backside.

"You had best watch yourself, baby brother. If I wasn't stove up, I'd kick your ass where you stand," Richard said, then limped up the trail in a hurry to catch the wagons.

Still wide-eyed and breathless when they started walking, Emma said, "Why is Richard so angry all the time?"

"Wish I knew," Abel said. "Slightest little thing'll set him off. He's always been inclined that way, but it's a whole lot worse since we left home. I reckon some if it is on account of you don't pay him no mind."

"The truth is, Abel, I do not like Richard very much. His foul moods—his drinking—his disrespect for your father—he is just not the sort of man I could come to admire."

Abel said nothing, just walked along. After a long silence, Emma said, "Do you think there is anything to what he says? About your father, I mean?"

It took Abel a while to formulate an answer. "I don't know.

Pa sure ain't like most men. When he feels something, it grabs him hard. And when he takes a notion, he won't let go. I don't understand much about the things he worries over—slavery ruining the States, and such." He thought some more. "I guess when all's said and done, I figure he's my Pa, and that's enough. I read in that Bible of his, 'Honour thy father and thy mother' so that's what I try to do. He might not be right all the time—but, like I said, he's my Pa."

Emma reached over and threaded her arm through Abel's and pulled him a bit closer as they walked. His face reddened again.

So did Richard's when he looked back to see Abel and Emma walking arm in arm.

CHAPTER THIRTY-FOUR

A morning came when the wagons rolled out and the world changed. Rather than the dense forests wrapped around intermittent parks of open country the Pates had known all their lives, they entered a land where the woods thinned out and the trees bunched up, surrounded by miles and miles of prairie and plains.

This was the Cross Timbers, a border region separating the green and well-watered East from the arid West. Towering hardwood trees that scratched the clouds and covered the ground—hickory, elm, ash, walnut, beech—gave way to smaller blackjack, post, and shin oaks along with other ground-hugging trees and tangled undergrowth continually thinned by fire.

The wagons stopped atop one of the endless rolling hills one morning to give the stock a blow. Melvin, enfolded in his own arms as if cold, said to Abel, "I don't like this. Feels kind of exposed—if someone was after you out here, they could see you from a long ways off."

Abel turned a slow circle, taking in the view. "You're right, brother. On the other hand, you can see 'em coming, too."

"I guess so," Melvin said with a shiver. "But I don't like it. Too big and empty."

"That's what I like about it. Feels like you can see all the way to tomorrow. Ain't a thing between a man and what he wants."

And there were buffalo. The train had encountered small, scattered herds along the way, but now they saw vast herds, stretching for miles. One afternoon they bunched the wagons when a herd passed as if they weren't there, flowing around them like ocean waves. The drumming hooves, the smell, the nearness of the giant beasts frightened the travelers and upset the mules, oxen, heifer, horse, and chickens alike.

But the tide passed and the wagons rolled on and any discomfort over the herds was offset by their presence as a ready supply of fresh meat. When first the buffalo started appearing in numbers, Abel took his father's long rifle and rode out to hunt—if hunt it was, in the circumstances. He rode to the top of a low ridge and in a swale below, well within range for an easy shot, a small herd of bison grazed.

Abel dismounted, checked his load, sat down, steadied elbows on knees, and took down a young female. The other animals in the herd raised their heads to look around but did not give up their feeding until the horseback man came down the hill toward them. They loped away, leaving the cow on the ground.

Unfamiliar with the means of dressing buffalo, Abel attacked the job as if he were butchering a beef—without the ease of a hung carcass. With lariat and saddle horn, he dragged the animal around until its head lay downslope and he used Uncle Ben's fancy knife to slit the throat to let it bleed out. He bunged the backside, then opened the belly and pulled out the entrails and pushed them aside after saving out the heart and liver. He slit the skin up the limbs and around the neck and peeled the hide with considerable effort, even with the help of the horse to shift the carcass around. After a rest, Abel went back to work, wielding knife and hatchet to carve out the hind quarters and separate the loins from the rump.

The horse protested, but Abel laid the buffalo hide hair-side down over the saddle and horse's rump and hefted the meat aboard, then wrapped and lashed the hide over and tied it off to any part of the saddle rigging he could find. He left the remains of the buffalo for the wolves, coyotes, and carrion birds. With the lead rope and bridle reins, he managed to get the skittish, shying horse to the wagons without it running off.

By the time he caught up, camp was made and supper in the works. But the women, excited at the prospect of turning their culinary skills to buffalo meat, immediately set to slicing out steaks to fry and filling cast-iron kettles with meat to roast overnight for the days ahead.

The cooking meat stimulated the appetites of the men. "If that buffalo tastes as good as it smells, we shall eat well this evening," Daniel said.

Melvin stood staring at the steaks sizzling in the skillets. "I reckon I could eat one by myself."

"You did well, Abel," Lee said.

Richard said nothing, but neither did he stray far from the smells of the cooking fires.

After parceling out the meat, Abel rolled the hide and lashed it under the wagon, thinking that, later, he might want to tan his first buffalo hide. Then he sat cross-legged on the ground cleaning and oiling the rifle, and honing Uncle Ben's big knife and the hatchet he'd used to butcher the buffalo. He was still sitting there when Emma carried him a steaming plate with a buffalo steak hanging over the edges and a biscuit, puddle of beans, and heap of rice crowding for space.

"Abel, here you are," Emma said.

He looked the plate over and smiled at Emma. "Thank you—but I can fix my own plate."

"Oh, I know. But since you brought in all that good meat, well, you deserve to be coddled a little." She handed him a cup of cold creek water. "There is coffee on, if you would care for some."

A hurried flurry of chewing and a hard swallow preceded his answer. "No thanks, Emma. I'll have some later. Can't wait till that heifer calves and freshens. Milk would sure taste good about now."

As the men and women sat and ate, they peppered Abel with questions about the buffalo hunt.

"Sounds about as hard as shootin' a hog in a pen," Richard said.

"Now, Son. . . ." Lee warned.

"Aw, hell, Pa! Abel as much as said so hisself."

"He's right," Abel said. "It was a whole lot easier than stalkin' a deer through the woods for the better part of a day. Funny thing was, them critters wasn't jumpy at all. Even after I shot the one, they just kept on eating as if nothing was wrong."

Melvin said, "Me, I'll just keep on eatin' too. That meat's right good. Ma? Got another'n of them steaks?"

"Yes," she said, banging a spoon against the rim of the bean pot. She wiped her hands on her apron, swept back a stray lock of hair from her forehead, picked up a fork, speared a piece of meat and lifted it from the skillet. "Well, you comin' to get it, or do you expect me to bring it to you?"

He grinned and held up his plate. Muttering under her breath to feign displeasure, Sarah carried the steak to him and slapped it on his plate.

Mary gathered plates from the other men, scraped them free of scraps and slid them into the dish pan. "Jane, I believe it is your turn to wipe. I will wash."

"Jane, it is your turn to wipe," Jane said, mimicking her older sister as she minced her way over. She slid her plate into the wash water and exaggerated a curtsey. "At your service, your majesty."

A few day's travel left the Cross Timbers behind. The wagons rolled and rolled across the treeless plains and vistas spread on every side for more miles than the Pates ever imagined possible.

"You ever seen anything like this?" Lee said to Daniel one

day after they unhitched and unyoked their teams for the midday break.

Daniel lifted his hat, pulled a handkerchief from his pocket. He mopped his forehead as he gazed at the unchanging scenery. "As a matter of fact, I have, Lee. The monotony of the seascape during our passage across the Atlantic Ocean was much like this. Very much so, indeed." His face dulled like a clouded sun. "I hope this crossing does not bring so much grief."

Chapter Thirty-Five

Lee Pate tossed and turned in his bedroll, begging sleep to return but troubled by a recurring dream that kept him awake and overwrought. When finally the stars dimmed in the east and a ribbon of gray eased onto the horizon, he threw off the confines of his covers and stirred up the campfire and slid the coffeepot with last night's leftovers nearer the flame. Sarah soon joined him, sitting on a packing box near the fire, staring into the flames.

"What's troubling you, Lee?"

He sat poking at the fire with a stick and continued as if he did not hear.

"Lee?" Sarah said again.

He flinched, as if surprised at her presence.

"Sorry, Sarah. Lost in thought, I guess."

"What's got you thinking?"

He reached out and tapped the coffeepot to test its warmth. "Can you get me a cup, Sarah?"

She fetched two, and Lee filled them both. They blew the steam off their coffee and sipped in silence for a moment.

After a time, Lee said, "It's a dream, Sarah. A dream I keep having."

Sarah chuckled, but without mirth. "Not the first time you've let a dream take hold of you."

"This one's different. It wakes me up nights, and if I can get back to sleep, it wakes me up again." He sipped at his coffee and thought for a minute. "I don't know, Sarah. It must mean something."

"Oh, Lee. . . ." Sarah shook her head then stared at the contents of her coffee cup. "Your dreams and your notions have caused this family enough trouble. Let it go. If you can't, don't let it talk you into doing something foolish. I don't think we can stand it anymore. Whatever it is, leave it lie."

By now the Lewis girls were up and about. Soon they would be rattling skillets and kettles and rooting around in the kitchen boxes, laying out the fixings for breakfast. Abel rolled out of his bed and checked the livestock. Melvin shuffled to the fire, scratching and sniffing. Sarah found another cup and filled it for him. Richard sat in his bedroll bleary-eyed, waiting for wakefulness to overcome his torpor.

Abel walked up to the fire with a wide grin. "Good news, Pa, Ma. That heifer finally dropped her calf. Good-lookin' little bull. We'll have to make room for it in the wagon for a while—but in another three, four days we'll be drinkin' milk!"

Sarah swirled the now-cool coffee in her cup. "Good. I could sure use a squirt or two in this coffee. It's bitter as Job's soul." She tossed the dregs into the fire, raising a hissing cloud of steam, then raked a hank of hair away from her face. "Guess I best get to fixin' breakfast. Can't leave it all to them girls."

Lee placed a hand on her arm. "Hold off a minute, Sarah. I'd like to talk to you and the boys. Richard, come on over here."

Richard mumbled and grumbled but stumbled to the fire.

Lee let his family stew for a moment. Richard said, "C'mon, Pa. If you ain't got nothin' to say, I'm goin' to see a man about a horse."

"Sit tight, Richard." Lee stood and paced a short track beside the fire. "The thing is," he finally said, "I'm worried." He made another circuit, stopped again. "I been havin' this dream—"

"—Oh, shit," Richard said. "Here we go again."

Sharp glances from Lee and Abel stilled Richard's protest.

"This dream has me worried," Lee said, picking up the thread of his story. "It makes me fear for my family. For you-all."

Again, Richard. "Aw, hell, Pa—it ain't but a dream. No matter what, it's only a dream."

"Stop it, Rich," Abel said. "Let him talk."

Lee said, "It's fine. I know dreams don't mean much to some folks, but I put a good deal of store in mine. I believe they have meaning, and it would be foolish to ignore them."

"Yeah, sure. And it's just as foolish to follow them. Look where your dreams has got us so far," Richard said.

"I know you see it that way, Son. And that's what this dream is all about, I do believe. I ain't sure exactly what it means, but like I said, it's got me worried." Lee paused, and his eyes lost focus as his mind went elsewhere.

When the silence became uncomfortable, Abel said, "What is this dream, Pa? Tell us what it is."

Lee returned, and in a low voice said, "We—the family—we're on a journey in some far-off place. It don't look like anyplace I ever seen—don't even look real, somehow. And yet it does. It don't matter. What matters is, there's this river. It's a wide river—not Mississippi wide, but wide enough.

"Some of us has crossed over—we're there on the bank with the wagon. But you-all," Lee said, wagging a finger back and forth at Richard and Melvin, "are back on the other side. We're a-standin' there on the river bank—me and your Ma and Abel—waving you-all to come on over. But you don't. You-all just stand over there lookin' at us."

Lee knuckled away a tear. "The side of the river we're on, it's a fine place. Grass and trees and cattle and sheep and deer and songbirds and all. 'Bout as beautiful as anyplace could ever be. The other side, over where Richard and Melvin still are, it ain't but dirt and rocks and thorn bushes. Don't seem like any kind of place you'd want to be. Still, Richard and Melvin won't come on across the river. You-all just stand over there watchin' us—but it's like you can't even see us." Tears flowed freely down Lee's cheeks, dripping off his jowls.

The rest of the Pates sat, unsure what to say, and so said nothing.

"Missus Pate," Jane Lewis said, interrupting the silence. "Missus Pate, Ma'am—Mary says to tell you we got things ready to cook breakfast and wants to know, can we get started?"

CHAPTER THIRTY-SIX

The farther he rode from the Canadian or the creeks that fed the river, the more the wide-open spaces disconcerted Richard. Like his brother Melvin, something about the emptiness made him uncomfortable. The farther west the wagons rolled, the more the sun absorbed the humidity, and on days of powerful heat his very breath seared his throat. With no trees to stem the wind, it rolled across the prairie like a tide, rippling the grass before it in waves. Thunderstorms sometimes boiled up in the afternoons, flashing across the plains and down-pouring rain so intense it raised a dust. With no real shelter anywhere, he would seek a low spot in the rolling terrain and hunker down beneath the horse. Fortunately, the storms passed quickly and he was soon back in the saddle, with a fresh smell and thin layer of mud the only reminders of the rain.

Despite the loneliness, the emptiness, and the ever-present perception of danger, Richard took to the saddle at every opportunity, often finagling Melvin out of his turn to scout or hunt. Richard saw buffalo frequently, but seldom shot one unless close enough to the coming wagons to get help with the butchering. He bagged an occasional deer and once took a shot at a lone and distant pronghorn, unsure what the strange animal might be.

But mostly he rode aimlessly. And brooded. His inability to please his father befuddled him. Try as he might, his every effort soon deteriorated into a useless contest of wills. He wondered at Abel's ability to please their father—a gift he lacked and did not understand. Lee's recent dream offered no encouragement; rather it added to his feelings of hopelessness and helplessness. *Hell, even in the old man's dreams I ain't no good,* he thought. He worried over Emma, and her ambivalence about, even dismissal of, his interest in her. And her attraction to Abel, despite his brother's apparent lack of intentions where she was concerned. He stewed about what they would find in Mexico, and what kind of life, if any, he could build there.

And he wondered when he could get another drink.

One day, he sat in the saddle, stopped atop a low rise and lost in contemplation. He did not hear the approach of the Indians and ignored his horse's warnings. And so he was startled, even terrified, to find a mounted man on either side of him. He raised the rifle from where it rested across the fork of his saddle, but the Indian to his left grabbed the barrel and held it still despite Richard's best efforts to move it—he jerked and yanked and twisted, but could not wrest the gun from the Indian's grasp.

The man holding the barrel said something in a language Richard did not understand and the other man laughed. After a moment, the Indian said, "Stop it. I will not let go until you do."

Richard's eyes widened at the Indian's words and the smile on his face. "You speak English!" he said.

"Yes. Yes I do."

The man's smile and the grin on the other Indian's face convinced Richard he was in no imminent danger. He stopped pulling at the rifle and after a moment the Indian let it go and Richard lowered it to rest on the saddle. "What do you want?"

The man spoke to his companion in whatever Indian language they spoke, and again the other rider laughed. This time, he spoke. "You were so still here for so long, we were worried you had turned to ice." He waved an arm across the landscape. "And yet it is summer and the sun is hot. Maybe you slept—or maybe you were dead, we thought."

"Well, I ain't. So I reckon I'll be moving along."

"Wait," the first Indian said. "You are with the wagons? The two drawn by oxen and another with mules?"

After a moment, Richard realized it would do no good to lie as the men obviously knew the answer.

"We saw your wagons. The chickens. The cow and calf. The women gathering buffalo wood and the men driving the teams."

"What of it?"

The Indian dismissed the question with a wave of his hand. "We mean you no harm—nor your people. But we do not see many travelers here. We will ride with you to your wagons for a visit. Catch up on the news from the East."

Skeptical, but realizing any objection would be wasted, Richard reined his horse around and started toward the distant river.

"Wait."

"What is it now?"

The Indians laughed. "If you go there, you will not find your wagons. They are far past there by now. You slept too long."

"I wasn't asleep."

The Indians laughed as they rode off. "This way," one said over his shoulder with a grin. "Follow us."

The wagons, so far ahead it surprised Richard, had already halted for the day when the trio arrived. They rode up and stopped, met by Abel, pistol in hand, Lee with the other revolver, Daniel with a rifle, and Melvin with a single-shot pistol that belonged to Daniel.

"Put the guns down," Richard said. "These men don't mean no harm."

The men lowered their weapons and the women stepped into

the open. The travelers studied their guests. They looked to be well mounted. Their dress was much like their own, but embellished with some beadwork and other decorations. One of the men had a tattooed face.

"Might as well step down," Lee said. "We'll have a fire going soon and you-all will be welcome to coffee."

"Do you have sugar?"

As Richard had been earlier, the people in the camp were surprised to hear the question in English.

"Why, sure," Lee said. "A little."

"Good!" the Indian said with a smile.

Melvin led the unhitched mules to water, Emma following along leading one of the oxen with the other three plodding behind. Sarah untied the milk cow from the wagon and shooed it off in the direction of the oxen, knowing it and the calf would follow. Mary kindled a fire and piled on buffalo chips as Jane wrestled kitchen boxes out of the wagons.

When the coffee was ready, the men sat and talked while the women went about their work preparing food.

"How come you-all to speak English so good?" Lee said.

"Our people have lived among the white men since beyond memory. We are from what your people call the Five Civilized Tribes."

"Cherokee?"

"Chickasaw."

"Ah," Lee said. "I remember you-all comin' through Memphis a couple years back. On your way to here, I reckon?"

"That is so. It took years to negotiate our 'removal' with your government. But we were forced out of our homeland and sent here to the Indian Territory to live on land leased from the Choctaw. It is not what we would have chosen." They talked some more about the removal; the difficulty of transplanting nearly 5,000 tribal members, more than a thousand slaves, and thousands of well-bred horses that attracted thieves and rustlers every step of the way and ever since.

Daniel said, "We have seen no other Indians for donkey's years. Where are the rest of your people?"

"You passed our settlements long ago. While this is Chickasaw land, most of our people live near the Choctaw. We two—well, we were stricken with what you people call 'cabin fever' and are out here seeking a cure. Just to look over the country, maybe do a little hunting."

Melvin said, "There ain't much to look at in this country. It sure is different from home."

The Chickasaw men nodded agreement, and the conversation turned to the emigrants, who explained their intention to settle in Mexican Territory. Lee preached his sermon on the evils of slavery and the pending destruction of the United States in recompense for the sin. The Indians only laughed.

"Our people have hoped for the demise and departure of the white men for hundreds of years and it has yet to happen. Perhaps your prediction will finally bring it to pass," the most talkative of the two said. "But I am worried it may come to our harm as well, if what you say about slaveholding is true. The Chickasaw have kept black slaves for many, many years, as have the Cherokee, the Creek, the Choctaw. It is a practice we learned from your people."

"Well, I reckon there may be some forgiveness for you-all on account of that," Lee said.

Mary approached the men, wiping her hands on her apron. "Now that you-all have emptied the coffeepot, you may want to put something more substantial on your stomachs. Supper is ready."

Talk continued as the men ate. Their guests assured the travelers there was no danger from relocated Indians, as they were well past the settled areas and even the possibility of a chance encounter—such as theirs—was remote.

Before they rode away, the Chickasaw visitors warned that Comanche raiding parties from the south sometimes crossed the Red River, and as the wagons traveled west they would be passing through Comancheria, crossing lands frequented by wandering bands of the tribe. They would not find the Comanche so good-natured.

Chapter Thirty-Seven

The wagons threaded their way through the Antelope Hills and at some unrecognized place crossed out of Indian Territory and into the panhandle of Texas. Soon, they reached the breaks of the Canadian River, the gorge deepening as they wended their way west. Climbing out of a rocky ravine one afternoon a rear wheel of the Pate wagon slid sideways off a boulder and dropped, the rock snapping the axle as if it were a stick of kindling and leaving the wheel spinning in the wind.

Lee stooped under the wagon and studied the broken axle and backed out on his hands and knees. He stood and dusted off his pants legs, shaking his head, then turned to the family circled around. "It's gone. Busted clean through."

Sarah said, "Can it be fixed?"

Brushing his hands together, Lee shook his head.

"So what do we do?"

"Don't know. Have to think on it some. We'd have carried a spare had I known."

"We're in a hell of a fix, then, is what you're saying."

After a moment, Lee said, "That ain't exactly how I'd put it, Sarah, but I suppose that explains it."

By now, the Lewises had parked their wagons on the plain above and were walking back down the slope to see what the matter was. Lee explained the situation. "Thought about bringin' a spare, but didn't," he said.

"Nor I," Daniel said. "What is to be done?"

No one offered an answer until Abel crawled out from under the stalled wagon. "We'll make a new one."

Richard laughed. "Two things, baby brother. First, we ain't seen a tree for weeks except for cottonwoods in the river bottom. That wood ain't stout enough to make a crutch for a three-legged coon hound. And second, you don't know one damn thing about makin' a wagon axle."

All eyes turned to Abel, awaiting his response and knowing Richard's contention, while crude, was logical. "We've got it to do," Abel finally said. "I'll find a way."

He chocked the front wheels of the wagon with rocks. "Pa, you might unhook the team." He untied the milk cow from the tail of the wagon and handed the lead rope to Jane. "Would you mind leading her on up?" She started up the hill and the calf followed. He lifted out the endgate and set it aside. "Rich, Mel—load up. We'll have to tote most all this stuff to the top. Anyone else cares to lend a hand, well, your help is sure welcome."

It took most of the afternoon to carry the wagon's goods and pile them on the rim. With that job nearly done, Abel gathered up the axe and rode the saddle horse down the ravine and into the gorge. He came back after a while with two six-foot lengths of cottonwood limb stripped smooth of twigs and branches tied to the saddle skirts alongside the horse.

"What the hell's them for?" Richard laughed. "Looks like Mel's been whittlin' on your poles there."

Abel swung out of the saddle and loosened the load, dropping the limbs beside the wagon. "What you said about a crutch gave me an idea. You'll see."

Richard looked on while, with Melvin's help, Abel set up the wagon jack on the side of the wagon with the wheel still on the ground, removed the linchpin and pulled the wheel. Trusting the stability of the jack, he crawled under the wagon, dragging one of the lengths of cottonwood with him and wedged it between the hounds and bottom of the wagon box and lashed it in place with the tail end poking out behind the wagon.

"I get it," Richard said as Abel got the process underway on the other side of the wagon. "It's a crutch." He laughed as if it was the funniest thing he had ever seen. "A wagon crutch! You're a bigger fool than I thought, little brother."

"Why's that?"

"How far you think you can drag that wagon on them sticks?"

"Only have to get to the top of the hill." The other wheel, spinning idly in the breeze, came off easily. But finding a place for the jack and lifting that side of the wagon, high-centered on the rock, proved a challenge. "Rich, why don't you get off your butt and lend a hand. Sooner we get this prop put on and the wagon up top, the sooner we can figure out a more permanent fix."

It took a considerable amount of straining and groaning and grumbling and swearing, but they eventually got the wagon off the ground, the boulder out of the way, and the prop installed. Melvin backed the mules to the wagon and saw to their hitching. He urged the team forward and Abel watched the props gouge shallow trenches in the dirt and bounce over rocks, hoping with every jolt they would hold. The poles were uneven, causing the wagon to list, and it didn't track straight, but the props held and with much screeching and scratching and creaking and cracking the wagon finally lurched over the rim.

Supper was on the fire and the Pate boys ladled generous portions of venison and gravy over biscuits, saving room for a sweet rice pudding with raisins. Lee and Daniel, under Sarah's direction, had arranged the unloaded wagon goods under a canvas fly staked to the ground and lashed to the side of one of the Lewis wagons. With the other supper dishes already done, Emma and Jane played singing and hand-clapping games as they waited for the Pate boys to finish eating. Mary sat on a rock a ways off from the wagons with a book in her lap.

Richard handed his plate to Emma, and held on to it for a second or two when she tried to take it. With a sigh, she rolled her eyes and stopped tugging and waited for him to let go. He grinned and loosened his grip and, after she walked away, lifted himself to his feet and walked out to where Mary sat.

"You don't look to be readin' much—you holdin' that book for some other reason?"

Mary caressed the open page then closed the book on her thumb to mark the place. "No. I meant to read, but my mind wandered." She looked off into the distance. "The sun is down now. It will soon be too dark anyway."

"Me, I never took to reading much."

"I enjoy it. Martha was the smart one, though. Had her nose in a book any spare minute. She wouldn't go to the privy without book in hand." Mary realized what she had said, ducked her head and giggled behind her hand.

"What is it you was reading? Or meaning to?"

Mary studied the cover of the book. "It is a book of poems Martha left. By an Englishman named Wordsworth."

"Poems. We had to learn a poem by heart in school. I don't remember mine anymore. What's this English fellow's poems about?"

"Oh, many things. Nature—death—philosophy—his feelings." She opened the book to the marked verse and read the first stanza:

I wandered lonely as a cloud
That floats on high o'er vales and hills,
When all at once I saw a crowd,
A host of golden daffodils;
Beside the lake, beneath the trees,
Fluttering and dancing in the breeze.

Richard laughed. "Daffodils? Ma had some of them flowers planted at our place. Come up ever' spring." He laughed again. "Sure as hell that feller who wrote that wasn't wandering around this country. Ain't no daffodils here."

For a long moment, Mary studied Richard. He squirmed, embarrassed. Then, "Wordsworth writes more about the flowers," she said. "But I do not believe it is the flowers themselves he finds important. It is the beauty they represent, and that beautiful things stay with us, in our hearts. And the pleasure such memories bring."

Her thoughts brought only a blank stare.

"Listen, Richard, to the end of the poem":

For oft, when on my couch I lie
In vacant or in pensive mood,
They flash upon that inward eye
Which is the bliss of solitude;
And then my heart with pleasure fills,
And dances with the daffodils.

Again, no response from Richard. Mary smiled and closed the book. "Richard! Do you not ever remember beautiful things you have seen?"

"Don't know. Never really thought about it."

"Oh, come now! Surely your thoughts turn from time to time to beauty! Do you never think of Emma in a quiet moment? Does not her image 'flash upon your inward eye' when you are in a 'pensive mood'?"

Richard blushed. He had no answer for Mary's teasing. She stood and smoothed the front of her dress. "Come," she said. "It is dark. We should be getting back."

Chapter Thirty-Eight

Abel was under the wagon at first light, studying the break in the axle. It looked more snapped or sheared than shattered. The break was just outside the through-bolt that joined the axle, hound, and bolster. He could see where the sharp edge of the boulder had bitten into the bottom of the axle, with gravity and the weight of the wagon doing the rest. Other than a few splinters at the edges of the break, very little wood was missing. He did not know why, but Abel thought that a good thing.

He unhooked the brake linkage and pulled out the brake beam. He called the other men to help and they lifted off and set aside the wagon box, laying bare the running gear. The buffalo hide he'd tied atop the reach was still there and he cut it loose. Abel looked the works over to determine how best to get to the broken axle, and removed the hound braces and through-bolts and each end of the axle dropped free in turn. He laid the ends together on the ground and, squatting with forearms on knees, stared at them as minute after minute after minute passed, as if they would magically rejoin.

"Any ideas yet, Abel?" Lee said. "You been staring at that axle for a long time."

"Not yet, Pa."

"Wish I could help. Don't know what to do."

Richard yelled from where he sat in the shade. "I do. I got an idea if you-all want to hear it."

"What's that, Son?"

Richard walked over to the wagon box. "Cut the damn thing in half. There ain't nothin' wrong with the front end."

Lee pursed his lips and wrinkled his brow and after a moment said, "So we make a cart." He thought some more. "It's an idea."

"Won't work, Pa," Abel said.

Richard stuttered and stammered and finally spat, "What the hell do you mean, little brother? Just 'cause it ain't your idea? 'Course it'll work!"

Abel stood. "Sure. We could build a cart, all right. But what you fixin' to leave behind? We ain't hardly got enough of what we need to get started somewheres as it is."

"We could put stuff on the Lewises' wagons!"

"Some, maybe," Abel said. "But not half a wagon load or more."

Daniel said, "We will be happy to take what we can—but Abel is right. Our wagons are fairly well stuffed."

Lee weighed the arguments. "Abel's right, Richard—but so are you. Let's give Abel time to fix the wagon." Then, to Abel: "Son, we ain't got a whole lot of time to waste. If you don't come up with an idea soon, well, I don't see as we got any choice other than cut down the wagon like your brother says."

Abel and Richard locked eyes and held the gaze until Abel turned away. He walked over to the camp equipment under the wagon sheet fly and rummaged around in the bags and boxes. When he came out, he carried a narrow canvas bag. He squatted near the axle and dumped the picket pins from the sack, selected one and laid it next to the axle.

Lee and Daniel walked over as if hoping to read Abel's thoughts. Richard and Melvin stood by as well. After a moment, Abel stuffed the picket pins back into the bag and tossed it aside.

"What do you have in mind, Lad?" Daniel said.

"Don't matter. Won't work. Steel ain't strong enough."

"Tell us," Lee said.

"I thought I could make holes in the axle and stick a steel rod in there to span the break—but one of these picket pins would only bend. If only I had a steel rod that was thicker, stronger. . . ."

Daniel perked up after a moment and stabbed the air with his forefinger. "By George!" he said. "I might have just the thing!" He quickstepped to his lead wagon and climbed over the seat into the box. They watched the canvas rustle, heard the shifting and moving of boxes and bags and after a few minutes Daniel emerged from the wagon with a wool blanket rolled around something and tied with string.

He dropped the bundle and untied the lashings and unrolled the blanket to reveal a rifle. "Gentlemen, this is a Baker rifle, manufactured in Enfield. Carried by my uncle—a member of the 'Prince Consort's Own Rifle Corps'—at the Battle of Waterloo."

The rifle's stock was split and half was gone; only a splinter of the forestock still adhered to the barrel. The ramrod was missing altogether, as was the lid of the butt-trap patch box. The still-elegant scrolled trigger was twisted, the folding rear sight broken off, the cock and frizzen bent.

Richard said, "What the hell happened to it?"

"Our home was attacked by mobbers in Missouri. This is some of their work. I kept it for sentimental reasons, hoping one day to have it restored, but I am a right pillock to think so. I fear it is damaged beyond repair. Abel—will its barrel suit your purpose?"

Abel squatted over the broken rifle and tipped his hat back. He felt the steel of the barrel, running his fingers along its length. "I believe it will, Mister Lewis. Are you sure you want to sacrifice it?"

"Oh, its value is nil, even for sentimental purposes. If it will solve your problem, it will have died an honorable death."

Abel rose and clapped and clasped his hands. "All right, then. Melvin, will you gather up some rocks and build a kiln like they did with bricks at the brickyard—only has to be maybe two feet—and lay a fire in it. We'll have to haul up plenty of wood from the river. I'll need a tub of water as well."

The men and the women went to work, trooping down the ravine to the river and hauling back buckets of water and bundles of wood. No one of them was certain exactly what Abel planned—nor was Abel—but the work went on.

Richard, hefting a bucket in each hand and a load of wood strapped to his back, complained every step of the way, heard mostly by no ears other than his own. Melvin walked with him after building his stone beehive, but did not join his brother's complaints. Mary and Sarah teamed up, as did Emma and Jane, each pair sharing a bucket between them and carrying another. Lee and Daniel each drove a harnessed mule down and dragged heavy logs back to camp.

Abel stoked a fire in the makeshift kiln and recruited Jane to keep it fed. He filled a washtub with water and shoveled in several spadesful of ashes from the cookfire and stirred them in. He unrolled the stiffened green buffalo hide and worked it into the tub, and when immersed weighted it down with rocks.

"Well, folks, that's all I can do for now. May as well have supper. If we take turns to keep the fire in the kiln goin' all night we can go to work again in the morning."

Daniel said, "If you do not mind, Abel, can you explain what it is you plan to do?"

Richard laughed and said, "I don't think he has any idea what he's up to. Whole lot of work for nothin' if you ask me. And when he's all done foolin' around and wasting time, we'll cut that wagon down and be on our way. Mark my words."

"Now, Richard, we chose to give Abel a chance," Lee said.

"*You* chose. Not me. You're as big a damn fool as he is," Richard said and walked away.

Abel let the dust settle for a few minutes. "Here's what I'm thinking. We get a hot enough fire in that kiln, we can heat up that rifle barrel enough to trim it down to a proper length and narrow one of the ends into a sort-of point. Then we keep it hot enough to burn a hole half as long as the barrel into each one of the busted ends of the axle. Then we stick the barrel in and join the axle ends together. I'm hopin' that steel will be strong enough to support the wagon."

Lee nodded, thought a minute, and said, "What about the buffalo hide?"

"Once we get it fleshed and scrape the hair off, we'll cut it into strips and wrap it around the axle. That rawhide should shrink up tight and dry hard as the hickory in that axle. Leastways I hope so. All I can do now is break down that rifle so the barrel will be ready. Come mornin' we'll put some fire to it. We should know in a few days if this idea has any chance of working."

Abel thought a minute, lowered his head and shook it slowly. "Could be Rich is right." He wandered off into the brush, absent-mindedly knocking leaves from the brush with a stick as he thought. Later, he returned to camp and sought out Emma.

"Miss Emma, I've got something for you."

The girl studied the sparkle in his eye through the blush shading his face and took note of the cookie tin—biscuit tin, to her—in his hands. "Whatever could it be, Abel? Biscuits—or cookies, as you call them?"

Confused by the question, it finally dawned on Abel what she meant. "Oh, no! This can—well, it's just somethin' I saved years ago to keep trinkets and treasures and such in—you know, arrowheads and marbles and pretty rocks and a lead soldier I found. Such like that."

"So it's a treasure you've brought me?"

Again, her question disoriented him. "Oh, no," he said. Then, "Well, maybe."

With that, he thrust the can into her hands. She smiled, further perturbing him, then worked loose the lid. With its grip released, she lifted the lid and looked inside to see a hairy brown spider the size of her hand scrambling around the bottom of the tin. Despite using all eight legs in the attempt, the tarantula was unable to find a way up the side and out of the container.

Rather than the hysterical scream Abel expected, Emma slid the lid back into place. She clutched the can to her breast and flashed her widest smile. "Why, Abel, it is a treasure indeed. How will I ever thank you?"

Abel watched in horror and confusion as Emma walked away.

Chapter Thirty-Nine

Abel's attempt to repair the wagon proved slow and laborious. The deep bed of coals in the kiln, fanned by whatever came to hand to increase the heat, took time to turn the end of the gun barrel from black to red to orange to yellow to white. Alex estimated—guessed, really—an acceptable length for his axle patching rod and, hammering a hatchet blade for a chisel, using a flat rock for an anvil, cut the barrel. The end was reheated and hammered and drawn to a square-sided point. Then, slowly, slowly, he used the rod to burn—drill—a hole into each broken end. Despite gloves, the palms of his hands were soon blistered and raw from gripping the metal, hot as it was even at the unfired end. He tried wrapping the rod with strips of wool blanket saturated with water, but the resulting steam burned all the more. Dry blanket strips proved a better barrier, but working the metal without proper smithing tools took its toll.

Abel took his time to experiment with the best combination of heat, pressure, twisting, and cooling water to confine the fire as much as possible to the diameter of the hole. Keeping the holes straight and centered in the axle also required care and concentration.

Richard's frustration eventually glowed as hot as the gun barrel. "Pa, how much longer are you going to put up with this nonsense? We been sittin' here for days while Abel plays around and we still ain't got any idea if it will work. Had we cut the wagon down like I said, we'd be miles from here by now—and that many miles closer to wherever the hell it is we're a-goin'."

"Son, so far as I know we ain't late for anything. It says in the Good Book, 'The patient in spirit is better than the proud in spirit.' You might take a lesson from it."

"Oh, the hell you say. Abel don't know a damn thing about fixin' a wagon and you know it. Me, I been patient with him long enough. Far as I'm concerned, Abel is the only one bein' proud here, thinkin' he knows what the hell he's doing. And you—you're willing to go along with it!"

"Be that as it may, Richard, we'll all be better off with your help. Look at Melvin—he's helpin' out."

"Oh, hell, yeah. Stoking the fire and stirrin' that smelly damn buffalo hide Abel's got soakin' in the tub. Ain't much he's doin' that a pickaninny couldn't do."

Richard ducked his head to avoid Lee's look. After a moment, his father said. "I'll brook no more of that kind of talk, Son. You know my feelings on that subject. Besides that, it's hateful toward your brother."

Richard turned and walked away. He was standing on the verge of the gorge when Mary found him, tossing pebbles into the void. She did not say anything, just walked up and, arms folded across her chest, stood beside him.

Richard tossed three pebbles one after another then turned to her. "You ain't going to read me another damn poem, are you?"

Mary swallowed hard. "No. I just thought you might enjoy some company. Someone to talk to."

He tossed another pebble and watched it disappear. "Well, I won't."

She waited as he scooped up another handful of pebbles and continued pitching them over the side. "Who is it you hate the most, Richard—your father or your brother?"

All the pebbles sailed away in a single toss. "What the hell do you care?"

"I do not care. Not really. I just wonder how you can harbor so much hate. They are your family, after all."

"You'd never know it. To Pa's way of thinking, Abel's the only son worth having."

"Why do you say that? According to my observations, he treats all of you well. You, Melvin, and Abel. Your mother shows no favoritism, either, that I have seen."

Richard said nothing.

Mary reiterated her jealousies where her sisters were concerned—the way men failed to notice her whenever Emma was present; Martha's superior intellect that had always seemed to find answers to most any difficulty; Jane's favored treatment—by all of them—as the "baby" of the family. And, of course, her resentment at filling her late mother's role in the family. "But, still, Richard, they are my family. Envy and jealousy must be set aside as inferior to family ties."

"It ain't the same," Richard said. "Your father and sisters, they expect you to step up on account of you're the oldest. With my Pa, it's just the opposite—he gives all the responsibility to Abel, never mind that he's the baby in our family."

"I have seen that. But I have told you before that Abel makes it easy. You are forever challenging your father. Can you blame him for just wanting things to get done without a fight?"

He gathered up another handful of pebbles and resumed his attempt to fill the gorge as if Mary was not there, nor ever had been.

Richard did not return to camp for dinner. The other men sat together over their plates, spooning up beans with pemmican stirred in. Daniel sopped his plate with a hunk of corn dodger, then scraped what was left with his finger and licked it off.

"Tell me something, Abel," he said, licking his lips. "How did you come to this approach to mending the axle?"

Abel swallowed the last of his milk and set his cup on his plate and the plate on the ground at his feet. "Truth be told, Mister Lewis, I don't really know. I looked the thing over and thought about it and nothing come to me. Then, all at once, it was all there. Don't know how or why or where it come from—it was just there."

"Are you confident it will work?"

"I think so. I hope so. The holes I burned in the axle are 'bout deep enough—should be done by evening. When I slide the ends together there's some play in them, not as tight as I'd like, but I think binding it up good with rawhide will take care of it."

With the need for rawhide drawing near, Abel and Melvin pulled the saturated hide from the tub. The weak lye solution from the ashes and water with the added catalyst of summer heat had done their work, and hair slipped easily from the hide. They rinsed the buffalo skin with clean water then draped it flesh side up over a log. Abel pulled Uncle Ben's fancy knife from the scabbard and showed Mel how to scrape away the stray bits of fat and meat. When clean, Mel was to turn the hide over and scrape off the hair. After rinsing in three tubs of clean water, Abel figured the hide was ready.

By fire and lantern light that evening, Abel honed the Damascus steel of Ben's knife blade to a razor edge and sliced the hide into long strips a couple of inches wide. He stuffed the strips back into the tub of water and turned in for the night. Come the morning, he would wrap the axle, stretching the rawhide tight, knowing it would shrink and tighten as it dried, hoping it would dry tight enough to hold the reinforced axle together and strong enough to carry the wagon.

He had just turned in when Richard came back to camp and collapsed onto his bedroll.

CHAPTER FORTY

The men spent the morning standing around sipping coffee in the early morning sun as Abel put the finishing touches on the holes in the broken axle ends where he would insert the stabilizing rod. The talk wandered far and wide, with Richard intervening now and then to complain about Abel's unhurried wielding of the heated steel to burn the holes to the exact depth that brought the broken ends together.

Lacking anything better to do, the men did much the same through the afternoon and early evening as Abel wrapped the reinforced axle with layer after layer of the rawhide strips. When finally finished, he set the axle in the wagon bed to dry, which would take a few days. He said, "Well, that's that, you-all. Nothin' to do now but wait." He wiped his damp hands on his shirtfront and said to Daniel, "You was going to tell us about what happened to that rifle."

Daniel invited the Pate men to fill their cups, as his story would be a long one. They knew he came from England. They knew he came to America to be with the Mormons. They knew he was in Missouri before they met his family in Fort Smith. But he had told them little else, and now he would fill that void.

"We lived in the west of England," he said to start the story, "near a town called Preston—not far from Manchester, nor Liverpool. The Lewises farmed there for centuries, but being the fourth of six sons, my prospects lay elsewhere. I kept a public house and we prospered, but depression came to

Lancashire and future prospects looked dim. The wife and I were casting about for a better situation, you see, before the money was gone.

"We were invited one evening to hear a preacher at a neighbor's house. Lizzie—my wife, Elizabeth—enjoyed a good sermon so we attended. Heber Kimball, that was the man's name, from America, preaching for the Church of Jesus Christ of Latter Day Saints—the Mormons, most would say; they would say Saints. He preached a fine sermon to my way of thinking, but my Lizzie, she was infatuated beyond reckoning. In days to come, we listened to more of his preaching, and that by others he traveled with. To make a long story short, given there was nothing, really, to hold us, and Lizzie's yearning to meet the Mormon prophet Joseph Smith, we sold out and emigrated—about the first Britons to do so to join the Saints, so I believe.

"As I have mentioned on other occasions, my Lizzie took ill and died aboard the ship. The girls were as committed to the Mormons as their mother, so when the ship arrived in New Orleans, we took a river steamer up the Mississippi and another up the Missouri to Independence. The Mormons had long since been evicted from that city; exiled to the northern part of the state, so we outfitted ourselves with these wagons and joined them.

" 'Twas a city called Far West they were building. Joseph was there, recently come from Kirtland, in Ohio—one step ahead of the law, some said. Be that as it may, the old settlers in that section of Missouri were at odds with the Mormons, much as they had been in Independence."

Lee reached out a hand and placed it on Daniel's knee. "Why, Daniel? What was the cause of the troubles?"

"Oh, the rough-hewn people of Missouri—'Pukes' as they were called—had a litany of complaints, and no shyness about voicing them. They disliked the Saints' air of superiority, the 'chosen people' and all that. They took issue with Mormon notions of a communal economy—primarily, I must say, because by pooling funds the Saints could outbid them for property. Joseph taught that Indians were remnants of the House of Israel and worthy of conversion, and the Pukes believed any congress or alliances with the Indians dangerous. The Saints, originating mostly in New England, were more inclined toward the abolition of slavery than not, which did not sit well in that section of the country.

"But, as is often the case, much of it came down to politics. The Mormons tend to vote as one, and take direction from their leaders when they cast their ballots. When, of course, enough Saints settle in an area, their political influence becomes a concern to others. And if it was not politics that started the Missouri troubles, it gave the savagery a place to start."

Daniel paused to refill his cup and catch his breath. Lee fidgeted at the interval. Abel looked to be lost in thought and Melvin whittled at a stick with his jackknife. Like his father, Richard fidgeted—but for different reasons.

"The story we were told," Daniel said, "was that Mormon settlers in Daviess County—north of where we were at Far West—went to the county seat at Gallatin to vote and were turned away by the Pukes in the community. A brawl ensued, and our boys got the best of them. The result being ballots cast by the Mormon men and bruised pride among the Missouri boys. Afterward, as the Scotch are wont to say, it was 'Katy bar the door.'

"Night riders from both camps took to their work with a vengeance—mobbers for the Missourians, Danites for the Mormons. They plundered and burned and stole almost at will, with the government turning a blind eye for the most part, but favoring the old settlers when necessary. For a time, the

Mormons gave as good as they got—and sometimes got the best of the Pukes. But not for long.

"One night, my family was roused from our beds and attacked. They destroyed furniture, slashed our bedding, stole stock and some provisions. That night, my arm was fractured and the rifle, as you have seen, smashed and broken. Fortunately, the Pukes were interrupted in their riot before they could harm the girls or cause further damage to our property. The very next day, we loaded the wagons and left the Saints behind, bound for Texas.

"The rest I know only from letters from friends still living among the Saints and from newspaper reports, which are not always to be believed. In the end, the Mormons were overcome by superior numbers and by the government. When a mob—under the guise of a militia—murdered seventeen of the Saints—including women and children—at a place called Haun's Mill and dumped the bodies down a well, the wind went out of Joseph's sails.

"That, and the governor's order that the Mormons be driven from Missouri or exterminated."

"Is that so?" Lee asked.

" 'Tis. An official order signed by Governor Lilburn Boggs, I learned from reliable authority. Joseph ended up jailed for a time. One of his Elders, Brigham Young, spent the winter arranging the Saints' exodus to Illinois. They have settled peaceably and built a city there on the Mississippi they call Nauvoo. But I fear the peace will be short-lived, as the same peculiarities that upset the Missouri Pukes still hold with the Mormons—and soon enough the people of Illinois will likewise object."

Lee let the story settle, then said, "Well, now, that's quite the story, Daniel. I never imagined. Oh, things would come out in the newspapers now and then about the Mormons. But I never knew much. Are you-all glad to be shed of them?"

Daniel thought for a moment. "The violence—even the threat of it—for certain. I never held with the beliefs as much as my Lizzie did, but did not find them objectionable, either. For the most part the Saints hold to good Christian teaching, with a few embellishments here and there. Time will tell if it is but a passing fancy."

The sun slid below the plain as the men swallowed the last of their coffee or tossed the dregs into the fire. Richard stood and stretched his elbows over his head and yawned. When he opened his eyes, he pointed across the gorge and said, barely above a whisper, "Sonofabitch! Will you look at that!"

There, silhouetted on the far rim, sat a lone Indian on horseback.

Chapter Forty-One

The Indian sat watching from across the gorge. Daniel ran to his lead wagon and found his brass telescope in the jockey box. He pulled the end caps off the leather sheath and extended the tube.

"He is much different in appearance from those Chickasaw gentlemen we met," he said after watching the sentinel close up. "His garments are not of cloth, as theirs were—in fact, he wears very little clothing at all. Moccasins, leather leggings and a breechclout, and a few feathers in his hair. Nothing more."

Lee said, "Is he carryin' a gun?"

"No. A spear or lance of some sort. Something at his waist—a knife, I assume. He seems to have a short bow strung over his shoulder."

"Let me get your huntin' rifle, Pa," Richard said. "I reckon I can hit him from here."

Abel said, "No need for that."

"Shut up, Abel. Pa?"

Lee thought it over, all the while watching the Indian watching them. "I don't believe so, Richard."

"Damn! There ain't but one of him now—we let him go, there'll be a dozen of them on us come morning. Maybe more."

"Yes, Son, and if you shoot at him and miss—which ain't unlikely at this distance—they'll be back for sure, and they won't be on friendly terms."

"What makes you think they'll be friendly anyhow?"

"Nothing. But it could be they'll leave us alone if we leave them alone."

Daniel collapsed his telescope. "What tribe do you think he is?"

"Can't say for sure," Lee said. "From what folks told me, I guess Comanche. Kiowa, maybe."

"If he's Comanche, we're in trouble for sure," Richard said. "Them Chickasaws said the Comanches ain't got no use for white men. I say we just shoot him and be done with it."

Richard's proposal proved pointless as the Indian reined his horse around and rode away.

"Well, that's that. We'll likely be dead in our beds come morning," Richard said.

Lee and Daniel talked it over and determined that setting a guard for the night was advisable. Lee said, "Mel, you take the first watch. We don't expect any trouble, but we best keep an eye on the stock just in case. If Indians come, they'll most likely come after the cattle or the mules."

"Like hell," Richard said. "If they come, it'll be for your hair. God knows what they'll do to the women."

"Now, Richard, there ain't no use in gettin' all stirred up over what ain't likely to happen," Lee said. "You take second watch. Abel, you relieve Richard."

The men did not inform the women of the sighting. But when Sarah watched the teams picketed near the camp after supper rather than hobbled to wander loose, she grew suspicious. "Lee, what is going on?"

"What do you mean, Sarah?"

"Oh, come now. I'm not blind. You-all have staked out the mules and oxen for some reason. What is it?"

Lee did not answer for a moment, watching Sarah let her hair out of its bun at her nape and start plaiting it into a braid for the night. Then, "Well, we just thought it might be wise to keep the animals close tonight."

"Why, damn it?" Sarah said, pulling the strands of her braid tighter than usual. "What's wrong?"

Again, Lee hesitated.

"Lee!"

"I don't want to worry you none, because it probably don't mean anything. We saw an Indian watching us."

"So? We've seen Indians before."

"True enough—and most likely this ain't no different. But away out here, they maybe ain't so used to seein' white folks. Won't hurt to be cautious, just in case."

As the rest of the camp rolled into their blankets, Melvin sat with his back to the fire to keep his eyes adjusted to the dark. The glow gave him just enough light to keep his knife working on the stick of wood he whittled on to pass the time. The barrel of one of Abel's revolvers, stuffed in his waistband, poked at his thigh and he shifted it to a more comfortable position. After his mother's raised voice stilled, he listened for a while to the Lewis girls talking and giggling softly but could not hear their words. Soon, they, too, were quiet.

The moon shed enough light that the stock was visible, if dim. Halters rattled from time to time when the mules or the horse shook their heads. The oxen and the milk cow lay on their bellies chewing cud. The calf, staked away from its mother, lay curled up on the ground looking as much like a rock as an animal.

When he judged from the position of the big dipper that his watch was up, he toed Richard awake through his blanket and handed him a cup of coffee from a pot long gone bitter.

"Damn, that's nasty," Richard said after a sip. But he set the cup carefully aside while he scoured his eyes with the heels of his hands. "Anything out there?"

Melvin said, "Nah. Saw an owl fly over, huntin' food. Ain't

heard nothin' but some coyotes yapping. Leastways I think it was coyotes."

Richard yawned. "I sure as hell hope so." He rolled out and gathered his coffee cup and shuffled past the fire to take up his place on the box vacated by Melvin. Rather than going to bed, his brother followed him and squatted to sit cross-legged on the ground.

"Rich, you really think that Indian means trouble?"

He took another sip of the coffee, screwed up his face, and dumped the rest into the dirt. "Don't know, Mel. I sure don't think his interest in us was social."

"Here," Melvin said, handing Richard the revolver. "Forgot to give you this. Hope you don't need it any more than I did."

Richard set the pistol on the ground beside the box. He chuckled. "I'm surprised Abel let us have the borrow of one of his precious damn guns."

Melvin tossed a split cottonwood log on the fire and flames flared up briefly, then gently licked at the wood. "You think that business with the wagon will work? You know—what Abel done?"

Again, Richard laughed. "You ever known our baby brother to know anything about wagons?"

"No, I reckon not."

"Damn right you reckon not. He don't know no more about wagons than me or you."

"Still, he thought of something to do. Maybe it'll work."

"Sure. And maybe that mule over there will figure out how to throw Thoroughbred colts. Ain't neither one of 'em has the wherewithal."

"I don't know, Rich. Me, I hope it works."

Richard yawned. "I wouldn't get my hopes up, was I you." He yawned again. "You best be gettin' some sleep."

"Nah. I ain't done enough these past days to get tired. I'll just set here with you for a while. Keep you awake."

It was Melvin who awakened Abel for the last watch. For the past hour, Melvin had wondered how Richard could sit on the box and not fall off despite being fast asleep. Now, he and Abel giggled and watched Richard snore for a minute. Abel reached out and grabbed Richard's shoulder and gave it a shake and held on when Richard jerked awake.

"What?" Richard said, looking around to figure out where he was. "What is it?"

"Might as well go on to bed, Richard," Abel said. "You'll sleep better there than sittin' on this box."

"I wasn't asleep," Richard said, stifling a yawn.

"C'mon, Rich," Melvin said with a smile as he hooked his brother's arm and lifted him up. "I'll help you find your way."

Richard jerked away, and stumbled toward his bedroll, mumbling something indecipherable.

"Ain't seen a thing all night," Melvin told Abel.

"That's good."

"There's coffee, but it ain't fit to drink. Reckon I'll turn in."

"G'night, Mel," Abel said. "Thanks."

Abel picked up the revolver and blew the dust off it then slipped it into the holster at his waist. After a minute, he took it out again, pulled the hammer to half-cock and removed the cylinder, checked the load in each chamber and the seating of the caps, reassembled the pistol and returned it to the holster. He walked into the night, out past the animals, and circled the camp before taking his seat on the box to await the dawn, wondering what the new day would bring.

Chapter Forty-Two

Sarah dumped the thick sludge from last night's coffee from the pot, rinsed it out, filled it with fresh water, and hung it over the fire to boil. Mary hung another coffeepot and while she waited for it to heat, filled a pan with meal and added salt and fat, to which she would add the boiling water for corn dodgers. Emma sliced thick slabs of bacon. Jane prodded the cow to its feet and took care of the milking then turned the calf loose for its share. Sarah drained off a cast-iron pot where dried apples had soaked overnight, tossed in some rolled oats and poured in some milk and a touch of cinnamon and sugar and set it on hot coals and heaped more on the lid to make a porridge.

Abel, already awake owing to his shift on guard duty, was first in line for fresh coffee. The other men, awakened by the activity, made their way to the fire one by one, Richard filling his cup when the others were already on their second.

"Well, Richard, it seems we are alive and well and ready to meet another day," Daniel said with a smile.

"Can't argue with that," Richard said. "But you might be singin' a different tune before the day's over."

Lee said, "Sarah knows about the Indian. Got it out of me last night. So, I reckon the girls know by now." He took a sip of his coffee. "I think it best if we don't upset them with any more loose talk."

Richard glowered, Daniel nodded in agreement.

"Nothing out of the ordinary in the night?" Lee said.

Melvin smiled, said, "One thing kind of strange. Never seen such a thing done before, but Rich fell asleep sittin' upright on that there box over there and didn't fall off. Kept expectin' he would slump off, but darned if he didn't sit there still as can be—'cept for a lot of snorin' that is."

All the men—save Richard—had a good laugh. The furrow in his brow deepened and when the jest died down, he said to Abel, "You goin' to get the wagon put back together today so's we can get the hell out of here?"

"No. The rawhide wraps on the axle are still dampish. They're drying and shrinking up good, but need some time. We'll see how it looks after another day in the sun."

"If we live that long. I ain't about to trust that Indian's done with us."

"Now, Richard," Lee said. "That's enough of that talk."

"Damn it, Pa, we've wasted enough time here. Could—should—have moved on days ago! Now look where Abel's foolishness has got us. I swear the boy's as harebrained as you are!"

Lee's face turned gray but he did not speak. Daniel lowered his head as if hoping to discover something new in his coffee cup. Melvin shifted his weight back and forth on his feet.

"Here—hold this," Abel said, and handed Richard his coffee cup. Then, with his brother holding a cup in each hand, he launched a fist that landed flush on Richard's lower lip.

The blow did not stagger Richard—before his body had time to effect any such move, he was on his backside in the dirt, hot coffee soaking his shirtfront and dribbling off his face and dripping out of his hair making tiny puddles in the dust. He cast aside the one cup he still held and felt his smashed lip and looked with surprise at his bloody fingers. As he scrambled to his feet he said, "Why you sonofabi—"

Before he finished the curse he found himself on his backside again. This time it was his father who put him there, grabbing a shoulder and forcing him back down before he could rise. Melvin stepped behind Abel and wrapped his arms around him but the younger brother offered no resistance.

"You sit right there, Son, and calm down," Lee said, sounding more sad than angry.

"I'll kill him! By God, see if I don't!"

Abel said, "You're welcome to try. Anytime, brother. I don't much care what you say—or do—to me, but you show Pa some respect."

The women stood silent, watching, as still as if time had stopped. The sound of bacon in the skillet sizzled its way back into Sarah's consciousness and she said, "Breakfast'll be ready soon. You-all had best get cleaned up and come to your senses if you-all want to eat."

Little else happened during the day. Lee and Daniel fussed and fretted with organizing and reorganizing the camp equipment and supplies. Melvin and Sarah, as much to stretch their legs as water the stock, led and drove the cattle and mules and horse down to the river for a drink. Emma and Jane upset their father's organizing to shift and stack boxes and trunks to create a corral for the chickens to let them scratch and dust their feathers. Mary sat in the shade and occupied herself with needlework, repairing rips and snags and tears already repaired and darning socks already darned. All the women took turns stirring beans that didn't need stirring. Richard sat at the edge of the gorge, tossing pebbles into the defile.

Throughout the day, Abel rotated the drying axle to put the sun on each surface. The progress of the repairs pleased him—the rawhide setting up stiff and hard as iron and the axle itself seeming rigid and strong. He checked the firmness of the spokes and felloes on the wheels, the tightness of the fasteners on the reach and hounds, the security of the tongue and doubletree, and otherwise tinkered with the wagon to pass the time.

Later, Lee and Daniel set their Bibles aside and called a halt to debate and discussion when called to supper. As the families sat around the campfire eating, Lee allowed that again setting a guard for the night was advisable and offered to take the first shift. Daniel volunteered for the second. Neither Melvin nor Richard spoke up, so Abel said he would take the last watch as he wanted to be up early getting the wagon back together anyway.

When the low-hanging sun dipped below the horizon, Richard called attention to the mounted Indian across the canyon. As the day faded, everyone in the camp stood for a time watching the lone rider watching them.

Chapter Forty-Three

The night passed too slowly for Abel. With a bitter cup of tepid coffee in hand, he perched on the accustomed box and studied the animals for any sign of alarm. The clock hands of the big dipper read around about four-thirty when he heard footsteps. He turned toward camp and saw Emma coming his way, lifting the skirt of her nightgown out of the dust, and stood to greet her.

"Abel," she said.

"Emma. What are you doing up?"

"Oh, I don't know—couldn't sleep." She lifted her eyes and caught his gaze. "Mostly, I wanted to talk."

She could not see Abel's blush in the dark. "Here," he said, "sit," then held her arm for balance as she lowered herself onto the box.

Emma sighed. "I guess we shall be moving on tomorrow. I must say I am looking forward to it."

"Me too," Abel said, and sat on the ground next to Emma. "I just hope we can keep going once we start. If that axle don't hold. . . . Well, we'll be moving on with half a wagon, like Rich said. And half our goods."

"It seems to me your brother Richard says a lot of things."

"Oh, he's got his opinions on just about anything, for sure," Abel said. "Including you."

"Whatever do you mean?"

Abel laughed. "I reckon you already know, Emma. Rich thinks

the sun rises and sets on you. He'll likely be askin' your pa for your hand 'fore too long."

"Well, it will not do him any good. He will not be getting my hand or any other part of me, no matter what father says—not that he would agree to any such arrangement." Emma paused, drew in a long breath and let it out again slowly. "When I marry, it will be to a much different sort of man."

"What kind of man would that be?"

This time it was Emma's turn to laugh. "I think you know that, Abel. You may be quiet and shy, but you are not blind. Nor stupid."

Silence stretched on for minutes, interrupted only by night insects and the rustling of the nearby animals. Then, in the distance, the yapping of coyotes.

"What was that?" Emma said. "Coyotes—or Indians?"

"Coyotes, I hope."

"Do you fear the Indians, as your brother does?"

Abel pondered for a moment, then said, "You'd be a fool not to fear them. But they can't be all that different from any other folks, at least in most ways. I suspect if we leave them be, they'll leave us be."

"Why do you think that one was watching us?"

"Just curious, maybe. Wondering what we're doing a-way out here. I don't blame him for keeping an eye on us—I'd do the same, if I was him."

They sat without talking for a few minutes until Emma said she had best be getting back to bed as it would soon be time to start breakfast and morning chores. Abel jumped to his feet and offered a hand to help Emma up from her seat on the box. She stood, rose on her tiptoes, drew Abel's head down with a hand on the back of his neck, kissed him on the cheek, then turned and walked quickly back to the wagons.

Abel, wide-eyed, sat down on the box and touched his cheek,

still feeling the caress of Emma's lips there. The sensation remained as dawn lightened the sky, past breakfast, and well into the day as he reassembled the wagon. Every time he thought of it, his face flushed and both his mother and Mary asked at times if he felt all right. He assured them he felt fine.

The wagon went back together without incident, and the axle felt sturdy as he attached it below the bolster and hounds with the bolts, and hooked up the hound braces. Melvin helped block up the wagon high enough to put on the wheels. Abel coated the axle spindles and clouts with tallow as well as the boxing inside the wheel hubs. The wheels, affixed to the axle with their leather washers and linchpins, showed an acceptable amount of play but not an excess.

After hanging and hooking up the brake beam, Melvin raised the running gear off the blocks with the wagon jack and lowered it to the ground. Abel held his breath, but the repaired axle did not appear to move. He knew, however, that the real tests would come later when the box was installed, when they filled the wagon, and when it lurched over the bumps and rattled through the potholes on what passed for the trail.

By the time the men lifted the wagon box and set it inside the bolster stakes and lashed the canvas over the bows, Sarah and the Lewis girls had the kitchen trappings packed in their boxes, foodstuffs bundled, and beds rolled. When the sun reached its midpoint, the wagons were loaded, mules harnessed, oxen yoked, and the train was on the trail.

Lee and Abel walked behind the wagon, watching the rawhide-wrapped axle. After an hour or so and rough couple of miles, Lee said, "Son, it looks like it's going to hold."

"I sure hope so. Time will tell, I guess."

"Well, if it gets us to the Mexican settlements we ought to be able to find a new axle there."

The train moved along without incident, Sarah driving the

mules and Daniel prodding the oxen on the lead wagon. Mary kept pace with the oxen on the second wagon. Jane and Emma walked along beside the wagons talking while Melvin ambled along on the other side. Richard rode ahead to scout the trail.

But it was Melvin who spotted the Indians.

"Pa!" he yelled, and stopped while Lee caught up.

"What is it, Son?"

Melvin pointed to the opposite rim.

"Oh, my," Lee whispered. Across the canyon, nine Indians rode in single file keeping pace with the wagons. Behind them, six women and an assortment of children walked along, some leading horses pulling heaped travois.

"Damn it, Pa, what do we do now?" Melvin said.

Lee offered no response.

"Pa!"

"Let me think, Melvin. For now, we just keep going."

"You should of listened to Rich and let him shoot that first one what came. Now look at the fix we're in!"

Lee glared at Melvin, then hurried ahead to catch up with Daniel.

Melvin turned his anger toward Abel. "This is all your fault, little brother. Had you not come up with your crazy notions about fixing the wagon we'd of been miles and miles away from here. These damn Indians wouldn't even of knowed we was here."

"You don't know that Mel. Could be they've been watchin' us even before the wagon broke down."

Melvin scoffed. "Don't try to weasel your way out of this. You and Pa put us all in danger. Rich ain't goin' to be happy, that's for sure."

"Truth is, Mel, I don't care anymore if Rich is happy or not. Fact is, I can't remember the last time he was happy."

"We should of done like he said with the wagon."

"Pa chose not to."

Melvin stewed for a moment. "I think Rich may be right about Pa. He's gone and wrecked our lives. Maybe we should of just stayed in Tennessee."

"Well, we didn't. Pa wanted to move on and we did. We're a family and we go where he says."

"Some family. Half the time even Ma thinks Pa's crazy," Melvin said. Then, "Rich says he'll be leavin' soon as he can. Could be I'll go with him when he does. Other than wantin' somebody around to help with the work, I don't think Pa would even care if we was gone."

Up ahead, Daniel and Lee talked over the presence of the Indians and Daniel agreed going on was the best—the only—course of action.

And so the wagon train lumbered along, the string of Indians keeping pace across the gorge. No one in the families could help but wonder how long they would keep their distance.

Chapter Forty-Four

Richard never did return to the train that day. Although riding scout, he had not spotted and warned of the presence of the Indians. He had not found and reported the most painless route for the wagons. Nor had he located and guided the wagons to that night's campsite. He was, it appeared, missing.

As night fell, Sarah fretted over where he might be, fearing the worst. Lee worried something might have happened, unsure what it might be—an accident, a scrape with Indians, a thrown horseshoe. Melvin feared he might have quit the family and ridden away and left him behind without so much as an invitation. Abel wondered if Richard could have gotten lost, even with the Canadian River right there to show the way. But he dismissed the notion, berating himself in the instant for thinking ill of his brother.

Morning came with no sign of the prodigal son. They found him midmorning the next day. The wagons encountered a clear trail coming out of the river bottom and leading off to the north. Lee and Daniel opted to follow the trail down to the river to see if it followed the Canadian upstream, as the river bluffs were now lower and the valley between wider. A mile or so upriver, Abel allowed as how he smelled smoke.

Rounding the base of a ridge revealed the source of the smoke—a dying campfire—bonfire, more like—in a still-occupied camp. Two two-wheeled carts with tall wooden wheels, heaped with hide- and canvas-covered loads, rested on their shafts. Nearby lay a disorderly pile of rawhide panniers and wrapped bundles. Scattered in the grass between the campsite and the river, four mules, as many horses, and two bony oxen grazed. Tethered by the bridle reins to a scraggly mountain juniper, the Pate saddle horse stood, still under saddle and head hung low.

No people were immediately evident, but as they neared the camp they determined the buffalo hide and canvas lumps strewn about covered sleeping men. Closer still, they identified Richard's boots at the end of a pair of legs reaching out from under one of the carts. The reason for the inactivity revealed itself in the whiskey bottles, some whole and some broken, spread around the campsite, some so recently deposited the earth beneath them was still damp.

The wagons halted at the fringe of the camp. The Pates and Lewises lined up beside their wagons and looked on in silence, unsure of their next move. Only Abel acted, untying the horse and leading it to the riverbank to drink. He let the horse quench its thirst but not drink its fill before leading it back to the camp, stopping on the way to deliver a swift kick to the bottom of one of his brother's boots.

It took two more blows before Richard drew back his leg in defense. Frustrated, Abel grabbed the still-extended leg and dragged his brother out of the shade and into the sun. The next encouragement, more prod than kick, landed in Richard's ribs. He raised himself on his elbows, opened his eyes, slammed them shut again, then opened them in a squint.

"Abel? What the hell you doin' here?"

"I could ask the same of you, Rich."

Richard sat up, wagged his head back and forth, ground at his eyelids with his knuckles, scratched his fingers through tousled hair, and coughed and hacked and spit.

"You done?" Abel said.

A half-hearted kick missed Abel's leg.

"You never said what you were doin' here," Richard said with a thick tongue. "Damn, I need a drink. Find me a canteen."

"Find one your own self."

The look Richard gave Abel could have frozen the contents of a canteen. He rolled over to his knees and pushed himself upright, staggering and grabbing the cart for balance. After propping himself up for a moment to find some sense of equilibrium, he walked the few steps to the horse and unslung the canteen hanging from the saddle horn. He swished a mouthful of water around and spat it out, took a couple of long swallows, then dumped the remainder of the water over his head. Dripping, he wiped the water from his eyes and looked around, noticing the three wagons and his family and the Lewises lined up in a row watching him as if he were on exhibit at a county fair. Taking a deep breath, he attempted to smooth his hair back and walked with delicate steps toward them, making a brave attempt not to wither under their gaze.

"Well," he said, clearing his throat. "I see you-all made it."

Lee wondered at that. Then, "Where, exactly, have we made it to, Son?"

Richard wrinkled his brow and wondered at that. Then, with a sweep of his arm at the surroundings, "Why, here. You-all made it to here."

Every spectator in the line laughed at that, if with little humor.

Some of the heaps on the ground were stirring. Thrown-back covers revealed rough-hewn men, all dressed at least in part in buckskin, most with beards or mustaches—whether from design or lack of grooming. All—those who showed themselves, at least—were dark-haired and dark-complected, looking to be of Mexican descent.

All, that is, save one, who was as pale as death and just as wasted. Unlike the others, who sat on their bedding and scratched and snorted, he stood, brushed off his buckskin trousers and smoothed the front of a black swallowtail jacket. Beneath it was a ruffle-front shirt so stained and discolored its former whiteness was barely evident. A limp and frayed string tie rounded his collar, and he stooped and picked up a stove-up beaver-felt stovepipe hat with a silk ribbon and plopped it on his head, covering a stringy and thin tangle of oily blond hair. He stared, one-by-one, at the Pates and Lewises with eyes so pale a blue-gray the pupils looked almost white in contrast to the bloodshot rims that should have been white.

Sarah could barely speak but managed to say, "Richard—who are these people?"

"They're traders, Ma. They're comin' up from a place called *El Paso del Norte* to trade with the Indians—Comanches, mostly, so they are called *Comancheros.*"

Sarah sniffed.

Daniel said, "We were concerned that perhaps the Comanches had captured you—even killed you. You were so concerned with those who were watching us, we feared the worst."

"Oh, them," Richard said with a wave of his hand. "No need to worry. Turns out them Indians is on their way to meet up with these men and other Comancheros to do some trading. They'll meet up at a place a ways north of here called *Cejita de Los Comancheros*—I think that's how they say it, somethin' like that. Meet up there a couple times a year, they do."

The pale man walked over to join them, trying his best to present a dignified air. "You must be Rich's family."

"Yes," Lee said. "We are. I don't believe I caught your name."

The man tugged at the lapels of his jacket and tilted his nose into the air. "Names do not amount to much out here. The Mexs and Comanche call me *Ojos Blanco.* It means 'White Eyes' in the Spanish tongue. You may call me the same or not, as you wish. Asking for identification beyond that will be considered bad manners."

Daniel said, "I believe I hear something of the Continent in your voice—German, if I am not mistaken."

With a slow gaze in Daniel's direction, he told him that where a man came from was also of little consequence and not discussed.

Lee asked if it was bad form to know what was in the carts and the mule packs. "Just curious is all," he said.

"About what you would expect," came the answer. "Fabrics, metal goods such as cooking pots and hatchets and knives and other tools. Tobacco. Flour. Glass beads and trinkets. Alcohol. Powder and lead and guns if we can get them, which is not often."

"And in return?"

"Hides and skins, primarily. Horses. On occasion, captives."

Lee cocked his head, questioning his hearing. "Captives?"

"Captives. Yes. When the Comanche raid other tribes or Mexican settlements—even the white settlers in Texas—they take prisoners. Treat them horribly, I must say. They are sold to other tribes or Mexican *rancheros* and *hacendados* who use them as servants, or as laborers for the mines or other work. Young women, as you might imagine," he said with a nod to the Lewis girls, "are put to other uses. If there are likely looking captives when we meet the Comanche to trade, we may barter for them."

Lee stiffened. "You are little more than slavers, then!"

White Eyes glared at him cold-eyed. "We are traders. We exchange things of value for other things of value. To the benefit of both parties, I might add."

"But you are buying and selling human beings!"

White Eyes nodded. "At times. At other times, you could say we have rescued human beings from a terrible fate. We locate the homes and families of wives and children of Texians, especially, taken by the Comanche, and sometimes those captured from wealthy Mexican families, and offer to return them."

"For a price, I suppose," Lee said with disgust.

"For a price, of course. We are, after all, traders."

"It is a sorry business you engage in."

White Eyes shrugged. "It fills a need. And it turns a profit."

Lee turned on his heel and walked toward his wagon. "Come along, folks. We had best be on our way."

Richard stopped his father with a shout.

"What is it, Son?"

"Don't leave. Not now."

"Why not? Ain't you had enough to drink yet?"

Richard's wan complexion reddened, first in embarrassment then anger. "Maybe not. But that ain't none of your damn business. What you need to do is forget your foolish pride and silly notions and talk to this man—listen to him, more like. He knows the country and the people hereabouts—not just the Indians, but the Mexicans and the Americans too. Could be he can help you find what you're looking for—if you even know what the hell that is."

Lee looked at the sun then turned to his family and the Lewises. "Too early for nooning. But I reckon we had best stop here a while and see what this man has to say. Unhitch and turn the stock out to graze." He watched the Comancheros still struggling out of their sleep. "Best stake them—I don't know as they're safe here. Abel, unsaddle that horse and give it a rubdown if you will." He glared at Richard. "Treatment he's been given, likely he's saddle sore and cinch galled."

Richard walked away, picked up a whiskey bottle, and held it up to the light. Seeing it still held an inch or so of liquor, he tipped the bottle up and drank it down, his eyes never leaving those of his father.

Chapter Forty-Five

The Comancheros were disappointed the Lewises' hens weren't laying. But constant travel and continuous upheaval are not compatible with egg production. The traders did, however, enjoy fresh milk and butter from the Pate's milk cow and, as a result, Sarah's supplies of flour and corn meal were somewhat replenished from the stores of the Comancheros.

Mary, Emma, and Jane stayed out of sight behind the wagons as much as possible, uncomfortable with the long, leering looks of the traders and ill at ease with comments they could not understand and the sneering laughter they spawned. While the women went about their business and tried to stay out of sight, White Eyes, the Pate men, and Daniel huddled in the shade of riverside cottonwood trees talking.

They learned from the Comanchero something of geography and government. He recommended leaving the Canadian not far from where they sat, when it veered northward toward its source, and to strike a course more directly westward to the Gallinas River, which they should reach in three or four days.

"On the Gallinas you shall find civilization again. There is a new town called Las Vegas. Here, you will find the Santa Fe Trail that will lead you to that city. And there you must go if you are to settle in New Mexico as that is the seat of government and has been for longer than your United States have existed. Without incident, you should reach Santa Fe within two weeks; perhaps less."

Lee and Daniel asked questions about the terrain to and travel on the Santa Fe Trail. They wondered about wagon parts, and learned abandoned wagons littered the trail between Las Vegas and San Jose on the Pecos River; some broken, some burned, some intact. Perhaps a replacement axle—or spare, if Abel's fix continued to hold up—could be found there.

"What's the chances of Americans findin' a decent place to settle down?" Lee said.

White Eyes thought it over for a moment. "There is no shortage of places here. Endless miles of unsettled land that would serve. The government is of two minds on granting any of it to Americans. I do not know what whims drive the decisions. As you can imagine, the nature of my business, while legal for the most part, is not considered legitimate and so we do not deal with the officials in Santa Fe if we can avoid it.

"A few years ago there was a rebellion of sorts here concerning the constitution and tax laws drafted in the City of Mexico and the *Jefe Politico* sent to enforce them. He—Perez—was killed by the rebels. Now the governor is Manuel Armijo. He is supportive of trade with the Americans, and pays little notice to the government in the City of Mexico. He has granted large tracts of land, I am told, to some American traders."

"So we may be in with a chance," Daniel said.

"Perhaps. One difficulty. You know, of course, of the Republic of Texas which claims independence from Mexico."

The men nodded in agreement.

"The Texians claim all the land to the Rio Grande for their Republic. That includes the ground upon which we sit, and, in fact, Santa Fe itself. Needless to say, the Mexicans are having none of it. It is possible it will take a war to decide it. I say this only because it may color Armijo's attitude about allowing settlers from the east."

"We will assure him we have no connection with Texas, and

have left the United States behind," Daniel said.

Lee said, "We're obliged for the information, Mister White Eyes." He stood and offered his hand. The trader did not rise, but extended a limp hand. As they shook, Lee said, "We'd best get on the go. We can put a few more miles behind us before the day's over."

White Eyes sat and watched the men dust themselves off. As they started for the wagons, he said, "All best wishes to you." Then, "Keep a sharp eye on those young ladies."

Abel spun on his heel and took a step toward the smirking Comanchero but stopped when his father called his name.

While waiting for Melvin to bring up and hitch the mules to the wagon, Abel sat down under the tailgate and gave the repaired axle a few hard jerks. He detected slight movement at the repair site, but imagined it solid enough to go on. To stay here—in the presence of the Comancheros—for a day or two to soak the rawhide to stretch and rewrap around the axle and wait for it to dry and harden was unthinkable.

"Richard," Lee said, "the mules have had a good rest so I want you to ride the wagon with your Ma and drive them. You don't look to be in any shape for walking—and I don't want you ridin' off again."

"I'm a grown man, Pa. It oughtn't be up to you no more to be tellin' me what to do or where to go."

"It pains me to do so, Son. But ridin' off and gettin' liquored up when you're supposed to be scouting for a place to camp and watchin' out for trouble is plumb irresponsible. Ain't no way for a growed man to behave."

Richard held his tongue, his lips set in a thin line. He walked away and helped Melvin finish hitching the mules. They exchanged a few words, then Melvin looked around and, seeing everyone in the party occupied with preparations to leave, hustled over to the Comanchero *carreta* where they found Richard sleeping earlier. He reached under the cart and fetched a cotton flour sack that clinked when hefted. After hurrying back to the wagon, he lifted the canvas cover and stuffed the bag behind the seat.

Atop the seat, Richard watched Abel help Emma hitch the oxen to the Lewises' second wagon. They laughed and talked as Abel lifted the yoke above the animals' necks and held it while Emma hung the bows and slipped the keys into the holes. With the wagon tongue in place, Abel untied the saddle horse from the wagon, snugged up the cinch, stepped into the stirrup, and swung a leg over the cantle. He said something to Emma, which prompted a giggle, then heeled the horse into a walk and headed up the trail.

Emma stood with hands on hips and watched Abel ride away. Richard sat with his chin propped on the fist of an arm propped on the knee of a leg propped on the top of the wagon box and watched Emma watch Abel. He cursed under his breath, took out his pocket flask and sipped at the whiskey. The flask went back into the pocket when he felt the wagon shift as his mother grabbed the box and stepped on the wheel hub and lifted herself to climb onto the seat.

"Still got your eye on young Emma, I see," Sarah said as she tucked her skirt under her thighs and settled herself on the seat.

"What?"

Sarah smiled. "I saw you watching her. I ain't blind, you know." She paused, then said, "I saw what you got in your pocket there, too."

Richard squirmed on the seat but did not respond.

"You know, Son, you're wasting your time mooning over that girl. Any fool can see she ain't got eyes for nobody but your brother Abel."

"Yes'm. But she could change her mind."

"Not likely. And she won't be lookin' your way so long as you keep on actin' so peevish all the time. That, and filling your gullet with that foul liquid like you do every chance you get."

"Well, hell, Ma—what do you expect a man to do? Here we are out in this godforsaken place with nothin' but the hot sun for company. Don't know where we're goin' or when we'll get there. Had I knowed what was in store, I'd have hogtied Pa back home in Shelby County to keep him from leadin' us on this merry chase."

"Now, Richard—"

"Aw, Ma, I know you think the same."

Sarah considered her response. "Your Pa don't know how to be anybody but who he is. The fact that there ain't a day go by that I don't curse your father and his cussed notions that brought us out here don't change a thing. We are his family and we owe it to him to go along."

Richard snorted. "You sound just like Abel."

"You may not like to think so, Son, but sometimes Abel is right."

Another snort. "Damn right he is—to Pa's way of thinkin' the little turd is always right."

"That's as it may be. Me, I think you're more jealous of your brother than you got any call to be." Sarah lowered herself off the wagon seat. "I believe I prefer to walk along with Melvin for a spell."

Richard did not reply. He looked ahead to where Abel was now little more than a jot or tittle on the horizon. He released the brake lever and slapped the lines on the rumps of the mules as the Lewis wagons rolled. "Get up, mules!" he said. "Time to follow baby brother farther down the road to hell."

Several times as they lurched along the trail, Richard turned to look back at the Comanchero camp. After one such look, he found his father sitting beside him on the wagon seat. "What the hell, Pa! You like to scared me to death!"

"All I did was climb onto the wagon, Son."

"What for? You come to remind me that it's rollin' down the trail just like new, thanks to Abel's handiwork?"

Lee studied the wrath on Richard's face and flinched at his own inability to soothe his son. "Difficulties among brothers ain't no new thing, Son," he almost whispered. "Been goin' on as long as there's been brothers—take Cain and Abel—but don't be taking what Cain did to *his* brother Abel as a worthy pattern. Firstborn sons feeling done by by younger brothers ain't new neither. Look at Esau and Jacob . . . Ishmael and Isaac. . . ." A pause, to clear sniffles from his nose and mop the corners of eyes threatening to overflow.

"Come to that, I never much got along with my own brother Ben—from the time we was boys he lorded it over me that he was bigger and stronger, never mind he was younger. Even as growed men, he never passed up a chance to remind me he had amassed more of everything than me—more land, more livestock, more money. More of darn near everything—but sons. That stuck in his craw, but there weren't nothin' he could do about it."

Now it was Richard's turn to study his father. "I knowed you two never got along. Didn't know it was that bad."

Lee chuckled but there was no humor in it. "Bad enough we're here 'stead of back in Shelby County where we belong."

Richard's brow furrowed as he wondered what his father meant.

It took Lee a moment to choose his words. "Ain't nobody else knows this and I'll ask you to keep it as such.

"Now, it ain't no secret that I don't hold with slavery, and that evil practice would have driven me out of Tennessee sooner or later. But it would have been later and under better circumstances had it not been for your Uncle Ben."

Again, Richard's lack of understanding painted his face.

"The day we left, you'll recollect I had business in town. On the way home, I happened across one of Ben's 'nigras' as he called them—the one named Jefferson. He was herding a dozen or so market hogs to town. One of them hogs took a contrary notion and went off into a cornfield. Jefferson chased him 'round and 'round and tore up that crop no end. 'Course them other hogs took the opportunity to root around and made the damage even worse.

"Anyhow, I was tryin' to help Jefferson get them hogs out of that field and back on the road when Ben come along. Didn't even bother to whoa-up his buggy horse 'fore he jumped out of that shay and lit into the boy with his whip.

"I'm ashamed to say my temper went the way of Ben's. I grabbed his shoulder and spun him around and struck a blow that sat him on his backside among the ruined cornstalks. I never bested him with my fists but once or twice in our lives, but I did that day. Ben was as surprised by it as me. He cursed me. I cursed him in turn. We carried on like that at cross purposes while poor Jefferson looked on. Even the hogs was so shocked by all the ruction they stood and watched.

"The gist of it is that Ben swore he would set the law on me for interfering with his 'property.' And he reminded me that if it come down to his word against mine, there wasn't a lawman nor officer of the court in all of Shelby County that would take my word over his. Then he laughed at me. He dusted himself off, climbed into his buggy and as he drove away warned me to expect the sheriff to be paying a visit, as he fully intended to file charges."

Wide-eyed, Richard said, "And that's why you came home in a dither and told us to start loading the wagon."

Lee nodded and then ducked his head, searching for something of interest on the wagon's toeboard.

"Why didn't you say?"

After a long look at his son, Lee again ducked his head and Richard strained to hear him say, "Ain't no man likes to get outdone by his younger brother."

Chapter Forty-Six

The train made good time and two days after leaving the Comancheros, they were miles away from the traders. Melvin, riding as scout, located a suitable campsite and the wagons hove to for the evening.

Reliving their days as laundresses, Mary and Emma walked up from the nearby stream, each with a full bucket in hand and sharing a third between them. They would use the water to further the revival, washing clothes for the camp while Sarah and Jane saw to supper.

"I wonder how Martha is doing," Emma said as they knuckled clothes against the washboards.

"Oh, you know Martha. Smart as that girl is, she will figure a way to deal with any problem that might come up. But, I don't suppose she and Peter—Mister and Missus Neumann," Mary said with a smile, "will encounter many problems. Fort Smith and his employment there seemed to suit Peter. Martha will adapt, I am sure."

Emma held up the wet shirt she was cleaning—one of her father's—saw the stain on the sleeve had faded but still needed attention and dunked the shirt back in the tub and scrubbed some more. "Do you think we shall ever marry?"

Mary paused in her washing, wiped a damp brow with an even damper forearm, and studied her sister. "Why ever do you ask, Emma? Should you desire to marry you shall have no difficulty attracting a suitable mate."

"Do you think so? I am not so sure."

Mary smiled. "Oh? And why is that?"

Emma scrutinized the soggy shirt again, saw it was suitably clean, wrung it out and tossed it in the tub of rinse water. "It's—it's—well, it's Abel."

"What about Abel?"

Neither girl noticed that Richard was listening. He had taken a seat on a boulder near the washtubs but behind the girls, eavesdropping on the conversation and nipping at his whiskey flask.

Emma bowed her reddened face. "I believe he knows how I feel about him. But he shows so little interest in me."

"It seems clear that he is fond of you."

"Maybe. But it seems he sees me more as a cousin, or just a friend."

"He is young, and inexperienced. One day it will dawn on him that what he feels for you is much more than friendship."

Emma pulled a pair of drawers from the laundry bag and pushed them down into the wash water and scrubbed vigorously against the knurled washboard.

Richard pushed the cork into the lip of the flask and slipped it into his pocket. He cleared his throat, startling Mary and Emma.

"Richard!" Mary said. "What are you doing here?"

"Just passin' the time. Thought I'd spend some of it visiting with you-all."

"Surely there are more important pursuits requiring your attention."

Richard only smiled.

Emma, her blush more florid than before, said, "How long have you been here?"

"Long enough to hear you moonin' over my baby brother."

Emma attacked the garment in the tub with more vigor than

its soil required. Mary stood and used her apron skirt to wipe her hands. "Please," she said. "Show some consideration."

Richard retrieved his flask and took a sip. "Just want to make sure Emma don't make a mistake."

Mary sniffed. "A more likely explanation would be that you are jealous."

He raised the flask to Mary as if making a toast and took another sip, then plugged the flask and dropped it in his pocket. "Fact is, you-all don't know what Abel's really like."

Emma wrung out the washed drawers and sloshed water out of the rinse tub when she threw them in. She riveted Richard to his rock with her fixed stare. "What are you talking about?" she hissed through clenched teeth.

After a moment, Richard recovered from her acrimony and smiled. "The boy's got blood on his hands." He paused. "You-all was talkin' about Peter. Ask Abel how Peter come to be with us back in Fort Smith."

Emma's face paled.

"While you're at it, ask him where he got that fancy knife he carries."

Mary lowered herself to her knees and steadied herself on the edge of a wash tub.

Richard talked on. "Might just as well ask about them pistols he prizes so, and that linen duster rolled up and stashed in the wagon."

Emma and Mary looked at each other, then back at Richard.

"Hell, while you're at it, ask him about his hat. He never come by that stuff honestly, I can tell you that." With that, Richard stood and brushed off the seat of his pants and left the women kneeling next to their tubs full of water, now stilled.

When Emma came to herself, she said, "Mary? What do you think he is talking about?"

"I do not know. Cannot even imagine. Peter never mentioned

anything untoward back in Fort Smith. If he said anything to Martha, she did not mention it."

Emma sighed. "I suppose I shall have to ask Abel. There must be some explanation."

The girls finished the washing and hung the clothes to dry on makeshift clotheslines strung between juniper trees. Emma said nothing during supper. Abel felt her eyes on him, but she lowered her eyes whenever he looked her way.

After the meal, Jane excused herself to answer the call of nature—or "take the air" as she called it. "Emma? Mary? Care to come along?"

Neither did. Daniel said that as it wasn't full dark yet she should be safe enough, but advised her to be careful and not dawdle, then watched Jane walk out into the brush toward the stream. She had not been gone long when a scream brought the camp to its feet.

"Jane!" Daniel yelled and ran after her.

Abel rushed to the wagon and pulled one of the Colt revolvers from the holsters draped over the wagon wheel and followed Daniel. Jane shrieked again, but the scream ended as suddenly as a cork stopping a bottle. Lee grabbed his rifle from the wagon and checked the load, told Richard to stay at the camp and watch Sarah and Mary and Emma, grabbed Melvin by the sleeve to break him out of his seeming stupor, and they ran out of camp.

"Good Lord," Sarah said, trembling and hugging herself. "I hope that girl ain't come to some harm."

Richard said nothing; only stood gazing out into the waning light.

Chapter Forty-Seven

The willows and brush grew thicker the closer to the stream he got. Daniel thrashed through the growth, shouting Jane's name over and over and over.

Abel caught up, and grabbed Daniel's shoulder, jerking him to a halt. "Stop, Daniel! Listen!"

Daniel's heavy breathing subsided in a moment and the two men listened in the silence. Off to the left, they heard faint rustling and what sounded like grunts and groans. But the noise was overwhelmed by the approach of Lee and Melvin crashing through the brakes. Abel halted his father and brother when they drew near. The men huddled together and Abel sent each of them off a few yards to either side with instruction to move slowly in unison through the willows, in some places so thick only deer trails penetrated.

A short-lived scream sent Abel rushing ahead. He broke through a stand of willows into a small clearing to find Jane in the clutches of a man with one hand covering her mouth and nose and the other arm wrapped around her waist. He struggled to hold her still and keep ahold of the skinning knife in his hand. Jane strained against his grip, whipping her head back and forth and kicking at his legs and stomping and pushing against him whenever her feet touched the ground. A wide-brimmed sombrero lay in the dirt, apparently lost in the struggle.

Abel pulled back the hammer on the revolver and the trigger reached down to find his finger. He sidestepped around the small clearing, Jane's captor rotating with him, using Jane as a shield. The man looked like one of the Comancheros whose camp they had visited.

Daniel broke into the clearing and charged. The buckskin-clad man let go his hold on Jane's face and grabbed instead a hank of hair, yanking her to the ground as he released her waist. He slashed at Daniel with the knife. Daniel stumbled as he skidded to a halt and fell on his backside, crabbing his way backward on hands and feet. The Comanchero stepped toward him, dragging Jane with him, but she resisted, opening a gap between them the length of the man's outstretched arm.

Seeing the gap, Abel pressed the trigger. The powder flashed, and the bullet smashed into the Comanchero's upper arm, turning him and breaking his grip on Jane's hair. The man grunted and turned aside from Daniel swinging the knife toward Abel. Abel took a step back, yelling at the attacker to stop but he kept coming. The next round from the revolver smashed through his moustache, tearing his nose aside and shattering teeth and jawbone. He pitched forward and landed without breaking his fall, dead before hitting the ground.

Abel lowered the pistol and waved at the powder smoke. Jane had crawled to her father, and they huddled at the edge of the clearing, embracing one another and sobbing. Sometime during the confusion, Lee and Melvin had come into the clearing, and stood watching the dead trader, Lee pointing the rifle at him as if he might rise and attack again.

Once he saw everyone was safe, Abel dropped to his knees. His breath came in gasps and his stomach heaved and saltwater flooded his mouth. He feared he would vomit, but swallowed back the urge.

Lee reached down and grabbed the Comanchero's unbloodied arm and rolled him over. The man stared up at them with unseeing eyes, littered, like the rest of his bloody face, with bits of grass and leaves and particles of dirt. A puddle of blood muddied the soil where his face had lain, and chips of bone and shattered teeth shone white in the viscous bog.

"Lord, lord, Abel—you've done killed him," Melvin said as if coming out of a fog. "He's deader'n hell."

Jane moaned and Daniel held her closer. "He is one of those Indian traders, isn't he," he said.

"Was," Lee said. "He ain't tradin' nothin' now but barbs with the devil. But he was at that camp, for sure."

Rustling in the willows caused Lee to raise the rifle. He avoided—barely—pulling the trigger when Richard's face appeared above the blade of the front sight. "Damn, Pa! Put that rifle down!"

Lee lowered the gun and eased the hammer back down to half cock. "What are you doing here? I told you to stay with the wagons and watch over the women!"

"I heard the shooting—wondered what was goin' on." He stared at the dead Comanchero.

"The women could be in danger!" Lee said.

Richard spat. "When the shooting stopped, I figured the fight was over."

Lee could barely speak. "You fool! We don't know if this—this—*drinking companion* of yours is alone. There could be more of them still around!"

"Well, if they ain't they soon will be. Ojos Blanco and that bunch won't take kindly to you-all killin' one of their own."

Daniel blurted, "But he had my Jane! Abel had to shoot. What choice did we have?"

Richard laughed. "You think they're going to care about that?"

"Let them come," Abel said, rising to his feet. "They won't be carrying off any of Daniel's girls if I can help it."

"Listen to you, baby brother. But, come to think of it, you are an old hand when it comes to kidnapping—killing is gettin' to be a habit with you, too."

"That's enough, Richard," Lee said.

"What does he mean, Lee?" Daniel said.

"It doesn't matter."

Richard snickered. "The hell it don't, old man. Emma's got her sights set on Abel, but she don't know—and neither does her daddy here—that she'd be takin' up with a killer."

Abel bristled and took a step toward Richard, but Melvin grabbed his arm and held him back.

"Richard!" Lee said. "I said that's enough!"

"Shut up, old man! I'm done taking orders from you—you and your damn fool dreams and cockeyed notions!" Richard stepped forward and, with both hands in his father's chest, shoved him. Lee staggered, and as he stumbled, inadvertently raised the rifle in Richard's direction. Richard shoved the barrel aside and landed a fist on his father's jaw. Lee staggered again, the step this time causing him to trip over the dead Comanchero.

Abel jerked loose from Melvin's grasp and with the Colt revolver still in his hand swung a long arc that ended suddenly when the barrel of the gun reached the side of Richard's head. As he fell, Melvin again grabbed at Abel, but the younger brother spun away.

"Don't you touch me, Mel!" Abel said. "You do, and I'll slap you silly."

Lee got to his feet. He looked from one son to the other. "I guess we had better clean up this mess. Daniel, would you fetch some shovels from the wagons, please. Melvin, rouse your brother and help him back to the wagons. Then stay there and keep an eye on things—and I mean *stay there*. Here," he said, handing the rifle to Melvin. "Take this."

Daniel gave Abel a long, lingering look then wrapped an arm

around the still-weeping Jane and they walked off through the willows.

Melvin grabbed Richard by the front of his shirt, lifted him off the ground and shook him. "Rich!" he said. "Wake up!" He shook him some more and lowered him back to the ground.

Richard groaned, squeezed his eyes tight shut and felt the lump on the side of his head. He opened his eyes and saw Melvin looming over him, took the proffered hand, and his brother hauled him to his feet. Unsteady, he held onto his brother for support. Melvin held Richard's arm and led him shuffling toward camp.

With the others gone, Lee and Abel sat side-by-side on the ground. Abel looked at the dead Comanchero. He replayed the killing in his mind and followed it up with the fight with his brothers. As he sat, holding back tears, his father placed a hand on his back and gave it a pat.

Chapter Forty-Eight

Lee tamped the last shovelful of dirt on the Comanchero's grave, then he and Daniel scattered willow twigs and leaf litter over the bare ground. It wasn't much of a disguise, but perhaps enough not to call attention to itself in a cursory glance. After the grave was dug, Lee sent Abel on a circuit of the area in search of the dead man's horse, hoping he could locate the mount in the dark. It was unlikely, Lee thought, that the trader would have walked the nearly two days' journey from the trader camp, particularly in light of the fact that the Comancheros were probably already on the trail and the kidnapper would have to catch them up somewhere along the way.

Not long after Lee and Daniel stowed the shovels in the wagons, Abel rode in. He swung down from the scrawny mustang and pulled the Mexican *vaquero* saddle with its Spanish rig, slick fork, and horn nearly the size of a dinner plate. "What'll we do with this horse and gear, Pa?"

Lee, Daniel, Melvin, and Abel gathered around the campfire and talked over the possibilities. They could bury the saddle and turn the horse loose to wander. They could keep the saddle and turn the horse loose. Discard the saddle and keep the horse. Abel said, "I say we keep the horse and the saddle. The horse seems sound. The saddle's had rough use but looks to be in good enough shape."

"What if one of them traders finds us? Havin' that horse and saddle is as good as sayin' outright we killed their man," Melvin said.

"Me, I don't think they'll come after him," Lee said. "Leastways, not anytime soon. If we drive hard, we ought to be at that Las Vegas place before he's even missed. Maybe even Santa Fe. Them Comancheros ain't likely to show up there lookin' for him, if what White Eyes said is true."

Melvin thought that over for a minute. "Maybe so. But what'll folks there think 'bout a bunch of Americans with a Mexican horse and saddle?"

Abel laughed. "Mel, I reckon Mexican stuff is as common as ticks on a coon hound out here. We are in Mexico, you know. Even gringos like us havin' a Mexican outfit ain't likely to attract no notice."

"I believe he is right," Daniel said. "We do not know what we may encounter in the Mexican settlements, but with all the traffic on the Santa Fe Trail, I suspect we will find an admixture of cultural influences."

Melvin shrugged. "Suit yourselves. Rich ain't goin' to like it."

Lee shrugged. "We had best turn in. It's late and we'll want to get an early start. Put all this behind us."

Daniel held up a hand. "One thing, before we depart." He bowed his head, rubbed his hands together, and looked at Lee. "It pains me to ask, but do you suppose Richard had anything to do with this?"

Startled, Lee sat upright. Melvin jumped to his feet, fists clenched, and leaned toward Daniel, looking as if holding himself back required some effort.

Only Abel could find words. "What makes you think so?"

"Please," Daniel said, raising his hand again. "I have no reason to believe he did. Only a suspicion, if even that." He paused, swallowed hard. "He did spend considerable time among those nasty blokes. Most of the time, pickled. Perhaps, while in his cups, he passed along information that proved valuable in the attempt to kidnap my Jane—or even planted the idea."

"I can't believe that of my son," Lee said. "He may be contrary and bad-tempered at times, and I'm troubled by his fondness for drink—but I don't think he'd be capable of evil such as that. Besides, those traders saw the girls for themselves."

Melvin still stood, jaws clenched, glaring at Daniel.

"Forget it, Mel," Abel said. "He don't mean nothin' by it. Mister Lewis is just worried about Jane."

"Can't blame him for that," Lee said.

Melvin huffed and fetched his bedroll from the wagon, rolled it out next to where Richard slept, his head wrapped in bandages.

Daniel said, "Well, to bed. I will check on Jane; make sure she is all right. Do you think we should set a watch?"

"I think that Comanchero came alone," Abel said. "I didn't see no other tracks out where he left his horse, nor any sign of anyone else. It was plenty dark, so I could of missed something, but I don't believe there's anyone out there."

Daniel nodded. "Good night, then, gentlemen."

"Pa," Abel said when Lee was out of earshot. "Do you think Daniel really believes Rich said something back there?"

"I hope not. I don't think Rich would do that. I hope Daniel believes me. Why? Do you think Daniel's right?"

Abel stood and untucked his shirt tail. "Nah. Not really. Rich is plenty mad at me most of the time, but I don't think he would cause any harm to them girls. I sure hope not."

Daniel found Jane in the moon shadow of the wagon, enfolded in Mary's arms. She slept, but still sobbed softly as she breathed, her tear-stained face pillowed against her older sister's breast. He squatted near where Mary sat propped against the wheel of a wagon and reached out and caressed Jane's cheek with the back of his hand, then stroked her hair gently.

"Is she all right, do you think?" he whispered.

Mary shook her head. "It will be quite some time before she is all right, I fear. I cannot imagine suffering such an ordeal—and at her age. . . ." Mary wiped away a tear of her own.

Emma, too, showed signs of weeping. She sat next to Mary with a quilt wrapped around her shoulders. "It's my fault, Father. I should never have let her go alone."

"Oh, Emma," Daniel said. "We are all guilty of that. But it is not the fault of any of us. We expected no danger."

"Jane said Abel killed the man."

"That he did. He saved Jane and, most likely, my life as well." He stroked Jane's hair once more then stood. "Try to sleep, girls. We will leave early in the morning. We all believe it best to be away from this place."

Mary nestled down against Jane. Emma rewrapped her quilt and lay down, her head on her older sister's thigh. Daniel rolled out his bed a respectful distance away and was asleep in minutes.

Everyone in the camp slept soundly until the faintest hint of dawn appeared in the east and Jane screamed.

Chapter Forty-Nine

Mary jerked awake when Jane screamed and she slammed her head on the spokes of the wagon wheel against her back. Emma, slower to rouse, sat up and scrubbed her eyes with her fists. Mary reached out and wrapped her arms around Jane and pulled her close.

"Jane," she whispered in her sister's ear. "Jane, what is it?"

Jane pushed herself away and looked around, unaware of where she was or what she was seeing. Then her eyes focused and she gasped and fell back into Mary's arms. Emma added herself to the hug, wrapping her arms around Jane and Mary.

Daniel ran to the girls and dropped to his knees beside them. Not far behind came Sarah and she squatted beside the girls and rubbed Jane's back. The Pate men came too, but held back with hands in pockets and shuffling feet.

"Jane, Jane, Jane," Mary said. "You are safe. We are here."

Sobbing, Jane said, "My dream—I dreamed that awful man had me again—It was awful—awful—"

Emma said, "I know, Jane. I know. But it is all right now."

No one moved for what seemed minutes. Then Abel put the revolver he held back into the holster and belt slung over his shoulder. Melvin walked to the fire, added a few sticks of kindling and, with this hat, fanned up flames from the ashes. Richard looked around, rolled his bed, laid it beside the wagon, and walked out of the growing firelight into the fading dark.

Lee watched him walk away, leaned his rifle against the

wagon, and helped Sarah to her feet. "Sarah, can you whip up something quick for breakfast, please. Let's be gone from here."

And so she boiled coffee, and boiled oatmeal with pemmican stirred in, but fixed no breadstuff. While the pot and kettle boiled, she boxed and bundled up the rest of the camp equipment. Lee loaded the wagons while Melvin and Abel brought in the mules and oxen. Sarah untied the calf and let it suck the cow to save the milking. Richard came back to camp and stood watching the Lewis family, still huddled next to the wagon. Melvin called him to help yoke the ox teams to the Lewis wagons while Abel harnessed and hitched the mules.

No one spoke as they ate, spooning up the hot porridge and sipping the scalding coffee. Some ate hungrily, most without enthusiasm, and Jane not at all, refusing even to hold a bowl or cup.

When Sarah finished, she said, "You-all just shake out your cups and throw them in this here box. Drop your bowls and spoons in the bucket—I'll give them a quick rinse, otherwise them oats will set up hard. Boys, get the horses saddled. We'll have this stuff in the wagon and ready to go by the time you-all are finished."

Jane climbed onto the seat of the lead wagon to be near her father as he walked beside the oxen with his goad and one of Abel's Colt revolvers in his waistband. Mary and Emma found places on either side of the second wagon's team. Richard, his head again rendering him in no shape for walking, albeit for a different reason this time, took his father's advice to help Sarah drive the mules. But Sarah, again this day, allowed she would walk alongside with Melvin. Lee mounted his horse to take the lead; Abel would ride the Comanchero pony and bring up the rear.

The sun had yet to reveal itself when the trace chains rattled and the wheels groaned and the wagons creaked into motion.

No one looked back at the abandoned campsite.

Jane did not get down from the wagon when the train nooned at a small stream and the clear, cold spring that fed it. Sarah stirred a handful of sugar into a cup of coffee and, climbing onto the seat beside Jane, encouraged her to sip at it. Mary fried some bacon, boiled water for corn dodgers, and stewed rice and raisins, providing something substantial after the hurried breakfast hours earlier.

"Lee, if you've a moment I have some questions for you," Daniel said after dropping his plate in the wash bucket. Mary followed the men a ways away from the wagons. They found seats on boulders and on the ground and the men sipped at their coffee as they settled in. After a few minutes of small talk, Lee asked what it was they needed.

Daniel set his cup aside and cleared his throat. "We want you to know—Mary and I, as well as Emma and Jane—how grateful we are that Abel saved our Jane. It is horrific to imagine what might have happened otherwise."

"Yes?" Lee said. "I see. But oughtn't you to be thankin' Abel?"

"No, no—it is not that. We shall, of course, I mean," Daniel said. "But, actually, it is something Richard said we want to inquire about. Something he said back there after Abel killed the Comanchero, and something similar he said to Mary and Emma."

Daniel paused, and Lee nodded him to go on.

"It may be nothing. A result of anger, or perhaps the alcohol talking. Or it could be codswallop, pure and simple."

"Yes, yes, spit it out, Daniel."

"Well, you know our Emma is fond of Abel. Richard has had his eye on the girl, and her attentions in Abel's direction appear to have caused a certain amount of jealousy and frustration." Daniel turned to Mary. "Mary, you go on. Say what Richard told you and Emma."

Mary did not hesitate. "He said Abel was not the man we thought he was. That Emma should be wary. He suggested we ask him about Peter. Then some nonsense about the origin of his pistols and knife. Even his hat and coat."

Daniel picked up the thread. "And you will recall, Lee, that when Richard arrived after the killing of the Comanchero, he implied that Abel knew something of kidnapping and murder."

"Yes?"

"I am sorry, Lee, but—solely in the interest of Emma's well-being, you see, should something of a more permanent nature develop between the youngsters—well, we—Mary and I—are curious as to his—Richard's—meaning, and whether his comments concerning Abel are related in some way. And, I suppose, what they mean."

Lee pondered for a moment, tossing the dregs from his coffee cup and rotating it around and around between his fingers, looking into its bottom. "You got three—four—girls, Daniel. I reckon they are about as different from each other in their ways as my boys. Richard, he's always been a contrary sort. Didn't matter if I'd tell that boy a hog has four legs, he'd argue about it. Challenged me at every turn.

"Melvin—well, Melvin's just Melvin. He's a hard worker, but the boy don't spend a whole lot of time thinkin' about what he's doin' or even if he ought to be doin' it. Mostly, he follows Richard's lead. Has done since they was little, and not always to his advantage.

"Then there's Abel. He's always been the kind of boy I wished those other two was. Smart, he is, and capable of doin' 'bout anything he sets his mind to. And he ain't got no quit in him. But I guess I'm kind of selfish about what I like best about the boy. He obeys me. If I was God and he was Abraham and I told him to slay Isaac, he'd do it. Might not be happy about it, but he'd do it."

Lee stood and set his cup on the rock seat he'd abandoned. He stretched his shoulders and massaged the small of his back. "Thing is, it just got easier and easier to ask Abel to do things I wanted done. Arguing with Richard over every little thing got too tiresome. It was a mistake on my part, I know, but I favored Abel and that upset Richard—as it ought to have done."

Lee paused to gather his thoughts. Then, "When we left Shelby County, we left a lot of things behind. I wanted no more of that life. Sarah wasn't happy about it, and she still ain't. Same with Richard." He laughed. "I guess that ain't no secret. Anyway, after we was gone, there was some left-behind things I wanted. Things my brother Ben had, but what belonged to me—left by our father to me as the firstborn.

"I sent the boys back to get them. Melvin and Richard went to my brother but he sent them away—give Melvin a good beating, too. Them two gave up and was ready to come back empty-handed, but Abel, he wasn't havin' any of that."

Picking up the empty cup, Lee sat again on the boulder. Daniel and Mary waited for him to continue. After a moment, he did. He told them about Abel happening on his drunken Uncle Ben. How Ben refused the request yet again and attacked Abel. About Abel killing Ben out of necessity. And the subterfuge he used to fool Peter and obtain the wanted property.

"He never intended to kill my brother Ben, nor to force Peter to come with us. It's just kind of how it turned out, I guess, and it's tortured the boy ever since. But Abel, see, he only did what I asked him to do—so if anyone's to be blamed for what happened, well, it would be me."

With that, Lee walked back to the wagons. Daniel and Mary sat and watched him go.

Chapter Fifty

Reaching Las Vegas was a revelation to the Pates and Lewises. The mountains, which first appeared as a sky-blue smudge on the western horizon many days ago, were now upon them. The town was a beehive of activity after lonely weeks on the plains. The low-slung, flat-roofed adobe buildings that fortified the central plaza looked strange to them. Dust and dung seasoned the air, spiced with sweat and smoke and the smells of unfamiliar foods.

Tall-sided, big-wheeled, lumbering Santa Fe Trail freight wagons rolled along behind six, eight, even twelve yoke of oxen driven by filthy, foul-mouthed bullwhackers whose popping whips kept the travelers' heads down and on the lookout for gunfire.

Mexican men led donkeys and pulled handcarts and pushed wheelbarrows burdened with loads of every description. Women spread colorful blankets around the edges of the plaza, displaying for sale baskets and pottery and silver jewelry and corn and chili peppers and other fruits and vegetables. Others squatted next to cooking fires where they flipped *tortillas* on *comals* and warmed clay pots of *frijoles* and *tamales* and stewed meats and other fragrant foodstuff, with *atole* and *horchata* and other beverages at hand to wash it down.

As soon as Daniel and Lee turned their wagons out on a side street and found a place to park, Jane jumped down from the wagon and slipped between it and an adobe wall, huddling in shade and fear. Emma, eager to explore the first settlement of consequence since leaving Fort Smith, instead crawled into the shadows and huddled with Jane, cuddling and whispering she had nothing to fear—never mind that many of the men milling about the town resembled the dark-skinned Comanchero who instigated her terror.

Lee left instructions for his boys to wait while he and Daniel located a safe place to camp but they had no sooner turned a corner when Richard led Melvin by the arm toward the plaza for a taste of what served to wet a whistle in New Mexico. Neither Sarah's nor Abel's entreaties served to stay their course.

Spying a flagpole hanging a limp banner, Lee and Daniel made their way to the doorway beneath it. The place had little to distinguish it from the other adobe buildings in the row, some of which appeared to house stores, others offices of one sort or another, still others residences. Ducking through the entrance, the men noticed the drop in temperature as they passed through the thick wall. A man seated at a desk pushed against a side wall saw them enter from the corner of his eye and held up a hand to stop them as he signed the bottom of the top sheet of a stack of papers before him. He put the pen in its holder, sprinkled powder from a pounce pot and gently shook the sheet for a few seconds before blowing away the excess powder. He put the page back on the pile and stood, tugging straight the lapels of the vest of his American-style suit.

"How may I be of service, my friends?" he said in accented English. He introduced himself as Hilario Gonzales, Justice of the Peace for *Nuestra Señora de los Dolores de Las Vegas.* " 'Our Lady of Sorrows of the Great Meadows' is the official name of our growing community, but it is simply Las Vegas by which it is known. Welcome, my friends, to New Mexico's newest city—it is only five years since our foundation, but already we are home to a few hundred souls, and, as you have seen," he said, with a wave toward the door and the plaza beyond, "visited by many, many who pass through on the busy trail. Now, how may I be of service?"

Lee asked about a safe place to lay over, and Gonzales directed them to a bow in the Gallinas River where they would be shaded by *los alamos* and have access to plentiful grass for their animals. He asked their business in New Mexico. "Only out of curiosity, you understand my friends, and in the event I am able to render assistance."

"We are looking to settle in New Mexico, perhaps," Lee said. "But we don't know much about the place or the prospects. Could be we'll go on to Alta California, if we can't find what we're a-lookin' for here."

"Aah, yes. Americanos have been trickling in to our country since the opening of the great Santa Fe Trail years ago. Not so many people, you understand, but some. Two of your countrymen—brothers—have become citizens and were awarded land here in our valley, near the hot springs." Gonzales paused, his brow furrowed. "I feel it my duty to inform you that many of our people resent the intrusion of Americanos. Some accuse them of—how do you say it?—*la estafa*—swindling native New Mexicans out of lands that have been in their families since the old days of Spanish rule. Not all will welcome you, I am afraid."

Gonzales advised their best course would be to continue on to Santa Fe and seek an audience with Governor Armijo, or perhaps Guadalupe Miranda, another government official, for advice on a land grant. They talked some more, then thanked the man and left.

"Where's Richard? And Melvin?" Lee said when he and Daniel returned to the parked wagons.

"Left near 'bout the time you-all did," Sarah said. "Couldn't dissuade them, though I tried."

Lee huffed. "Told them boys to wait here!"

Sarah's face sagged. She shook her head, then said. "I know it. But I do believe them two boys is about done listenin' to you."

He grasped the wagon wheel with both hands and leaned down until his head touched the iron tire. "I don't know what's to become of them two."

"Nor do I," Sarah said, laying a hand between her husband's shoulder blades. "They don't hold with your ways, Pa, and now that they're growed and got minds of their own—well, I guess they mean to go their own way."

He stood upright and sighed. "Don't know what I done wrong, Sarah."

"You did what you thought best. Them boys don't think it's best all the time." She chuckled. "For that matter, neither do I. Made no secret of it, neither. Fact is, you are a man prone to take on a lot of fool notions. Let your heart get the best of your mind."

"I know you think so, Sarah. But I'm bound to do what I believe I'm meant to do."

After a moment, Sarah said, "So are them boys, Pa. So are them boys."

Lee wiped the corners of his eyes with a thumb and forefinger, then said, "Well, I reckon we best get on to where we can camp. I'll deal with Richard and Melvin later." He snugged the cinch on the saddle horse and stepped into the stirrup and lifted his leg over the cantle. Finding the opposite stirrup, he rocked himself into the seat. Seeing Daniel ready to go, he nodded to him to get up the oxen.

Before riding ahead to lead the way, he said, "Abel! Drive the wagon if you will." He heeled the horse into motion, knowing full well Abel would obey.

Chapter Fifty-One

No mirrored back bar graced the dim and smoky *cantina* and the rough-cut bar held no polish; no sparkling fixtures dispensed beverages nor did a brass rail prop feet off the floor. Rather than sparkling glassware, Richard and Melvin drank from coarse clay mugs.

Richard signaled the bartender to refill his cup with the fiery *mezcal* from the earthen jug, watching his brother sip *pulque* as he waited. "I don't know how you can drink that sour crap," he said. "It's thick as vomit and smells about the same."

Melvin smiled, took a sip, and licked the residue off his upper lip. Richard shivered and shook his head, fluttering his cheeks and lips. Melvin smiled again and hoisted his mug, signaling the barkeep to fill it with another dipperful from the crock.

The man behind the bar, a filthy apron wrapped around his waist, had yet to speak a word to the brothers, words which would have been wasted as he had no English and they no Spanish. Instead, the Pate boys each dumped a handful of coins on the bar and sampled the limited *aguardiente* on offer until choosing their poison. The bar man fingered the coins, scratching out the necessary denominations and sliding back change.

"Pa ain't goin' to be happy to find us gone."

Richard sipped his drink. "I don't give a damn if he is or he ain't, Mel." He took another drink. "Fact is, brother, I think this may be as far as I go with Pa."

Melvin's forehead wrinkled and he cocked his head to one side. "What is it you're sayin', Rich?"

"I'm sayin' it's time for us to go."

"Go where? What do you mean?"

"Don't be an idiot, Mel—I been saying it for weeks—months. I thought you was with me. I'm sick and tired of followin' Pa and his fool notions. We've followed him clear the hell to Mexico! Ain't that far enough?"

Melvin worried the mug in his hand, sloshing the heavy pulque around, staring into the swirl and suds. "I don't know, Rich. It's hard to feature bein' away from the family—Ma especially. What would we do?"

The wood on the bar resounded like a gunshot when Richard slammed down his mug. "Dammit, little brother, grow up! We light out of here, we can do anything we want!"

"Yeah, but what do you want to do?"

"One thing's for damn sure—I don't want to work my fingers to the bone for Pa only to have him fritter it all away again. Besides, there's Abel. Hell, you know as well as I do that Pa don't care nothin' about me bein' the oldest and you bein' older—it's always Abel he favors. Every damn time. And it's that way even with Pa knowin' how hard it is havin' a younger brother lordin' it over you all the time. That only makes it worse, to my way of thinkin'."

Melvin wondered at his brother's words about Pa, worried it over for a moment, then shrugged and swallowed another mouthful of pulque.

The longer the brothers stayed in the stuffy cantina drinking Mexican alcohol and breathing stale air that had the taint of being breathed too many times before, the more Richard chipped away at his brother's uncertainty. They bandied about retracing their steps to return to Arkansas, or Tennessee, or elsewhere in the States. They mulled over going west to California, or north to the Oregon country. They talked about going south, deeper into Mexico.

Then Richard presented a plan that appeared fresh to Melvin, but was well measured in his own mind. "Comes to it, Mel, we don't have to go somewhere—leastways not any place in particular. Say we hook up with one of these freight outfits and be teamsters. Hell, if we didn't want to do that we could find that Cejita de Los Comancheros place and travel with them Indian traders. What do you think?"

Melvin pulled off his hat and ran his fingers through his hair. "I don't know, Rich. I'm too tired to think."

"Whatever we do, now's the time to do it."

"Well, I've got to sleep on it. I can't make up my mind about nothin' right now." He drained off the pulque in his cup and rolled forth a satisfying belch. "Let's go find the wagons and get some sleep."

The brothers were unsteady, propping one another up when needed as they walked back to where they left the wagons. They stopped in the little side street, looking out into the darkness and wondering which way to go.

Squatting in the shadows against the adobe wall where Jane had sought refuge, Abel watched his brothers for a few minutes, amused at their wobbly legs and unruly tongues as they argued about the most likely course to take. He would rather be with the wagons, rolled in his bed and resting. But his father asked him to try and locate his brothers, so here he was. He spent the evening hours in the plaza but did not see his brothers among the roving bands of bullwhackers who had long since left town. Nor did he find Richard and Melvin in any of the drinking establishments he ferreted out. But he did not find the dumpy little out-of-the-way *taberna* where the boys sacrificed sobriety for pleasure.

The brothers jumped at a voice out of the darkness. "You

boys lookin' for something?" They spun in slow circles seeking out the source of the sound. Abel stood and stepped out of the shadows. "Over here." Again his brothers started, then found him.

"Abel. Should've known it was you. Nobody else'd hide out just to scare us," Richard said.

"Yeah," Melvin said with a giggle. "Damn near made me pee my pants."

Abel shook his head. "It ain't like I was hiding. If you-all wasn't blind drunk, you wouldn't of had no trouble seeing me."

Melvin wobbled a bit, belched, then bent over and with hands on knees, puked in the dusty street. He heaved several times, unloading his stomach, then wiped his chin and mouth with his fingers and attempted to fling the residue aside.

"Damn!" Richard said. "That pulque smells as bad comin' up as it does goin' down. I told you not to drink that crap."

Melvin belched.

"C'mon, you-all. We best get Mel to bed. Sleep wouldn't hurt you any, either, Rich."

Richard swept off his hat and cocked it across his waist as he took a deep bow, stumbling and almost falling as he did. "As you wish, your Highness."

Abel led the way to the wagon camp by the river, Melvin and Richard following behind but urging him, again and again, to slow down.

Lee hauled himself out of his bedroll when he heard his sons coming.

"Evenin', Pa," Melvin said.

"Son."

"Pa."

"Richard."

Abel stood aside and watched as his father and brothers watched each other.

Lee broke the silence, saying, "Did you-all not hear me when I asked you to stay with the wagons?"

"We heard," Richard said. "But we didn't see no need. Didn't want to sit around. Been so long since we saw a town we wanted to have a look-see."

"What about the wagons? What about our goods? The stock? The women?"

Richard laughed. "Aw, hell, Pa! Abel was there. Abel, he can take care of anything, can't he?"

Lee searched for the right answer. "I don't know as he can take care of *anything.* But I know when I ask him to take care of something he generally does it. Never found him shirkin' his duty in no grog shop."

Melvin stood scratching at the dirt with the toe of his boot while Richard bristled. "Well, Pa," he said. "I'm sure glad you have such a fine son as Abel. More than makes up for the disappointment of me and Mel."

"Oh, Richard, don't say that!" Lee said with strained voice. "You're all my sons. We're a family." Then, in a moment, "But I do you wish you two would abide by my wishes."

"Wouldn't dream of takin' over Abel's job," Richard said. "I'm goin' to bed. C'mon, Mel. We got to get a good night's sleep so we can get an early start on disappointing Pa all over again."

Chapter Fifty-Two

Sarah found Lee sitting by the low campfire when she arose to start breakfast. He sat on the ground, his back against a kitchen box, wrapped in a blanket. Despite the bowed head, hunched back, and stillness, she knew he was awake. She stuck some sticks of kindling into the fire and watched the flames enfold and enflame them, then added split wood to build up the fire.

"What is it, Lee?" she said, settling atop another of the boxes near the fire, tightening the braid in her hair and twisting it into a bun at her nape.

He did not respond for a moment, then looked at his wife as if unaware of her presence. "Sarah," he said. "Couldn't sleep. Well, I did sleep but then that dream came back. Woke me up and wouldn't let me sleep no more."

Sarah smoothed her hair then leaned over and laid a hand on his shoulder. "Oh, Lee. You and your damn dreams. Ain't you got troubles enough in daylight without allowin' silly dreams to upset you?"

"You know I don't find dreams silly. There's meaning in them if you look for it."

Sarah sighed and patted his shoulder. "Yes. I suppose. And there's trouble in them if you look for it." She stood, lifted the coffeepot, shook it, then poured the sludge onto the edge of the fire, raising a cloud of steam. "Which dream is it? What's troubling you?"

"Richard and Melvin. The same one I told you-all about, the

one that keeps comin' back, where they're on one side of a river and me and you and Abel is on the other. We're in a pretty country, but their side of the river is a forsaken place, not fit for humans." He paused, shook his head, and went on. "Bad as it looks over there, them boys won't come over to us. We beckon and call and urge them on, but they just look at us. But with empty eyes, like they don't even see us."

"What do you think it means?" Sarah said as she continued filling the coffeepot with water, throwing in grounds, and setting it to heat over the fire.

"Don't know. I guess that's why it troubles me so. But I don't think it means anything good." He stood and wrapped the blanket tighter around his shoulders even though the weather didn't merit it. "I'm worried about those boys."

Mary walked into the firelight, ready to do her part in the breakfast preparations. "Good morning," she said. "Emma will be along. Jane wanted to milk, but asked Emma to go with her to stand watch."

"Poor child," Sarah said.

"She is improving, although still frightened to be alone. But she is sleeping better, thank the Lord."

Lee left the women to their work. He found Abel sitting up and pulling on his boots; Richard and Melvin, who had dragged their bedrolls to the other side of the wagons, were unmoving lumps of canvas. Lee asked his youngest son to take Daniel and ride out the Santa Fe Trail toward the toll station at San Jose and see about salvaging an axle from the wrecked wagons said to be there. The Comanchero White Eyes had mentioned, and Gonzales verified, that the trail was littered with abandoned wagons, some burned, some intact.

Years past, they had learned from Gonzales, New Mexico taxed trade on the Santa Fe Trail according to the goods on the wagons. But when inventory became cumbersome, the government assessed a flat tax of 500 dollars on each freight wagon regardless of what or how much it carried. One result was the large wagons that now plied the trail. Another was the practice of pulling off the trail ahead of the port of entry and consolidating loads in wagons large and small, filling space freed up from the food and supplies consumed on the trail with trade goods from other wagons and leaving the emptied conveyances behind, sometimes under a cloud of smoke.

Daniel and Abel saddled the horses, and Abel loaded the wagon jack along with tools he might find helpful on one of the mules. They rode through the plaza at Las Vegas and followed the Santa Fe Trail out of town down South Pacific Street. Like the plaza, the street catered to the wagon traffic. Even at this early hour, occupants of the adobe houses lining the road displayed goods for sale on their covered front porches, or *portales.* Daniel determined on the way out that on the way back he would purchase a small wheel of aged cheese from one of the several homes showing it. He doubted he would find anything of the quality of cheddar that was part of his English upbringing, but any cheese with heft would improve on the occasional batch of pot cheese Sarah cooked up from cow's milk curdled with vinegar.

The farther from town they rode, the more wagons—or remnants of wagons—they passed. Some were heaps of ash and twisted metal, others torn apart and scattered, some nearly intact. Abel found what was left of a wagon that appeared suitable. The box had been stripped of its planks and boards and the tongue was missing, but the running gear looked to be intact. Best of all, the rear axle looked to be a replacement, showing less age than the bolster or hounds or wheels to which it was attached. The wagon had no brake.

The wagon frame went up easily over the jack and Abel pulled the wheels and washers, then the hound braces and through-bolts and dropped the axle. The clouts were in good shape with essentially no wear. He examined the wheels, but found them no sturdier than the ones they already had so let them lie. With the axle and tools lashed to the mule, the men mounted up and headed back to town.

They rode into camp to find Richard pointing Abel's spare Paterson Colt at his Pa. Abel dropped the mule's lead rope and hurried his mount between his father and brother.

"Get the hell out of the way, Abel. This don't concern you."

"Don't be a fool, Rich." Abel turned to his father. "What's going on, Pa?"

"It ain't nothing, Son. Just a little spat."

"Spat? He's pointin' a gun at you!" He turned to Richard. "My gun." Rather than pulling the pistol's mate from the holster hanging from his saddle, Abel slipped his foot from the stirrup, lifted his leg and planted his boot in the middle of Richard's chest with all the force he could muster.

It was enough. Richard's feet left the ground and he tipped backward, the air leaving his lungs in a whoosh when he lit. The pistol fired, but the bullet went harmlessly upward. Abel hoisted his other leg over the saddle horn and slid out of the saddle and was on Richard before he could catch his breath. He tossed the pistol aside, rolled Richard over and wrenched one of his arms behind his back.

Before Melvin could insert himself into the fight, Sarah placed a hand on his arm. It was enough to hold him back.

"Rich, hold still," Abel said between clenched teeth when his brother struggled. He forced the twisted arm up between Richard's shoulder blades and applied pressure until the thrashing diminished to squirming then stopped.

"Let me up, you sonofabitch!"

"What's goin' on with you and Pa?"

"None of your damn business." More pressure on the arm.

"All right! I'll tell you. First, let go of me."

Abel let go and took a step back. Richard rolled over, raised himself to his knees and launched himself at his brother. Abel sidestepped and landed a boot in Richard's ribs as he hit the ground. He grabbed him by the collar and lifted him to his feet, spun him around and grabbed his shirt front with both hands. Abel shook Richard until his head rattled then pushed him back against the wagon and pinned him there.

"Now, big brother, tell me what's goin' on."

Lee laid a hand on Abel's shoulder. "Let him go, Son. Like I said, it's nothing."

Abel looked at his father in disbelief and let go his hold on Richard. Richard flexed his strained arm and tugged the disarray out of his shirt front.

Abel said, "It had to be something, Pa. It looked like he was about to shoot you!"

"Oh, he wouldn't have shot me. It was just his way of saying him and Melvin didn't want to unload the wagon if you come back with a new axle." Lee looked from Richard to Melvin and back again. "That looks like an axle on that mule's back. What do you say you get the wagon unloaded and help Abel get it put on."

Richard huffed, but signaled Melvin over with a nod of his head and lifted the tailgate out of the wagon box.

Daniel, still horseback, held up the sack he carried in his lap. "I say—would anyone care for a bit of cheese?"

Chapter Fifty-Three

The wagon came apart and went back together without incident. The new axle fit well and Abel was pleased to see his repaired axle was serviceable yet, with very little play between the broken ends. He lashed it under the hounds before the box went back on, thinking to save it in the unlikely event it should be needed again. By suppertime, the wagon was loaded and would be ready to roll come morning.

Richard and Melvin sat off by themselves during the evening meal, Richard periodically rotating his wrenched shoulder and glaring at Abel. Mary carried the coffeepot over to where they sat, each leaning against a cottonwood tree.

"Would you gentlemen care for more coffee?"

"Thank you kindly, Miss Mary," Melvin said. "I would enjoy another cup."

She filled his cup then did the same for Richard. She stood over him for a moment, watching him watch the steam rise off his coffee. She set the pot on the ground and folded her legs under to sit. "I guess we shall move on in the morning."

Richard finally looked at her. "Guess so," he said.

"What do you suppose we will find in Santa Fe?"

With a sniff, Richard said, "Don't know. Don't care."

"Mel, would you return the coffeepot to the fire, please? No sense in letting it grow cold."

After he left, Mary smoothed the skirt of her dress where it lay across her thighs. "Richard, it is your future we are talking about. Have you no interest in what your life may become?"

He thought a moment. "Not much, to tell you the truth. I just know I don't want it to go on the way it is."

Mary smiled. "That is good. I should think you would want to stop being so contrary and grow closer with your family."

Richard snorted and tossed out the coffee in his cup. "Put some distance between me and them, more likely."

The hard look on Richard's face startled Mary and she stood, took the cup from Richard, and started back to the wagons. She stopped when he called her name.

"Yes?" She turned to find Richard a step away.

"What you said about growing closer—how about you and me get a little closer? Sometimes you act like it ain't such a bad idea."

His hands shot forward, grasping her shoulders. Mary cringed at his foul breath as he leaned in and pressed his wet lips to hers. Wrenching herself away, she shoved Richard aside, gathered her skirts, and ran toward camp.

Richard spat upon the ground as he watched her go.

With a long evening ahead and little to keep him occupied, Abel took the family Bible from the wagon's jockey box and unwrapped the sacking that protected it and Ezekiel Pate's old journal. He studied the worn and scuffed cover of the Bible that was the source of much of his sorrow. Richard, who seemed to have lost any interest in his family and his heritage, would, by right as the firstborn son, inherit the Bible and journal that was its mate. Abel wondered if the books would be safe in his brother's hands, and if another generation would hold the books.

Not knowing the answers to his own questions, Abel left camp for the riverbank in the opposite direction his brothers had chosen, sat against a tree and opened the book. He thumbed through the pages at random and read a few lines from Ecclesiastes.

I said in mine heart concerning the estate of the sons of men, that God might manifest them, and that they might see that they themselves are beasts.

For that which befalleth the sons of men befalleth beasts; even one thing befalleth them: as the one dieth, so dieth the other; yea, they have all one breath; so that a man hath no preeminence above a beast: for all is vanity.

A sound distracted him and he looked up to find Emma sitting before him. "Emma!" He closed the book on his thumb and scrambled to his feet. "I'm sorry—I didn't hear you come up."

"Sit," she said with a smile. "What are you reading?"

He sat and opened the book and looked again at the passage he had just read. "Not sure," he said, thinking that was often the case when he read the Bible. "I think this part is about me and my brothers. Says the sons of men are beasts—at least no better than."

Again, Emma smiled. "I do not think you are a beast. Richard, he may well be, though. But somewhere else in that book, as I recall, it says something like, 'A wise son maketh a glad father.' I believe that does a better job of describing you."

Abel blushed at the compliment.

Emma said, "I don't know if you have been properly thanked for rescuing Jane. Without you, a terrible fate surely would have befallen her."

"Oh, it weren't no big thing. I just did what had to be done." He paused and hung his head. "Just wish I hadn't of killed that man."

Emma reached out and placed her hand on his arm. "Oh, Abel! Don't say that! As you said, you only did what had to be done."

He looked into Emma's eyes. "It seems to come too easy to me. I ain't but sixteen years old and already I've killed two men—one of 'em kin."

With no other comfort to offer, Emma raised herself to her knees and leaned into Abel, enfolding him in her arms. He grasped her shoulders and held her close for a moment, then gently pushed her away. He swallowed hard. "We had best be getting back to the wagons. It's coming on dark."

After the calf sucked, Jane tied it to the back of the wagon and led the cow out to a patch of grass, pounded a stake into the ground with a rock, and left it to graze. The oxen and mules and saddle horses were likewise tethered, the horses and mules and one of the oxen cropping grass, the other oxen lying on their bellies chewing cud. She looked around in the dim light and hurried back to the wagons and the light of the fire. She fetched the bucket of milk from where it sat and carried it to Sarah.

Sarah smiled as Jane passed her the bail. "Thank you, child. You don't know how much I appreciate your taking on the milking. It relieves me of a burden."

"I like it," Jane said. "It is so calm. And the cow is warm and soft where I lean against her."

From beside the fire, Daniel called, "Gather 'round all! I've a treat for you." Sitting before him on a cloth bag laid out on an upturned box sat the wheel of cheese purchased from town. With a kitchen knife he cut out a wedge and pared off slices, balancing them on the side of the knife blade to pass them to the others.

Melvin was first in line and gnawed off a bite. "That's good!" he said. "That don't taste like no cheese I ever had before."

"It is tasty," Daniel said as he continued slicing and serving. "Not English cheddar, you understand, but toothsome nonetheless."

Abel nibbled at his hunk, unsure.

Melvin said, "Don't you like it?"

"I don't believe I do," he said with wrinkled nose. "Reminds me of sweaty socks."

"I'll eat it!" Melvin said. Abel handed him the cheese and his brother bit into it with a smile.

Lee stood, pinching off and eating pieces of his portion. "Will you-all be ready to leave at first light?"

Mary said, "Our wagons are ready, save the kitchen boxes."

"Our wagon's all set," Abel said. "That new axle looks good and Rich and Mel got all the stuff loaded back up."

"Good," Lee said. "We'll roll out after breakfast and see if it's any easier traveling on that Santa Fe Trail. We've more or less made our own road up till now."

Sarah said, "It will be a comfort to have other folks around—even if they are Mexicans and them awful bullwhackers."

"I'm sure they're all fine folks in their own right," Lee said.

"Not all of them," Jane said with a shiver. At the thought of the Comanchero, tears welled in her eyes but did not fall. Emma moved close to her sister, wrapped an arm around her waist and pulled her close.

"You're right, of course," Lee said. "But I do believe most people are good at heart, thank the Lord."

"I concur!" Daniel said with a smile. "More cheese, anyone?" Melvin stepped up for another slice. "Now, to quote the Bard, 'To sleep, perchance to dream.' We must be rested for tomorrow's resumption of our journey."

Sometime in the night as the others slept, and perchance dreamed, Richard and Melvin saddled the horses and rode away forever into the night.

Chapter Fifty-Four

Up and around and preparing breakfast early, Sarah did not realize she and the Lewis girls would be cooking for fewer people that morning. It was not until Emma and Jane came into camp with the milk cow that anyone had any inkling this day was different from any other.

"Missus Pate?" Emma said. "The horses are gone. All the other animals are there, but not the horses."

Sarah wiped her hands on her apron and went to rouse Lee from sleep. There was no sign of Richard or Melvin or their bedrolls. "Lee," she said, shaking her husband's shoulder. "Lee!"

Abel heard his mother and sat up in his bedding with a sleep-smeared face, blinking bleary eyes.

Lee was slower to wake, but rolled to his side and raised himself on an elbow. "What is it, Sarah?"

"The boys are gone—Richard and Melvin. Emma says the horses are gone."

Stifling a yawn, Lee said, "I wouldn't worry. They probably went into town drinking. Wouldn't be the first time." His next yawn could not be subdued.

"No. Their bedrolls are gone. Unless I miss my guess, their clothes won't be here, either."

Sarah's opinion proved correct. Lee's rifle and shot pouch were missing as well. Everything else seemed intact, likely because the boys did not want to awaken anyone by rustling around in the wagon or camp boxes.

Abel pulled on his boots and walked out to where the stock was picketed. The horses were gone for sure. He found where his brothers had led them a ways away and tied them to a tree. *This must be where they saddled up,* he thought. A faint trail through the grass showed where they rode wide of the wagons and joined the road to town. Abel followed their tracks into Las Vegas, but the closer he got to town the more other traffic obscured the trail. By the time he reached the plaza there was no way to tell where their tracks went among the muddle of prints left by other horses, mules, oxen, cattle, goats, sheep, pigs, dogs, carts, carriages, wagons, boots, shoes, and bare feet left through the night and morning and for days on end.

Back at camp, Abel found Ma and Pa and the Lewises numbed. He told them of the lost trail and that there was no way to know where to even begin looking. Sarah wept and Lee could barely speak for the tightness in his throat.

Daniel sat on the same box as last night when he served the cheese, the upturned box still standing before him. "What ho!" he said. "The cheese! My cheese is missing." Despite the solemnity surrounding him, Daniel could not help but laugh out loud. "It appears your Melvin really did like that cheese!"

That jolted the women out of their languor and they all at once took up the preparation of breakfast. While Sarah and Mary fixed an over-large batch of fried bacon and corn dodgers to feed them this morning as well as on the day's trail, Emma scrambled a batch of fresh eggs acquired in town, and hoped it would remind the hens in their cages of their jobs once settled. Another unaccustomed addition to the meal was sliced peaches from trees planted by Las Vegas's first settlers and just beginning to bear. Jane milked the cow, leaving one teat for the calf. A supply of fresh corn and tomatoes and squash were also laid in to add variety to the meals in the coming days.

"Does this change your plans at all?" Daniel asked over breakfast.

Lee chewed on a chunk of bacon as he thought, swallowed, and said, "Don't know. Four less hands will make more work for breakin' ground or puttin' in a crop—if we can find farm land, that is. Hard to say. We could look more toward raisin' cattle, but that takes work, too." He thought some more, munching on a corn dodger. "My brother Benjamin, he had his fingers in all manner of business ventures. I reckon if I could find a borrow of money I could set up as a storekeeper—if there's a likely place for it."

"A saloon may require a lesser investment of capital," Daniel said. "Although I would never consider such a proposition for myself."

"Nor would I. I ain't opposed to drink in a general way, but I couldn't countenance encouraging it."

Daniel spooned up some eggs and once they were swallowed, said, "The girls and I have some money laid by. Their laundry business was more profitable than we anticipated. Perhaps at some juncture we could consider a partnership of some kind."

"What would your girls think about you putting their money at risk?"

Daniel smiled. "Martha would have demanded a voice in whatever venture I contemplated—with or without partners, mind you. I would certainly consult the girls, but my feeling is they will bend to my wishes." Daniel sipped his coffee, and smiled. "I suspect my Emma will be keen on any prospect that will keep the Lewis and Pate families entwined. Unless I miss my guess, she has grown quite fond of Abel. Jane has, as well, since her noble rescue. But while Jane's interest can be described as hero worship, I believe Emma's leans more toward the romantic."

Sarah had suggested much the same concerning Emma and

Abel, so while it had not been spoken of out loud, their blossoming relationship was an open secret. Lee looked to the wagons, where Emma and Abel shared the chore of yoking the Lewis oxen. They smiled and laughed and talked as if the job were an enjoyable one. He realized with a start that without Richard and Melvin around, the mules were neither harnessed nor hitched. And while he knew Abel would get to it, he felt obligated to carry some of the extra weight.

"Well, Daniel, it seems we have a lot to talk about. But right now, I reckon we had best get on the road." With that, Lee ambled away to bring in the team.

By the time the oxen were yoked and hitched to the Lewis wagons and the mules harnessed and hitched to the Pate wagon, Sarah and Mary and Jane had the camp equipment packed and loaded. There was nothing more to do than get up the oxen and slap the lines on the mules' rumps and set out on the trail. Abel walked with Emma between the wagons. No more would he ride ahead to scout the trail or ride out in search of game. But, as his mother pointed out, horses could be replaced—sons could not.

As the wagon crossed the Gallinas River, Sarah grabbed a wagon bow and leaned out to look back across the stream toward their campsite, thinking it the last place she had seen the sons she would never see again. She tucked a stray strand of hair behind an ear, adjusted her bonnet, and said to the husband walking beside the lumbering wagon, "It finally happened, Lee. One of your damn dreams came true."

ABOUT THE AUTHOR

Author of the Western Writers of America Spur Award-winning novel *Rawhide Robinson Rides the Range* and Spur Finalist *Rawhide Robinson Rides the Tabby Trail,* **Rod Miller** also writes history, poetry, and magazine articles about the American West. The four-time Spur winner is also recipient of writing awards from Westerners International, the Academy of Western Artists, and Western Fictioneers.

Born and raised in Utah, Miller lived for a time in Idaho and Nevada before returning home. He graduated from Utah State University, where he rode bucking horses for the intercollegiate rodeo team, and spent more than four decades as an award-winning advertising agency copywriter.

Learn more about the author at writerRodMiller.com and writerRodMiller.blogspot.com.

The employees of Five Star Publishing hope you have enjoyed this book.

Our Five Star novels explore little-known chapters from America's history, stories told from unique perspectives that will entertain a broad range of readers.

Other Five Star books are available at your local library, bookstore, all major book distributors, and directly from Five Star/Gale.

Connect with Five Star Publishing

Visit us on Facebook:
https://www.facebook.com/FiveStarCengage

Email:
FiveStar@cengage.com

For information about titles and placing orders:
(800) 223-1244
gale.orders@cengage.com

To share your comments, write to us:
Five Star Publishing
Attn: Publisher
10 Water St., Suite 310
Waterville, ME 04901